The Suicide Killer

The Suicide Killer

Zach Lamb

Second Print Edition

First Green Girl Publishing Edition

Cover by Fabled Beast Design

Author Photo by Darlin Images

ISBN 979-8-9871527-1-3

This book is dedicated to the memory of my Dad, who taught me how to love books.

Chapter One

Bobby Cotton watched the clock on the wall. The cadence of the second hand lulled him to sleep. He had not been able to sleep much lately. There didn't seem to be any reason for his insomnia, but as he dozed, he contemplated taking the clock above the door home with him. Nobody would miss it anyway. The second hand crossed the eleven on the emotionless face, and Bobby snapped upright. It was twelve minutes until she would walk around the corner to the Daily Grind Coffee Shoppe and order a coffee with skim milk and lite sugar. He poured a full pitcher of coffee in the sink and started a fresh pot. Danielle had been coming to the coffee shop every day on her lunch break for the past six months since she began working as the secretary at Arkwright Construction. She would sit by the window while Bobby tried to busy himself with his mundane tasks. He would steal glances as she watched cars going down the street until her lunch break was over and she left him once again. He would then wait for tomorrow when he would definitely start a meaningful conversation with her.

11:45. Danielle walked around the corner. His breath caught in his throat as he ran a dry cloth across the spotless counter. The bell rang, and she walked into the coffee shop. The chime always seemed to be louder when she walked in. The reverberations ran through his entire body. Echoes bounced off her chestnut hair.

"Good afternoon. Welcome to the Daily Grind," Bobby said, a

little too eager. "What..." Bobby cleared his throat. "What can I get for you?"

Danielle looked up as she dug through her purse. "Hey, I'll take a regular coffee with skim milk and lite sugar, please."

"And a name for the order?" Bobby asked, already writing her name on the side of the cup.

Danielle looked down and brushed her hair behind her ear. "You know, I would think after all this time you would remember my name and what I order."

"Oh, I remember your name and your order, but I always figure the one time that I have your coffee waiting for you, you will change your order." He poured the milk and sugar into her coffee.

"So, are you afraid that I will change my name too?" she asked, blushing.

He laughed nervously. "No, I just wouldn't want to get your drink mixed up with everybody else's."

He looked around at the empty coffee house. Danielle laughed. He handed her the change and watched as she walked across the room to her usual table and stared out the window. He busied himself as usual by wiping down the clean tables when she spoke.

"I see you when I'm at the park, walking my dog."

The sudden change in routine caught him off guard, and he didn't hear what she had said.

"What? I mean excuse me?" he asked, correcting himself to sound polite. The kind of politeness that only comes from years working in customer service; fake and detached.

"My dog, Charlie. When I take him to the park, I see you there a lot. Do you live nearby?"

"Yeah, I live in the neighborhood beside the park. I like to go there when I get off work."

The truth was Bobby didn't really care for the park too much. He would use the long forgotten bike trail that ran from the corner of the park to the edge of the woods beside his house as a shortcut. By cutting through the park, he could walk to work instead of driving. Walking seemed more economical to him even though the drive was only a few miles. One afternoon after working late, he saw Danielle walking her dog. Ever since that day, he would hang around the coffee shop thirty minutes after his shift in hopes he would somehow muster up the courage to talk to her like it was a coincidental meeting.

Danielle smiled, and pushed her hair behind her ear as she looked down at the coffee on the table. Bobby didn't notice the awkward air between them and went back to wiping the finish off the counter. He looked up to say something to her, but the chime stopped him.

"Dani, I've been looking all over for you. I finally got somebody in that place to tell me where you went."

Danielle looked at Bobby and then behind him to the man walking toward her.

"I can't believe you were harassing them, Mike. Those are the people I work with."

Mike pushed past Bobby and continued to Danielle's table.

"Well, if they had just told me which way you went, I would have left. I told them we had a lunch date, but they didn't care."

"Lunch date? We broke up. There are no more lunch dates. You should have made lunch plans with your girlfriend."

"Come on, Dani. I told you I was sorry. I'm going to break up with her," Mike said, and grabbed the back of the chair in front of him like he was going to sit down.

Danielle stuck her feet between the chair rungs and pulled it against the table.

"You're going to? So, you still haven't broken up with her?"

"It's not that easy. We've been together a long time. She gets emotional when I try."

Mike puled the chair and Danielle yanked it back to the table.

"I can't believe I'm sitting here listening to this crap. Get out and leave me alone. I'm done with you. I'm not going to be your side girl, and even if you did break up with her, I wouldn't date you. If you would cheat on her, then you would cheat on me too."

"No, I wouldn't. You're the one I want to be with."

"Sir, I'm going to have to ask you to leave now," Bobby said from behind Mike.

"Who the hell are you? You're not part of this conversation."

"I'm the guy who works here. And you're being loud and obnoxious and bothering all of my customers," Bobby said, and spread his arms, surveying the empty room.

Mike laughed, and walked toward Bobby.

"Right. All of your customers may get upset." Mike pushed Bobby out of his way and walked to the door. Bobby twisted the rag around his palm and stepped toward Mike.

"Don't worry, Dani. I'll break up with her like I promised, and then I'll find you," Mike said, turning to face Danielle again and stopping Bobby in his tracks.

"Go home to your girlfriend," Danielle yelled as the door shut behind him.

The lunchtime rush was about to start, and he wouldn't have time to talk to her now. It was almost 12:15 and she would be leaving soon. He walked to the counter as a new customer entered. He watched her from across the room as he filled the new order. Danielle kneaded her forehead with her fingers. Stray hair fell from behind her ear and curled around the bottom of her cup. What was he thinking when he jumped into their conversation? Normally he would never have done that. He would have gone back behind the counter and waited for them to leave and be glad when it was over. This time was different though. He had gotten mad at the way this Mike guy was acting and treating Danielle. He wanted to stop him. He wanted to hurt him and had to hold himself back from hitting the guy. At first, he thought it was because of Danielle, but there was another reason. There was no label for it. He just wanted Mike to be in pain.

Danielle got up and walked toward the front counter. His heart beat faster as he watched her approach.

"Maybe the next time we're both in the park, we could walk together or something," she said, and smiled at him.

"Uh. Yeah." Was all he could get out before she turned, and walked out the door.

The rest of the day was a blur. He relived her invitation over and over in his head. He imagined all the things he wished he would have said, and should have said. In his mind he was suave, he didn't have to worry about how he sounded, or how he looked, he always knew what to say, and in the end, he would have her.

It was getting close to the time Bobby got off work when one of the baristas taking his place showed up early. It was Thursday and Danielle would be in the park this evening. His daydreams and busy afternoon distracted him from the real opportunity to spend time with her. His palms dampened, and sweat ran down his brow. He went to the back and asked Denise if she would mind clocking in early because he felt sick. With a concerned look, she agreed.

Bobby stepped outside the shop and panicked. Fighting to remain calm, he walked around the building, but as he approached the contractor's office, he picked up the pace and ran. He hoped she hadn't seen his cowardly flash go by the window. It was only two blocks to the park entrance. If he ran to the gate, he'd get a hold of himself and walk the rest of the way home. The sign for Rusted Lakes Park mocked him as if crossing its border could do anything to help him. After a few steps, he lost his nerve and ran. He cleared the gravel parking lot and the open field, and cut through the playground. Gawking children hanging from monkey bars and fire poles looked on. He reached the opening to the tired bike trail and stopped to catch his breath. After hiding in the foliage for a few minutes, the pulse in his ears dissipated, and his breathing became regular. Bobby wanted to run again, but didn't because the trail was overgrown and branches stuck out, ready to trip him. He knew she wouldn't be chasing him and felt foolish. He walked deeper into the woods, kicking at the loose pebbles that littered the path. The route sloped slightly to a curve where he would have to push into the thick brush and enter his neighborhood on the backside. The bushes never seemed to give. No matter how many times he pushed through, they always moved back overnight and lay in wait for him to return.

Bobby hiked out of the woods into a long forgotten cul-de-sac in the back of the Lonesome Pines subdivision. Cracks ran across the pavement, and once green weeds sprouted through the flaws in the surface. He walked into the house on the corner lot, entering the old turn around. He lived alone in the timeworn two-story house inherited from his grandmother. The house was still decorated in the outdated style as it had when his grandparents bought the place. He walked into the dimly lit kitchen and sat at the table with a glass of water.

Three hours later he was still sitting at the table, staring at the untouched water. His mind was blank. He no longer thought about his day and how he had been a coward for no reason at all. He was ready to fight Mike but was afraid to talk to the girl who thought he was helping. Calling out of work sounded like a good idea, but he never missed work. There was no reason to let the events of the day effect work. Work was all he had left. The mundane broke the trance, and he trudged up the stairs, past the fading wallpaper, to his bedroom. He fell on his bed, and went straight to sleep.

For the next week, Bobby didn't stay late after work. When it was time for him to get off at five, he waited patiently for Danielle to leave work, to go pick up her dog. Then he would hurry out the door and into the park. While at work, he thought everything was going fine. Danielle would come in, and he would make her coffee and suffer through small talk, then she would leave. After a few days, the tension he initially felt had subsided, and he almost felt like things were getting back to normal.

On Friday, Danielle walked into the shop, and didn't look like herself. She looked like she hadn't slept. Had she been crying? Bobby knew something was off before the door shut behind her. He tried to act as if everything was normal and greeted her.

"Good afternoon. Welcome to the Daily Grind."

She did not respond immediately. Instead, she chewed on her bottom lip. Bobby was getting antsy when she finally spoke.

"Bobby, have I done something wrong?"

She didn't give him time to respond; instead, she continued talking while Bobby reached for a cup, unsure of what to do. He felt cornered.

"I feel. Well, I just feel like you have been kind of short with me since the other day with Mike and I haven't seen you at the park either. Are you avoiding me?"

Bobby puffed out his cheeks and blew out a defeated breath.

"No. Everything's fine. I've just been distracted, I guess. I haven't been avoiding you. I thought we were just missing each other at the park."

His lie made him feel weak. There was no reason to avoid Danielle. There was no reason for him to act like a second grader with his first crush. Shame crawled up his spine and rested in his face, causing it to turn a dark red. Danielle either didn't notice or acted like she hadn't.

"Oh. Well, how about today then?"

"How? How about today what?" he choked out.

"How about today we walk in the park like we talked about?" she said, now smiling and staring directly at Bobby. Her emerald eyes lit up with a fire Bobby had never seen before.

"Uh... yeah," was all Bobby could get out before he turned around to make her coffee. Today was Friday. She always went to the park with her dog on Tuesday, Thursday, and most Saturdays. She was changing her routine for him. A surge of excitement welled up within Bobby. She had changed her schedule to be with him, she actually wanted to go with him, not just spend time with him because they were both there and had nobody else. Bobby got so flustered he almost spilled Danielle's coffee on her.

"Whoa. Sorry. My hand was wet."

Danielle laughed at him and turned to leave.

"I don't have time to stay today. We have been really busy next door, but I'll see you later. I'll meet you beside the playground at 5:30. Okay?"

"Sounds good." Bobby watched her walk out the door and pass by the window. The S in Shoppe perfectly silhouetted her head and neck. When she turned the corner, he sat down at the counter until the door chime signaled the beginning of the lunch rush.

Bobby watched the clock slide to five, said his goodbyes and shuffled to the door. Outside, the early spring air still had a wintery blade that cut deep, making people rethink not grabbing a light jacket on the way out the door. He kicked a rock from outside the coffee shop all the way to the park. He lost the rock when his last kick sent it sailing into the parking lot, mixing in with the gravel. He sat down on a park bench beside the playground. The older children ran through the soft sand, and climbed up the slide from the wrong end, blocking the smaller ones who were trying to come down. Suddenly feeling awkward watching the kids without one of his own on the playground, Bobby rotated on the bench in time to see Danielle letting Charlie out of the backseat of her car. She smiled and waved when she saw him. Charlie pulled at his leash, trying to escape. Bobby was still sitting on the bench when Danielle closed in on him. He attempted to stand, but Charlie jumped up on him and pushed him back down to the bench.

"Charlie! Get down. I'm sorry, Bobby. He usually doesn't do that."

"That's okay. I guess he likes me," Bobby said, rubbing the dog's head. "What kind is he?"

"He's a yellow lab. He's only a year old, so he still gets a little excited," she said and pulled the dog off Bobby so he could stand up.

They walked around the playground trying to ignore the delighted screams of the children for their mothers to "look at the doggy." They sped up their walking until they were safely away from the children. Bobby stopped at the entrance to the trail that would lead him home. First, he fought the urge to take off running up the path. Before she knew it, he would be halfway to his house. But he realized he didn't really want to do that. It had always been in his nature to flee from everything. Right now, all he wanted to do was to be with her. He realized she was watching him look at the path. She probably thought he was crazy.

"That's the trail I take to my house."

"Well, I was wondering. You looked like you were about to take off running."

"Nah, the thought never crossed my mind," he said, and walked past his escape route.

"It's a good thing. Otherwise, I would have had to sic Charlie on you," she said with a smile. "So do you live alone or have a roommate or something?"

"I live alone. I lived with my grandmother, but she died last year and left the house to me."

Bobby never talked about his personal life with anybody. He never really talked to anybody about anything, but he didn't feel uncomfortable talking to her about himself.

"Oh. I'm sorry to hear that."

"It's okay. It's life," he said with a shrug. "So do you have a roommate or anything?" Bobby asked, hoping to change the subject.

"No. I live alone too. I have an apartment in Valley Summit, off Red Rock Road. I like it. It's only five miles from work and the park, so that's nice too."

"Yeah, I know where those are," Bobby said.

They walked and occasionally engaged in small talk, but mostly they were silent, the way they were in the coffee shop. The silences they shared were the best Bobby could remember ever having with another person. There was no awkward feeling that somebody should speak, and when they did, it wasn't something completely off the wall because neither one knew what to say. It was comfortable. They watched Charlie as he rolled in the grass and tried to hold him back when a squirrel taunted him before it dashed off into the woods. They ended up back in the parking lot after walking the two-mile path that meandered throughout the park. After wrestling Charlie into the backseat, Danielle was about to get into the car when she stopped.

"I had a really nice time with you today."

"So did I. We should do it again sometime."

Danielle's green eyes lit up.

"Great. How about tomorrow?" Her face flushed. "Or I'm here every Tuesday, Thursday, and Saturday. But any day is fine. It doesn't have to be one of those days. Any day that is good for you will be great too." Danielle's face turned a darker shade of red.

Realizing she could not shut herself up, Bobby stepped in and helped her out.

"Tomorrow sounds great," he said.

Thrilled by his answer and for his help with her anxiety, she leaned in quickly and gave him an awkward hug. She climbed into her car.

"See you tomorrow," she said, and closed the door.

Bobby watched her leave. The hug had been unexpected, and weird. But it was nice. He walked home thinking about his time with Danielle and Charlie.

Chapter Two

She saw him kissing the other woman at the entrance to the park and sat in her car, motionless as the tears formed. She wanted to drive away, but she couldn't. She couldn't let him think he was getting away with this. Regaining her composure, she stepped from the car on trembling legs.

The slow, deliberate walk across the parking area was painfully long. The outsider watched, unnoticed, through blurred eyes. The scene in front of her was only disturbed once she purposely crushed the brush under her shoes. The sound caused the paramours to look up with uninterested eyes.

"How could you do this, Mike?" She could no longer hold the tears back. They ran down her already red face.

Mike stepped away from his mistress slowly, his hand up as if to reach for her. "I can explain," he said.

His voice had the slightest waver to it. She'd caught him in his lies and there was no way he could talk his way out of this.

With the shock now turning to anger, she said, "So... I guess this is where you say it's not what it looks like." He moved to speak, but she wouldn't let him have his say yet. "I just saw you kissing her. Don't even bother giving me any of your crap, Mike."

Mike looked off toward the woods. For once he seemed at a loss for words. How long had he been cheating on her? His arrogant ass probably knew this day would come, but didn't even care. Now that she had caught him, he was speechless. Conflicting emotions passed over his face, but she couldn't tell if he felt bad or relieved that he wasn't hiding it anymore.

The woman with Mike froze where she stood, like the police had caught her shoplifting. "I had no idea he was seeing somebody. I just met him last month," she finally said.

Last month? The words stung. Mike had been distant, but she thought it was because of the problems she was having.

"I'm not mad at you. You've only been his entertainment," she said with a surprising false bravado.

At that statement, Mike snapped out of his shamed state.

"Now it's not her fault. Amy didn't know anything about us."

"I ... I said I'm not mad at her. Stop trying to make this about somebody else. It's about you."

The small amount of confidence she had faltered, and she was once again letting the hurt take control. She became unsteady and knew she was going to be sick. She walked toward him. Their little scene started to attract an audience, and she feared he would lose his temper and forget he was the one at fault.

Mike regarded the whispering trail walkers and picnicking families as they watched. His face turned red, and sweat poured down his face. He yelled, but all of his words came out a jumbled mess. The audience shamefully looked in the opposite direction while some of the families closer to them started to move away with their children.

This was not going how she planned. She only wanted to come to the park and eat her lunch while she enjoyed the sun before the mild early spring turned into another spring day that might as well be summer. She watched as Amy, no longer wanting to be a part of this, walked hastily toward her car.

Mike advanced on her. Salty tears burned her dry, cracked lips as she looked around for help or a way out. Everything seemed to be going in slow motion. Mike was only a few feet away when his outstretched hand fell low and brushed against her floral spring dress. He tripped over a tree root and laid on the ground in a cloud of dust, his hand still reaching out for her.

She turned and ran deeper into the park. Her shoe came off, but she didn't stop for it and hobbled off balance through the grass. She had only seen him like this once before when, according to him, she had started a fight in front of his friends. She jumped into their conversation and told everybody he spent more time working on his stupid car than with her. All of his friends thought it was funny. They made more than a few crude jokes about the car's exhaust pipes. The jokes were horrible, but she wanted to be part of the group and forced herself to laugh. That is when he lost his temper and said if she was jealous of a car, she had bigger problems and warned her not to call his car stupid again. Later that night, when they were alone, he warned her never to embarrass him like that again and said that he should have smacked her for acting like that in front of his friends. He squeezed her elbow tighter with every word, leaving red marks where his fingers had been.

Halfway across the park, she stepped on a stone. Its jagged edge ripped into her heel, and she fell. Her arms reflexively reached out to brace her fall and park debris sliced into her palms and wrists. She lay on the ground for a short time before clambering to her feet. She looked back and expected to see Mike about to grab her. All she saw was a large cloud of dust as his car fishtailed out of the gravel parking lot.

Dizzy with the rush of all the emotions flowing through her, she didn't know if it would have been worse for him to catch her or the fact that he was now leaving her in the middle of the park. He was probably going to try to catch up with Amy. She hoped that he did. Maybe Amy would not be afraid and stand up to him.

She hobbled toward the back of the park under the dark canopy of trees. She kicked off her remaining shoe and ran as hard as she could. With her shoe gone, she could run faster and her breath became labored as a stitch formed in her side. She recalled the feeling of being a kid again. It had been a long time since she thought about being chased on the playground while the other kids pursued her with their stinging words and stones.

Mike had been different in the beginning; he had liked her for who she was. He was going to take her away from all the hurt this city had caused her growing up. In the end, he turned out to be just like every other guy she had trusted. She was an easy target for guys who only wanted to take advantage of her before they cast her aside for somebody new. Her stomach churned when she stopped at the edge of the woods. With her hands on her knees, she threw up her breakfast. It came up with a suddenness she wasn't ready for. As her stomach emptied, she choked, and could taste the vomit and feel it run into her nose.

The young woman crashed into the forest, one hand on her stomach, while the other pushed low-hanging branches from her path. She doubled over and dry heaved, but her stomach was spent. The pain in her sides became too much for her and she fell to her knees. Tears streamed down her red face, and she wiped her mouth with the back of her hand. Her head ached. She wanted to sit down, but ended up lying on the dirty soil. Questions swirled through her mind.

How could he have done this? Did he not know how much he meant to her? Was he taking that girl, Amy, to their spot?

She rocked on the ground and crushed dead leaves beneath her crumpled body. Her mind raced with all the previous events, but at the same time, it was hard for her to think of anything in particular.

A sudden flash of clarity illuminated her mind. She knew why he was doing this. It was the miscarriage she had two months ago. He acted like he was okay with it, almost relieved, but she knew it bothered him. He had been in a bad mood ever since, or at least, a worse one than his usual mood. He must have thought it was all her fault. Maybe it was. Maybe she didn't take good enough care of herself, and that's what had killed their baby. Maybe he thought she would never be able to have children. He probably thought she was damaged goods like everybody else did. Too much baggage to worry about. It was all her fault and Mike knew it. That's why he was trying to find somebody new.

She was going to be sick again. As she walked deeper through the forest, she looked down at her stained dress and absently patted her disheveled hair. Everything was like a dream. It happened, but could she trust what actually happened? Her head spun, and she stumbled to a tree perched on top of a cliff overlooking one of the lakes in the park. The stabbing pains in her side felt like her ribs were going to rip through her skin. The aching caused her to lose her bearing, and she tumbled off the edge of the rise.

Branches and vines pulled at her skin as she rolled down the hill. Her arms moved instinctively to cover her face like they had done so many times as a child. Thorns from the bushes ripped her flesh open like heaved stones. Blood dripped from the leaves as she hurled by.

She came to rest at the foot of the hill and tried to push herself up, but her arms were too weak. She fell back into the dirt. After what seemed like an eternity, she pushed herself to her feet and walked through the forest. Her whole body was on fire, but she barely registered any of the pain. She stumbled toward the goal she had originally been running toward. It was a fallen tree. It was fresh, still green and clinging to life when she and Mike found it last year. Now it was black and rotten. Mike carved their names into it with his knife. As she ran her hands across the letters in the dead tree, she looked out across one of the rusty lakes they named the park after.

A shattered wine bottle lay on the ground close to where they would sit together at night after the park closed. Looking at the glass, she screamed and shook uncontrollably; he had been here with her. Mike had brought Amy here before. That was the only reason the bottle could have been there. Mike always filled their bottles up with water and threw them into the lake. He left this one here for her to see the next time they came to their spot. He wanted her to catch him.

She bent down and grabbed the largest piece she could find and gripped it tightly. The glass bit into her hand. She stabbed the tree where Mike carved their names. The wood chipped away easily as the glass slid across her hand, cutting it deeply.

Blood splattered like red tears on her dress and the tree where their names had been. She screamed, and turned around. The release of all the pent up rage toward Mike and herself had left her faint. Lightheaded, she slid to the ground in a calm stupor. She looked at her hand as if it were from a foreign body. Blood oozed between her fingers as she squeezed her fists and fingered the slits in her palm. Her head swam, and her body was numb on the inside and out. Mike was going to miss her and everything she did for him.

She put the broken piece of glass to her pulse and dug into her skin and slid up her arm. Blood poured from her wound like a river overflowing its banks and mixed with the dirt of the floodplain surrounding her. She weakly transferred the glass to the other hand and slid the glass up that arm with no hesitation. The cut on this arm was not as deep or as long as the other one, but the blood still seeped out. She tried to fight the urge to close her eyes, but eternal sleep was taking over. She was calm and serene as she thought about Mike being the one to find her, perhaps with Amy or maybe another girl he had on the side. Then he would see how much he had meant to her.

As the blood ran down her hand, forming pools of red in the fallen leaves, she realized this was always going to be the way it ended for her. Even if she had never met Mike, her life would have concluded in the same manner. He had only prolonged the inevitable.

Chapter Three

Bobby sat on a swing, waiting for Danielle. He felt awkward being there without a child. The cautious mothers kept a casual eye on him but would be ready to pounce if he started showing too much interest in the children running around him. Usually, he wouldn't sit alone in or near the playground. The other side of the parking lot ran down a grassy hill into a creek that fed the largest of the three lakes in the park, and he didn't want to wait in the parking lot or too close to it and look like he was too eager to see her. So, he resided to being uncomfortable for a few minutes, alone with his thoughts. He swung, with only the melancholy squeak of the rusted chains to keep him company.

The past three weeks he and Danielle met after work and on Saturdays to walk around the park. He was content with the way their relationship was going, but he knew she wanted more. Two times she had told him she was having fun, but they could go and do other things if he would like. He had changed the subject on her and cut their walk short on those days. He didn't have a particular reason for being that way, though. He was enjoying their time together and didn't want to risk screwing anything up by changing their routine, but knew sooner or later, that he would have to do something or she would get bored and move on.

Danielle pulled into the parking lot. He could see the smile on her face even from afar. As he jumped from the swing and left the playground area, he thought he heard a collective sigh from the mothers, but when he turned and looked at them, they didn't seem to register his movement. When he got to her car, Charlie greeted him by jumping and pawing at his hands. Distracted by the dog, Bobby didn't notice Danielle until he felt her soft embrace.

"Hey. He was excited to get out of the house today. I think he gets more excited to see you than he does to go for his walks anymore."

"Yeah, he's the reason I keep showing up too," he said, and rubbed the bouncing dog until he sat and kicked his hind leg.

"Hey! Not nice," she said, and pushed his shoulder.

They walked through the gravel parking lot and down the hill, following the babbling creek. Silent, she walked beside Bobby. He sensed something different with her but didn't know what it was. Charlie seemed to notice the difference as well. Every day, they would walk past the playground and through the open green space. When they reached his path, they would follow the tree line until they reached the first lake and then they would turn back toward the front of the park. They would walk until they reached the creek and the hill and finally the parking lot again. Today, she led them in the opposite direction. They stopped and watched the small waterfall, and Danielle moved closer to Bobby. She laid her head on his chest and reached for his hand. It looked like she was trying to catch a snake, squirming to get free. Her sudden show of affection caught him off guard. He relaxed his hand, and hers fell into his. They stood watching the water run down the rocks and splash into the small pool, barely large enough for two ducks to swim in, as Charlie tried to play with his reflection in the water.

Danielle pulled her head away and, on tiptoes, kissed Bobby's cheek.

"That was nice," she said, and pulled him by the hand back to their walk.

Bobby didn't say anything. Her words confused him. Was standing there with him nice? Did she mean kissing him? Finally, he decided it didn't really matter what she was talking about. He wanted to enjoy the rest of his time with her and not get lost in thought over thinking everything.

"So, how's work?" she asked.

Bobby shrugged his shoulders. "It's okay, I guess. Same thing every day. Nothing too interesting seems to happen during the day."

"Oh. So you get all the normal customers? And the real crazies come out at night."

"Yeah. They're all too busy trying to get back to work, so I guess there's not too many weirdos besides you."

"Ha. I'm not weird," she said, and pushed his shoulder.

"Oh yeah? Then why do you come in every day and order the same thing and stare out the window until your lunch break is over?"

"You've been watching me and know my routine. Right. I'm the weird one."

Bobby pulled back, not knowing if it was an insult or not. Danielle laughed at him.

"Don't be so sensitive, weirdo," she said, and wrapped her arms around him.

He pulled her close. He could still smell the fruity shampoo she used. After a tight squeeze, he drifted away and grabbed her hand. They walked in silence around the lake. When they reached the woods, they continued the reverse course on their typical route. Hand in hand they walked, and she avoided the pinecones, while he purposefully crushed them beneath his foot. They stopped before they reached the path to his house when he slipped on a flattened cone.

"You keep stepping on those things and you're going to fall."

"Nah, you'll keep me up," he said, and threw their hands in the air.

"Or you'll pull me down with you."

She turned and faced the woods, but did not seem to be looking at anything in particular.

"Have you ever wondered what it would be like to live in the woods?"

"What?"

"The woods. Have you ever thought about living in the woods? I think it would be fun. Have a log cabin or something. Wouldn't have to worry about anything. Just live and be happy."

"Yeah, and work hard trying to grow food and chop wood so you wouldn't die."

"That's a morbid way of looking at it. I think it would be great."

"I've heard there's an old Korean woman who lives in the woods over there in her car," he said, pointing back to the where they had come from.

"Really? That's so sad."

"You just said it would be great," he said.

"Yeah, but in a cabin. Not in my car because I am homeless. I'm surprised they haven't arrested her for living in the park."

"I think they have a couple of times, but she comes back because there is nowhere else for her to go. Her car has been back in the woods long enough that the vines and branches have grown up around it. It's not worth the trouble for them to try and tow it out."

"How do you know?"

"Because I've seen the car. I've just never seen her."

"Oh. It's still sad."

"Yep," he said with a sigh.

They stared into the woods a while longer. Bobby looked toward the path that led to his house, but he didn't feel like fleeing. He wanted to stay like this with Danielle for as long as he could. Of course, he would walk her back to her car before they parted. He wouldn't just leave her in the middle of the park while he walked home.

Charlie's growl startled him and brought him back to reality. In all the time he had spent with the dog, he had never heard him growl before. Danielle looked uneasy too.

"Charlie. Charlie. What is wrong with you?" she asked, pulling on his leash. Charlie barked and pulled Danielle toward the woods.

"Maybe he smells the old woman," Bobby said.

"That's not funny. She can't help it, and he never acts like this," she said.

Danielle snapping at Bobby hurt. He hadn't meant to offend her. He was trying to lighten the mood. It was hard knowing what would offend somebody at any given time. The dog pulled harder at the leash. He twisted and tried to rip it from Danielle's hand. He turned his head and bit at the restraint and jerked it between his teeth. Danielle tried to calm the dog down, but her soothing voice was not helping. Bobby attempted to grab the leash, but his and Danielle's hands fought for the lead. Charlie lunged toward the trees, pulling the leash from their hands. Once free, he darted into the woods barking.

"Charlie. Come back here. Bobby, we have to get him. I can't lose him."

"I'll go and get him. Just stay here in case he comes back or pops out somewhere else."

Bobby pushed into the woods. They were having a great time, and the stupid dog had to ruin it. Now he was climbing through the dense growth after Charlie instead of being with Danielle. Why hadn't the dog decided to take off down the path beside them? It would have been much easier to follow him. Bobby could see the bushes in front of him thrashing around. The dog disappeared, but he could make out the bright red leash tangled in the branches. He stumbled to the bush and pulled at the leash. Charlie managed to wrap it around a thick branch, and hook another branch with the loop at the end. He pulled the leash in one direction and the animal pulled in the opposite.

"Calm down, Charlie," Bobby said, and jerked the leash hard. Charlie let out a strangled yelp and took off running again.

"Bobby. You didn't hurt him, did you?" Danielle said. Her voice was faint, and he couldn't tell which direction it was coming from.

"No. I didn't hurt him. His leash got tangled in a bush," he yelled back and continued his pursuit of the dog.

Bobby pushed into a small clearing on top of a cliff. He walked to the edge and leaned against a tree. From where he stood, he could look across one of the lakes in the park. He had never been in this part of the forest, but when he looked to the right, he could almost make out the clearing on the hill as it made its way to the back of his subdivision. Charlie barked, and he looked down the bluff. The bushes moved as the dog jumped forward and then backward again.

Bobby looked around for an easy way down the slope, but couldn't find one. The dog was still barking but seemed to have stopped his running. He had found whatever he'd caught a whiff of in the park. Bobby watched the dog creep toward something white on the ground. A fallen tree blocked his view and he couldn't tell what the dog found. He realized there would be no easy way to get to the bottom and slid down the Georgia red clay hill. When he got to the bottom, red dust and patches of mud covered his clothes.

"What you found better be worth all of this," Bobby said through clenched teeth.

Charlie ran to Bobby and licked his hand. Bobby ignored the dog and crept closer to what was on the ground. He walked around the tree and saw what Charlie had been after.

The girl was pale. She wore her hair in a ponytail. Black dirt running off of the tree she leaned against streaked her blonde hair. Dirt and debris from the surrounding trees covered her white sundress. Pink hibiscus blooms circled the bottom of the dress and green vines climbed toward the conservative neckline. The vines ended in pools of red on her stomach. Then he saw the deep gashes on her arms. Bobby stumbled back and tripped over Charlie.

"Oh shit. What the hell? She's dead," Bobby said to the dog, wagging his tail over his find.

Bobby walked back to the girl. He reached out cautiously toward her neck, slowly, in case she tried to move and scare the hell out of him. With two fingers he felt for a pulse. He didn't know exactly where he should be looking for it; he just knew it was somewhere on the throat. He couldn't find a pulse, but he knew from the cold, clammy feeling of her slick skin that she was dead. A slight tinge of recognition or maybe it was something else surged through his body as he brushed her bangs out of her face. He slid the back of his hand down her face. With his fingers, he traced her collarbone until it ended at the necklace on her chest. He carefully picked the golden cursive letters up.

"Emily. I guess that's your name," he said, and let the necklace drop.

He ran his hand down her shoulder and across the slits on her arm, stopping at her wrist. A cracking branch from the top of the cliff startled him, and he stood up straight. The hair on his arms stood on end. He searched the top of the hill for who had interrupted him and Emily.

He saw movement and Danielle broke through the brush. He had forgotten she was waiting for him in the park.

"Bobby? What are you doing down there? Did you find Charlie?"

"Hey, yeah, I got him," he said, and picked up the end of the leash from the ground. "He finally stopped running from me."

"Why did he stop?" she asked and moved closer to the edge, peering down at him.

"No. No stop there." Bobby yelled with outstretched hands. His outburst scared Danielle, and she jumped back from the edge of the cliff. At least she didn't fall down the hill. How would he explain Emily? And Danielle might hurt herself if she tried to get to him.

"What's wrong, Bobby? Is Charlie hurt? He looks fine from here."

"He's fine. Just back away from the edge. It's not safe. I don't want you falling and getting hurt."

"Oh," she said, and looked at the crumbling earth around her feet.

She appeared relieved nothing was wrong with either of them, but still looked at Bobby curiously. "Well, what was he barking at?"

Bobby looked around confused before he said, "It's nothing. Only a dead animal. I guess he smelled it from where we were and wanted to see what it was."

"Dead animal? I wonder what happened?" she asked.

"I don't know, but wait right there. Charlie and I are on our way back up," he said, then turned and cupped the girl's cheek in his hand and rubbed the dirt off with his thumb. He wiped his hands on his jeans and climbed up the hill, pulling Charlie.

"What are you going to do about the animal?"

"Just leave it where it is. Something will eat it."

"That's gross, Bobby."

"Nah, it's just the way of the world. Something dies, then something else cleans it up."

Bobby looked back down the hill. He could just make out Emily's bruised heel sticking out from behind the large tree. Charlie whimpered and pulled on his leash. Danielle looked over his shoulder.

"Are you sure everything is okay?" she whispered into his ear.

"Yeah, everything is fine. Let's go before we both end up down there."

He gave the foot one last look and turned toward the old bike path.

"Hey. Where are you going? The park is back this way."

"Sorry. I was headed back to my house. Force of habit."

Danielle looked past Bobby and smiled.

"Well, we could go back to your house, and I could cook you dinner. I'm a pretty decent cook," she said, and looked at the ground while she brushed her hair behind her ear.

"I ... uh, don't really have anything to cook."

"I could order you a pizza. I'm pretty good at that too."

Bobby realized this was the turning point he had been expecting. He knew there was only one answer.

"Okay, sounds good," he said. He tried to sound as natural as he could. He also had to figure out how to get Danielle to the path and not look down to try to see what he and Charlie had found. Finally, he grabbed her hand and led her back the way they had come. When he felt hesitation in her hand, he turned left and headed for the path.

"Trying to find an easy way out of here so we can get to the path," he said over his shoulder.

The tension in her arm eased.

As they walked up the path, he couldn't get the girl lying against the tree out of his head. Who was she? Did she do that to herself? Why? The questions stopped as they stepped into the cul-de-sac. His thoughts went back to the woman he was leading to his house. There was no turning back. He had already brought her this far. She walked up the hill to his house beside him, her head leaning against his shoulder.

Climbing the steps, he looked back toward the park. He stopped on the top step and a cool breeze blew through his hair. He slid the key in the lock but stopped from unlocking the door when he heard his name.

Bobby...Bobby.

The soft voice was barely auditable. He looked at Danielle, and she only smiled. It wasn't her. He looked back to the woods and could hear his name floating on the breeze.

Bobby.

It was Emily, she was calling to him, and she wanted him to be with her.

Bobby, don't leave me out here, it gets cold and lonely at night. I need you.

He froze at the thought of a dead girl trying to communicate with him. He was going crazy. She couldn't speak. She had been dead at least a day, maybe two. But still, he heard somebody calling his name whether they were dead or not. It was her calling to him.

He twisted the key in the lock and pushed the door open, hurrying Danielle and Charlie in before him.

Bobby.

Bobby shut the door on the voice and leaned against the solid wood. There, he couldn't hear her anymore. All he had to do was stay inside, and he couldn't hear her. He would just drive to work in the morning, and everything would be better once somebody found her. It was too late to call the cops. He didn't want to answer any questions, and Danielle would know he lied to her about what he had seen and she wouldn't want to see him again.

"Bobby?"

He jumped at the sound of her voice.

"Are you okay? If you're not feeling up to it, we can do this another time."

"No...no, I'm fine. Really, I just had a cold chill and wanted to get inside."

"If you're sure."

"Yeah, of course. I thought you were good at ordering pizza."

"The best," she said, and pulled her phone out of her back pocket.

Bobby walked into the kitchen, stared at the white and harvest gold flowers on the faded wallpaper, and drank a glass of water. He wasn't going crazy. Seeing a dead body was a traumatic experience. He had never seen a dead body. At least he had never seen one out in the open like that. He had only seen bodies after the mortician finished with them. Death looked different when it was natural. There was nothing natural about Emily's death. It was painful. Both physically and mentally for the poor woman.

"Okay, pizza is on the way. I hope you like chicken and pineapple. They said they'd be here in forty-five minutes. If you don't want Charlie in here, I can put him outside."

"He's fine. Do you want something to drink? I don't have any coffee. I get enough of that when I'm at work."

"I'm good with water," she said with a laugh. "So, you want to take me on a tour of this place?"

"Sure, but it's nothing special."

Bobby handed Danielle a glass of water and walked through the kitchen and back into the foyer.

"There's not much to see really, my grandparents never redecorated, and I haven't felt like it either," he said. "This is the dining room, and the living room is through there. It pretty much looks like this, wood paneling and all. Well, except it has a sofa instead of a table."

They walked into the living room and back into the light cerulean blue hallway. They stuck their heads into a room, and Bobby turned on the light.

"This is just a spare room, I don't do anything with," he said, turning off the light before Danielle could see the empty room. "And this is the ugly pink bathroom." Bobby turned on the light. Light pink tile covered the bathroom floor and walls. The grout used to be bright white, but years of neglect left it dirty with a light pink hue giving the bathroom a strange glow.

"Wow."

"I know, right? The twin is upstairs," he said.

They walked up the stairs as they squeaked in protest. Bobby turned on the light to a small hall that had three doors running off of it.

"That's the twin bathroom, no need to see that again."

"What about in here?" she asked and turned the knob.

"No. Don't," he yelled. "That was my grandparent's room. I don't go in there."

Danielle slinked back to the head of the stairs. She looked scared of him. It was the second outburst he had since Charlie had run off.

"Oh, I'm sorry, I didn't know. I shouldn't have just gone in."

"No, I'm sorry. I kind of overreacted there. I don't know what's wrong with me tonight."

He checked to make sure the door was still closed and walked to the end of the hallway.

"And this is my room," he said, throwing open the door like it was the grand reveal at the end of a murder mystery.

I'm waiting for you, Bobby. Don't be too long. I need you. I can't come in your room like her, but you can come to me.

"Shut up," he yelled and ran to his window and slammed it shut.

"Who are you telling to shut up? I didn't say anything."

"Sorry, not you. I thought I heard my neighbors. They can get loud when they argue."

"Oh. I didn't hear anything."

"Neither did I apparently," he said with a grin.

Before he could say anything else, the doorbell rang.

"Great the pizza's early. I'm starving, let's go," he said, and ran out of the room. He took the stairs two at a time and yanked the door open.

Come to me. I'm so lonely down here in the dark.

"Good evening. That'll be $21.76," the driver said, giving Bobby a strange look.

He fished his wallet out of his pocket and pulled out the cash without counting it.

"Here, keep the change," he said, and shut the door.

He walked past a bewildered Danielle, grabbed a couple of plates and sat at the kitchen table.

"Are you sure you're okay? I think you scared the hell out of the pizza guy."

"I'm fine. I think I gave him an $18 tip, so he'll be fine too. I'm just hungry. I haven't eaten today."

Bobby sat at the table and forced himself to try to eat the pizza. There were three loud knocks on the front door. Danielle didn't seem to notice them. She kept eating her pizza, playing with Charlie in between bites. The knocking grew louder. The old wreath his grandmother put on the door at the beginning of fall three years ago bounced, but still no acknowledgement from his guests. The banging finally stopped, and the door slowly swung open.

Emily walked through the door in her dirty white dress. Patches of moss squirmed in her hair as she checked herself out in the mirror. He looked to Danielle. This time she had to have heard her walk into the house. She'll turn around any second and freak out. Charlie sensed a change in the air. He growled, then whined, and ran into the living room to hide behind the sofa. Danielle looked past Emily as she watched her dog run off.

"I wonder what got into him," was all she said before returning to her pizza. She hadn't seen her. She turned and looked right at her and didn't even know the dead girl in the woods was in the house with them.

Emily brushed the dirt from her dress.

Hello, lover. I got tired of waiting for you to come to me, so I came to you.

She walked slowly to the table. Her eyes were solid black. There was no iris, only pupil, letting all the light in. Red rings around both eyes made her look like she had been crying at some point, but no tears were on her dry face. She hugged herself.

I wish we had met sooner. Before I was dead and before you met her. We could have had a lot of fun together, don't you think?

Emily pulled a chair out from the table. The deep slit in her right arm spread the graying flesh and exposed the red veins that her life poured from a couple of nights ago. Bobby couldn't take his eyes off the cuts. Emily bent her head in his line of sight.

Do my slits bother you, lover? I can cover them if you'd like. Or I could get rid of her and show you all of my slits.

Emily grabbed Bobby's hand, exposing the deep red valley on her other arm. She looked at their hands intertwined and smiled.

Do you mind if I have a slice? Emily asked and reached for the pizza on Danielle's plate.

"No, don't touch her," Bobby yelled and jumped up from the table. He moved toward Emily, but she disappeared. He only saw Danielle with a slice in her hand, looking at him like he had lost his mind. Charlie crept back into the kitchen and whined.

"I am so sorry. I haven't been feeling well lately. You probably think I'm going crazy."

"I don't think that. I think you may not be getting enough sleep. You look like hell. Charlie and I should probably be leaving now, anyway. Do you think you feel up to driving us back to my car?"

"Yes. Of course," he said.

Danielle stood with her plate and Bobby stopped her.

"Don't worry about cleaning up. I can get it later."

"Are you sure?"

"Yeah. No worries. I'll handle it when I get back and then get some sleep."

Danielle hesitated, but finally relented and joined Charlie at the front door.

They climbed into Bobby's old Bronco and drove to the exit of his neighborhood without talking. He drove down Hawthorne Springs

Road, and they both watched the coffee shop as he turned and drove to the park entrance. He parked beside Danielle's car and helped her and Charlie out of his. Danielle stopped before sliding into her car.

"I really did have a nice time tonight."

"Even when I started acting crazy?"

"Well, it wasn't my favorite part, but we'll work on it. Now you need to go home and get some sleep. Please," she said, and tilted her head to kiss him.

He stood still as she pushed up on her toes and their lips touched. He closed his eyes and pulled her into a tighter embrace. Her soft tongue parted his lips and slid into his mouth. As he kissed her, he didn't think of anything. All the previous events and thoughts of Emily melted away. His mind was clearer than it had been in a long time. He wanted to live in the moment as long as she would allow. He opened his eyes only for a moment, but in that instant above Danielle's head, he saw a car parked near the bushes at the entrance to the park. He was no longer fully concentrating on Danielle, and she could tell and pulled away from him.

"Sorry, that car spooked me. I don't remember it being there."

"That's why you don't open your eyes," she said, and kissed his cheek before getting into her car. "I'll see you later."

Bobby watched as Danielle pulled out of the parking lot and drove off down the road. After he was sure she wasn't going to turn around, he walked to the lone red car. Through the tinted windows he could make out a purse in the passenger seat, and a bright yellow ponytail holder around the gear shifter. It was surprising nobody had looked in the car and smashed the window to get the purse.

The car could belong to anybody. People left their cars parked under the no parking over night sign all the time. He resisted the urge to see if the car was unlocked. He didn't want his fingerprints on the car in case it was hers. The police would never believe he didn't know anything about the girl in the woods if they knew he'd been inside her car. It would be best to leave the car alone and go back home and try to get some sleep. He really hadn't been sleeping well lately, and that had to be the reason he was hallucinating. There's no way she was real. Not anymore.

He got back in his car and headed home.

When he arrived, he tried not to look at the woods as he headed to his house. The wind kicked up, and on the breeze, he heard her voice again.

Bobby, I've been waiting for you while you dropped off your other woman. Come and be with me tonight. I need you.

"I'm on my way," he said, and headed toward the trees.

Chapter Four

Bobby...Bobby, get up. Somebody is coming. Nobody can find you here. They will take you to jail, and we won't be together again. They'll think you did this to me.

A branch snapped, and Bobby came out of his trance. He searched the tree line in the direction of the noise and followed the doe like movements through the forest. He pulled himself out from under the fallen tree and tried to listen for the commotion again. His muscles ached from being inactive for too long. How long had he been in the woods? His mind felt like it was in a smoggy haze. The last thing he remembered was Danielle leaving and telling him to get some sleep. But before he could get inside, he heard a sweet sounding voice call to him from the end of the cul-de-sac. She was lonely and needed his company. He also thought he heard fear in her voice. He couldn't let her stay out there by herself in the dark.

More movement came from above. He looked at Emily, but she was no help. Her skin was grayer than he remembered. There was an overwhelming smell of decay in the air he had not noticed before. She was dead and rotting. But she couldn't be dead when she was talking to him. Everything was such a blur. He could still hear the softness in her airy voice. He tried to replay his time with Emily, but his muddled mind would not allow it. Memories flashed to him sitting on the tree talking to her as she patiently waited to tell her stories. Sitting with his back against the tree trunk, leaning against each other with her hand in his. Now all he saw was the lifeless body that was once the Emily he never knew. The white dress had the same graying effect as her skin. The open wounds on her arms looked thick and black.

Hurry, Bobby, you have to get away. They are coming.

She was still talking to him, but he didn't have time to listen to her. Bobby could see somebody walking toward him. They were trying to be quiet like they were sneaking up on him. The blue outline faded and ducked behind a tree. Bobby squatted and looked for the best way to escape. Whoever it was would never believe he just found her like this. *Run.* He turned to run in the opposite direction as the intruder.

"Bobby?"

It was Danielle. He couldn't let her find him like this. How would he even begin to try to explain the situation? What was the situation? Obviously, he had lost his mind and started talking to the dead girl in the woods, and she wouldn't leave him alone.

Bobby, you must leave.

Emily continued calling out to him, even though he was acknowledging the reality of her death. She was dead. There was no way she could talk to him. He didn't understand why he could still hear her. Maybe he had a special connection with this girl? Yeah, that or maybe he was crazy. At least that's what everybody would say when they threw him in jail. Or an asylum. Didn't they close the one in Midland? Maybe he had lost his mind, but he didn't want to stick around and find out what the final verdict would be. He turned to run, but his legs felt sluggish, and he stumbled forward. The repercussions from not eating or drinking anything for a long time wracked his body. It was like fighting to free himself from quicksand. He was slowly sliding deeper into the pit he was living in. The sound of crushing leaves was right behind him.

Now she was too close. He wouldn't be able to get away.

"Bobby? What are you doing out here?"

"Danielle. No—stay there. Don't come any closer," he choked out. His voice was raspy and dry. Flames of stomach acid licked the back of his throat. Rubbing the pain away didn't help to sooth the pain. He had gone too long without water.

"I don't understand. You haven't been at work for two days. I asked where you were and they said you had called and told them you were going to take a vacation—that you were exhausted and needed a break."

He didn't remember making that phone call. He must have made it sometime that night after Danielle left. Before everything went blank. The worst part was Danielle said he'd been gone for two days. Two days was a long time to sleep in the woods with no supplies. That explained the smell. Part of it, anyway.

"I don't really know what's going on. Let's just go back up to the house and talk there," Bobby said.

"You look horrible. You look like you need a doctor," she said, stepping closer.

"No, don't," he said, stumbling toward her. She ran to catch him.

"Bobby? What's wrong?" her voice caught in her throat as she saw the girl. She covered her mouth with her hand. Her frightened eyes looked at Bobby and then back to the girl.

"Oh my god, oh my god. Bobby, what did you do?"

"I didn't do anything. I swear I found her like this."

"Oh no. No, no. She isn't the dead animal that Charlie found down here the other day, is she?"

Bobby didn't know what to say. He watched as her horrified face turned to one of anger and disgust.

"Bobby, please tell me you just found her here this morning, and you were about to call the police and tell them."

"Please, calm down. It's not what you think."

"Calm down? You found a dead girl in the woods two days ago and didn't tell anybody. Then you disappear, and I find you with her. Have you been here since I left the other night?"

"Honestly, I don't know. I don't remember anything after you left."

That was mostly true. He didn't remember calling into work and telling them he needed a vacation. He didn't remember coming back down here in the dark, and he certainly didn't remember spending two days in the woods, sleeping under a tree.

"She's not an animal. She's somebody's loved one. You can't keep her down here like a science experiment, Bobby. Come on. We have to call the police."

"No. We're not calling anybody. They'll arrest me."

"They won't arrest you. We'll tell them you found her this morning. They'll never know."

"They'll figure it out."

Shoe tracks covered his camping spot. It would be obvious he didn't just get here. Broken glass littered the area. Had he been drinking? His hand went to his throat. It hurt like he hadn't had anything to drink. A shard of glass rested beside Emily's open hand. She busted the bottle. But were his fingerprints on it? Or on her? He checked her pulse when he first found her. Was that the only time he touched her? Bobby's gag reflex kicked in at the thought.

"We have to tell the police now. You don't know if the person who did this to her isn't going to come back."

"She did it to herself."

"How the hell do you know?"

"She told me. She said nobody would miss her."

"Bobby, honey, you're sick, you need to come lay down in a bed. You don't know what you're saying. Let me take you home. I'll call the police and tell them where she's at. Somebody does love her, and they are probably worried about her."

"I love her. Nobody is looking for her. They don't care. They're the reason she's dead."

Danielle's face changed. He could see her concern for him, but he couldn't let her tell the police. If she told anybody, he would never get to see or speak to Emily again. He had to convince her. Jail would be bad enough, but he couldn't risk never seeing her again.

"Bobby, you are extremely confused. You probably feel like that because you haven't had anything to eat or drink in a couple of days. Why don't you come with me and we will figure it all out after you've rested?"

"Do you promise you won't call the police?"

"I promise," she said.

Bobby. Don't believe her. She's trying to split us up. She's just jealous of what we have. She will tell them that you hurt me, and you will go to jail for it.

"No," Bobby yelled. "She's not like that."

"Bobby, please come with me. I'll take you to my place so you can get some rest. I promise I won't call the police until we have talked about it. I don't want you to get in trouble either. Okay?"

"Okay, I'll go with you. I'm really tired," Bobby said, and staggered to her.

Danielle walked to Bobby and avoided looking at Emily. Bobby stumbled and fell against her, pushing her back toward the girl. Her leg brushed against Emily's shoulder, and she screamed into Bobby's ear. He shook the ringing from his head and tried to focus on Danielle's face.

"You've got to help me a little bit here. I can't carry you up the hill, and I just touched the dead girl."

"Her name's Emily," he whispered.

"Okay, okay. I just touched Emily, and I can't do that. It's just. It just won't help us get up this hill."

Bobby, don't go. We aren't finished here. I still need you. She will only take advantage of you. She will hurt you and then toss you away.

Bobby wrapped his arm around Danielle's waist, and they climbed the hill. They had a good pace going when they started to slide back in the dead leaves. Danielle propped herself against a tree and held Bobby up. The scent of dirt and sweat surrounded them, but there was something else. Death's sharp fragrance floated in the air. She turned her face from Bobby. Was it the way he smelled or did looking at him disgust her? The angle gave her an open view of Emily at the bottom of the hill. She turned her head uphill and pushed Bobby forward. They continued up the hill and only had two more issues. She got her leg caught in a vine and tripped, sending both of them to the forest floor. After struggling with Bobby's rebellious limp body, she was able to continue moving. Once they were close to the top, they had another dead leaf slide, but only lost a bit of momentum. Bobby knew she was determined to get him to the top of the hill and would not leave him behind, no matter how difficult he made the situation.

Don't leave me. Don't let her take you away.

They stopped at the edge of the forest where the cul-de-sac began. Both of them started to walk toward the house. Now that they were on stable, even ground, Bobby was able to help Danielle a little more, and they made better time to the house.

She dropped Bobby into the passenger seat of her car and leaned with her head on the doorsill to catch her breath. After she had regained some of her strength, she looked between her arms at Bobby.

He leaned back in the seat and stared at her. Their eyes met, and he could tell she felt pity for him, but there was some other emotion he could not determine.

"I'm taking you to my apartment. You can stay there tonight, so I can keep an eye on you and make sure you're eating and drinking. I'm going in your house to get some clothes and other things for you. Promise me you will stay here and not try to leave. I can't carry you back up that hill."

"I promise," he said with extra effort.

She closed his door and walked up the steps to his house.

Don't let her do it. That bitch is trying to separate us, and you are letting her do it. Get out of the car and come back to me, my love. She won't be as good for you as I am.

Bobby drifted to sleep.

The car jerked into its assigned parking spot. The abrupt stop woke Bobby up enough not to be a complete hindrance as Danielle helped him inside her apartment.

Once inside, the scent of a fresh apple pie greeted him.

"Mmm, pie."

"Sorry, no pie. It's just a candle I left burning, like an idiot. Before you do anything, you have to take a shower."

She led him to the bathroom and started the water for him. He swayed back and forth on rubber legs. She grabbed the bottom of his shirt and helped pull it over his head. It felt more like peeling the label off an old beer bottle. Without too much fuss, she was able to get the whole thing off and throw it on the floor. Bobby only smiled. She stared at him with a contemplating look that said she didn't know what she should do next. The hot water steamed the mirror. She grabbed his belt buckle and pulled him to her and looked into his delirious eyes. This was not how he had expected this moment to go. She fought with the buckle before finally getting the better of it and slowly released the tension on the belt. As his pants slid to the floor, Bobby's eyes lit up. He looked down and pulled his pants up quickly.

"Ah. She was right. You are trying to take advantage of me."

Blood rushed to Danielle's cheeks, painting them dark red like she had been laughing for too long.

"Bobby, don't be ridiculous. I was only trying to help you into the shower. You are nasty and sick. I'm not letting you in my bed like that."

"Your bed? I see."

"Yeah my bed, but it's early so I'm not going to bed now and when I do, I'll sleep on the couch."

"Mmhmm. Likely story."

"Okay, you've put me through enough for one day. I'm going in the other room. You can try to finish up here."

Danielle walked into the hallway and grabbed the doorknob.

"Remember," he said. "You promised you weren't going to call anybody."

"I remember," she said, and closed the door.

Bobby stood and let the water hit him in the face and run down the rest of his body. His throat felt raw and hurt. He opened his mouth and drank water from the showerhead. He greedily lapped at the water until he had too much and coughed. The cough doubled him over and he threw up. The warm water poured from his mouth and joined the black streams as they flowed down the drain.

Danielle beat on the door.

"Bobby. Are you okay? Why did you lock the door?"

"I'm fine," he choked out.

He didn't remember locking the door. Emily must have wanted him to do it. That way the other woman would not try to join him in the shower. Until that moment, Bobby hadn't realized he was no longer hearing Emily speak to him. He became weak in the legs, and his knees buckled. She thought he left her there alone and wasn't going to talk to him anymore. Was she mad at him for coming home with Danielle? He hadn't really had a choice. Perhaps he was just too far away from her. He would have to get back to her as soon as he could so she would not worry too much. That had to be the reason. She saw how Danielle dragged him out of the forest. He was too weak to do anything. He had to go. Danielle would never let him leave until he had some rest. As he turned off the shower, he decided it would be best to play along with Danielle until he could find a way to sneak home. She promised not to tell anybody. He believed she would keep her promise as long as he played along with her.

He opened the door, and Danielle jumped off the sofa.

"How do you feel?"

"I feel a little better. I think I just need to lie down for a while."

"You sure you don't want to eat something first? You need to drink some water."

"I just had some. I'll be fine, but thank you."

"If you say so. You can go sleep in my bed and I'll be in here if you need anything."

"Thank you," he said, and walked to the bedroom.

The satin sheets felt cool and soft against his tired body. He closed his eyes and fell into a deep sleep.

Bobby awoke when Danielle came to check on him. She walked to the bed and felt his head. He felt normal. She put a glass of water on the nightstand and climbed into bed with him. She wrapped her arms around him and fell asleep. Bobby laid staring at the ceiling.

Chapter Five

Wake up. Wake up, my love. Just lie there and listen to me. Don't try to get up yet. You might wake her. I can't believe she would wait until you were asleep and jump into bed with you. Does she have no decency? She's trying to take you away from me. I know you were worried that I was mad at you and went away. That will never happen. I saw that woman force you to leave me. You wanted to stay with me by our tree, but she made you leave.

Don't worry, my love, I saw her drag you up the hill while you tried to fight against her, but she was too strong. Now that you have rested, she won't be able to stop you so easily. She doesn't know what's best for you. Only I know what you need. I know it's not your fault. I am still with you. I just had to find you again. And now that I have you, I promise you; they will never tear us apart again. But, before we are together again, I need you to do something for me. I don't have too much longer where I am.

She's going to end up telling somebody where I am hiding, or I'm going to wither away, and there will be nothing left of me. Then I won't be able to talk to you. Very soon I am going to need a new place to live. I am not picky about what the outside looks like. The only thing that matters is what's on the inside, and I will be on the inside waiting for you. This is the only way we will be able to stay together.

Now, get up, but don't wake her, or she'll try to stop you.

Good, now don't come to the woods. I need you to start looking for a new place immediately before it is too late and I never see you again. Leave her where she is. Don't worry about her.

Walk. Yes, help me, my love. We will be together again soon.

Chapter Six

She ran through the woods, trying to catch up with Bobby. He was too fast for her. He knew all the trails in the forest and could move without tripping or stopping to see where he was going. Danielle called out to him, but couldn't understand her own words. They were soft and hollow. They echoed and reverberated around her. He ignored her and continued to run.

She pushed herself to run faster and tripped over a heavily rooted vine and fell into a bush full of briars. She put her hands in front of her to brace for impact and screamed as the thorns tore into her flesh. The tangle of thorns dug deeper into her soft palms the more she tried to climb out. She yelled in frustration and snatched her head back. The vines pulled and twisted around her hair. The skeletal branches released her head and left a clump of hair swaying from the mocking bush. She called out for Bobby to help, but her voice sounded as muffled as before. She pushed herself up and pulled her foot loose from the twisted vine and lost her shoe in the process. Searching for the shoe wasted her precious time in catching him before he disappeared. She resided to leaving it behind and ran to catch up with Bobby. When she finally caught up with him, he stood in a clearing in the woods. Her foot throbbed from stepping on jagged stones and piercing thorns.

His back was to her, and he was bent down over something, but she couldn't tell what it was. She heard low murmuring, but couldn't make out what he was saying. What *they* were saying? Who was he talking to?

She crept closer to Bobby, and he turned to face her. Red lipstick smeared across his lips and down his chin. His eyes were solid black orbs. Every muscle in her body went numb. He moved toward her, and she saw he had been kissing the girl he found in the woods. Emily.

She was in a further state of decomposition. The skin on the left side of her face was missing. Dehydration pulled the remaining skin tight against her skull. Emily's teeth peeked through the shredded flesh of her cheek.

The teeth ground together, rippling the remaining strands of flesh. She was seeing things, but then the head slowly turned. The pallid face looked her over, but the eyes were no longer in the sockets. Only black holes watched her. Bobby turned back to face the thing on the ground. Emily's arm resting in her lap twitched and then rose.

The index and middle finger were missing from the right hand, so the girl pointed at Danielle with the ring finger. Bobby turned, and a loud screech came from the dead girl. Bobby laughed and moved toward Danielle.

When she tried to flee, low hanging vines fought to keep her in the dark. She grabbed the vines and pulled them from the trees. Danielle ran, not daring to look back. She was afraid she would see Bobby about to grab her. His haunting black eyes would swallow her in their whirlpool of darkness, and she would be theirs.

She ran until she could no longer move forward. Her foot and side hurt her too much to keep going. Bobby was nowhere in sight. She must have lost him, or he gave up trying to catch her. With hands on her knees, she tried to focus her breathing. She stood with her hands on her hips and breathed in the cool fresh air and tried to decide which way she should go. As she watched the leaves fall from the tall oak trees, the crisp air changed direction. The dry dew scent of the afternoon sun pounding on the pine trees no longer swarmed around her head. The smell of death and decay floated on the breeze, and it headed directly to her like it had followed her through the forest. She knew she needed to run again, but before she made her first step forward, Emily's pale, white, skeletal hand fell on her shoulder.

Danielle awoke screaming. She had been startled awake by the cold, boney fingers when they wrapped around her shoulder and pierced through her soft skin. Looking at the alarm clock, she wiped the sweat from her forehead and neck. It was midnight. She rolled over to wrap her arm around Bobby, but all she found were the cool sheets. She ran her hand across the sheets like she had made an error and was trying to erase it. He had to be there, and her nightmare-fueled brain was playing tricks on her. Numbing panic filled her body. The room provided no answers to help locate him. She jumped out of the bed, and a single second of clarity hit her. The bathroom. He was in the bathroom, and she would feel silly for freaking out.

She knocked softly on the door so he wouldn't think she was freaking out because she couldn't find him. When there was no answer, she knocked harder and then tried the knob. The unlocked door gave and opened to a vacant bathroom. She ran back to the hall and burst into the spare bedroom. Bobby wasn't in there either. Shaking, she walked back into the hallway and toward the front of the apartment where the living room and kitchen were.

He was in the kitchen. He woke up thirsty. When she found him, he had been dehydrated. That wasn't something he could easily get over. The hospital would have been a better place to take him instead of her apartment. But Bobby would never have agreed to go there. They would ask too many questions and he would be afraid she'd tell somebody about the girl in the woods, which she needed to do as soon as possible. Handling one issue at a time proved to be harder than she thought it would be.

This was all crazy talk. He just needed something else to drink and had not seen the glass of water she left for him. Sure. That made sense. She was overreacting.

As she moved down the hallway, a cool breeze wafted through the apartment and swirled through her hair. She turned the corner. The front door was wide open. Bobby was gone.

Chapter Seven

Detective Gregory Burns arrived at the house on Red Rock Court to a flood of churning lights. The pre-dawn morning helped the lights to bounce off every dark surface. He hated pulling up to a crime scene like this. The light hurt his eyes, and he felt like they were burning deep into his brain. All the fluorescent lighting at the crime scene would have a cobalt hue long after the flashing lights were out of sight. He got out of his car and surveyed the blue street. It didn't look like the media had arrived yet, but they would be there soon enough. The neighbors were beginning to crowd around the driveway.

A car pulled up behind him. He turned only to have the headlights blind him. The driver left them turned on, and a feminine silhouette stepped from the car and flanked the blaring light.

"Detective Burns. Can you tell me what's going on here? I heard there was a murder. A single, white, female. Can you confirm this?"

He knew the voice. He had heard it at so many crime scenes that he thought he could pick her voice out of a crowd before he could recognize his wife's. Morgan Cramer was a crime reporter for the Crystal Valley Times. The newspaper industry was going downhill, but the Times had managed to create a strong Internet presence. They still released a printed version every day, but had outsourced to another newspaper's print shop. The outsourcing of local jobs had given the Times a bad rap as they closed their downtown shop, but people still wanted their local news, so the impact had been minimal.

Greg got to know Morgan better when he worked on her sister's case. Her twin sister, Amanda, had been raped and tortured before her body turned up in Lake Oliver, across town from where she lived. He never solved Amanda's case, and now Morgan hounded him for information on all the cases he worked. He thought she did it because she thought he owed her for not finding her sister's killer. In a twisted way, he kind of thought he owed her too.

"Look, Morgan, I just got out of my car. At this point, it sounds like you know more than I do. But, as soon as we have any information, I'm sure somebody will leak it to you at the appropriate time."

He left her at the curb, fidgeting with her voice recorder. She didn't deserve to be treated that way. He felt bad about it and would make it up to her later. He ducked under the low-hanging branch of an aging oak tree.

"Get a perimeter set up," he yelled at the stationary police.

Greg walked across the front yard and into the garage. He ran his hand over the hood of the car. It was still warm.

"Good morning, Mark."

Mark Harper looked up from the body on the driver's side of the car.

"You're going to contaminate your own crime scene, Detective," Mark said, and snapped on latex gloves.

"Nah, it doesn't matter. They'd never leave any evidence on the hood, would they?"

"I'm not going to try and tell you how do to do your job, Detective, it would just seem—"

"Well, that's a good thing for both us. Cause if you thought you could do my job, well you wouldn't be the one in the car with the dead girl, and I'd be out of a job. Of course, they also wouldn't have woken me up so early this morning, so there is that."

"It would just seem like it would be easier if your fingerprints weren't on everything too," Mark said.

Greg extended his hand to the annoyed technician. Mark grabbed the plastic bag off the dash and handed it to him. Through the plastic bag, he could see a folded piece of paper with writing on it. He took the letter out of the bag and cleared his throat.

"*What is a few short years to live in hell when that is all I get around here?*" He read aloud. "That's an interesting way of looking at things. Signed, what is that? Maybe an N? What's the woman's name?"

Mark took a deep breath and let it out slowly. He was already reaching his limit with Greg, and he'd just gotten here. Greg grinned and extended on his tiptoes. Maybe waking up this early had its benefits.

"Rachel Martin."

"Doesn't look like it's one of her initials then."

"Unless it's her middle initial," Mark quipped.

"Yeah, there's always that. So, what can you tell me about how she died?"

"I can tell you it's definitely not a suicide. Full rigor hasn't set in, so I'd say she's been dead three or four hours at the most. Her roommate came home this morning and found her in the car with the engine running and the garage door closed."

Greg put his hands on the roof of the car and ducked his head through the open driver's side window.

"If everything looks like a suicide, how do you know it definitely wasn't one?"

"Because she has a wound to the back of her skull. She suffered a blow from something with a sharp edge, but I haven't been able to find anything that could have done the damage. The killer may have taken it with him. It's hard to tell if it was the blow she took or if the fumes finished her off. You'll have to wait until I get her back to the lab before I know which one actually killed her. But if I had to guess, I'd say it was the blow to the head. It's a pretty nasty wound."

Greg knew Mark liked for it to be quiet while he worked, so he walked around the car and looked over Mark's shoulder. The back of Mark's neck turned blood red as Greg scratched lines in his notebook and hmmed a lot.

"Don's inside with the roommate if you want to see what he has."

Normally Greg would have hung around to bother Mark a little more, but it was too early. There would also be a lot of pressure to solve this case in a hurry. They wouldn't want the city to panic because somebody found a girl with her head bashed in and made it look like a suicide. He went through the garage door that led into the kitchen and found his partner, Don Murphy.

Don looked ragged and tired, the gray and black stubble on his face made him look older than his forty-two years. He was still Greg's senior by seven years, but times like this caused the emotions of Greg's previous cases to reveal themselves, and he felt like the oldest one there.

Don empathetically put his hand on the roommate's shoulder. The act was a melancholic Norman Rockwell painting showing true life. Don was always better at that part than Greg. He was glad Don beat him to the scene. That way he got to talk to her first. Greg didn't want to talk to her at all if he didn't have to. Dealing with emotional people was not Greg's skill set. He was better when following the evidence to a logical conclusion. Don noticed Greg sulking in the doorway and gave one last reassuring pat on the crying woman's shoulder and walked over to Greg.

"What did Mark say?"

"I don't know. Something about not being a morning person."

Don huffed.

"Look. We all know he's the one that went to the captain, but you still have to work with the guy. He's the last one you want to be goofing off around. The more ammunition you give him, the steadier his aim will be."

"Aw, don't worry about me. I'm not goofing off. I'm serious at all times," Greg said, trying to hide a smile.

Mark Harper had it in for him since they first met. He didn't like Greg, and he didn't care who knew. He had gone to Greg's superiors on multiple occasions because *their detective* wasn't conducting himself in a professional manner. Mark told them Greg played around too much and was never serious. Greg wasn't trying to cause a scene or make light of the situations. He was only trying to keep the mood light. He could see it on everybody's face, including his when he dared to look in the mirror. The job was getting to them. Too many officers ended up turning their guns on themselves because of the job, and he didn't want anybody he knew to be another statistic. Including Mark.

As far as Mark knew, the upper brass had not said anything to him, and that was the way Greg wanted to keep it. If he thought nothing was being said, maybe he would let it go and find somebody else to worry about. He didn't think he went too far. It's not like he had ever picked up a victim's hand and done a shadow puppet show or anything morbid like that.

Both detectives noticed Rachel's roommate watching them, black tears running down her face, longing to understand, to know why this happened to her friend. The two detectives paused and slid into the living room so she couldn't hear what they had to say. She did not follow.

"He said that he definitely doesn't think it's a suicide. We'd have to wait for the ME's report to find out the actual cause of death, but he thinks it was the trauma she sustained to the back of the head and not from the exhaust fumes. He also said she's been dead for three or four hours."

Don stared at the wall like he was watching the roommate. It was another demonstration of his empathy. Looking for the hurting person he was speaking about. If it had been any other detective, Greg would be suspicious of the actions, but Don was the sincerest person he knew.

"The roommate didn't miss the killer by much. No signs of forced entry. Maybe she knew her killer?"

"Maybe. Do you have the girl's ID?"

"No, it wasn't in her purse."

"The killer may have taken it for some reason. You done with the girl?" Greg asked.

"Yeah, I've gotten all that I'm probably going to get from her right now. She's had a rough time. She and the victim knew each other since third grade, so they were pretty close."

Greg made a lap through the rest of the house before heading back into the kitchen. Only Rachel's bed looked like somebody had slept in it. The roommate worked the night shift. She was still sitting at the table when Greg walked into the room.

"Ms.—?"

"Jessica. I already told the other detective all I know. I'm sorry."

"Jessica, my name is Greg Burns. I only have two questions he didn't ask, and then I will leave you alone, I promise, okay? What was Rachel's middle name?"

"It's Marie. But I don't see the point in knowing that."

"Ah, just a routine question. Have you heard her talk about anybody or do you know anybody whose initial is an N?"

"No, not that I can think of. Is that another routine question?"

"Nah, sometimes it's another letter," he said. "Here's my card. If you happen to think of somebody or anything else, give me a call."

The girl nodded, and Greg walked back into the garage. The crime lab was still in the process of going over the scene. They brought in floodlights to provide more light, but they were attracting moths and various flying insects. Their shadows looked like bats as they swooped through the garage. At times they blocked the entire light until they fluttered off.

In the kaleidoscopic light, Greg saw an ashtray on a small table beside the sensors that kept the garage door from coming down and crushing whatever happened to be in its way. He picked up the ashtray. It was a rough cut square made out of heavy glass. An ash smeared smiley face stared up at him from the bottom. One of the corners had pieces of skull and hair embedded in blood. He took a few slow practice swings and noticed Don watching him. He smiled and slid the ashtray into the evidence bag Don held open for him. Greg walked into the cool morning breeze. The sun was just beginning to rise, and it was already a hot day.

The usual suspects were all standing behind the barricade. The media crying out for his attention, so they could get the scoop on everybody else. The curious neighbors looking on horrified and telling each other 'she was such a sweet girl,' and 'would help anybody if they asked her.' Then there were the people who lived on the various streets in the neighborhood, who woke up with an early morning phone call to tell them something 'they just had to hear.'

Greg put a cigarette in his mouth and stared lazily into the glowing flame of his lighter. He lit the cigarette and scanned the surrounding cars, looking for his target. Mark Harper stood beside his old government sedan. He was talking to an assistant with his back to the house. Greg walked up behind him and dropped the heavy bag onto the hood of the car.

"Found it."

Mark jumped and covered his head.

"What the hell? What is wrong with you?"

"Who knows? Maybe I'm just a little overzealous. But I thought you would want to know that I found the murder weapon," Greg said, and let smoke slip between his lips.

"Your behavior is highly unprofessional."

"Possibly, but it is also highly efficient. Not only was I able to find the murder weapon that you guys overlooked. I also was able to piss you off for no reason, and it only took like ten minutes."

Greg turned and walked back to the garage.

"Oh yeah, her middle initial is not N, it's M."

Mark didn't reply, and Greg looked back. The young assistant grinned, but Mark stared with a blank face. Greg imagined Mark hiding his hand behind his clipboard and giving him the finger, but that would be *highly unprofessional* and Mark would never do anything like that.

"I don't know why you antagonize that guy," Don said.

"Neither do I. It's a compulsion."

The truth was, he hated the guy. If he were straight out mean to him, Mark would go to the captain and complain about bullying, and Greg would get in trouble. They'd probably write him up. The department started to crack down on that a few years ago when the hazing of a rookie went a little too far.

They were doing home breach drills. The rookie was the first one through the door. The officers who were with him backed away and let him enter the room alone, and the superior officers lying in wait opened fire with multiple beanbag rounds. He was wearing protective gear, but many of the bags hit unprotected areas, leaving large bruises and torn skin. The whole incident was recorded. Laughing could be heard in the background. Somebody was also heard yelling "Damn, he's taking it just like RoboCop."

The lieutenant was fired, and everybody else involved were disciplined. Greg wasn't doing anything like that, though he wouldn't mind taking a shot at Mark with a beanbag-loaded shotgun. He was only being mildly aggravating to him, and they hadn't outlawed being a smartass. Yet.

"Anyway, the only other thing I have is the suicide note. I asked her roommate, and she doesn't know anybody with that initial," Greg said.

Don held the bag containing the letter up to the light.

"I don't know. Are we sure it's an N? The ends on both sides are extended further than normal. Maybe it's a red lightning bolt or something."

"Maybe," Greg said. "But we're pretty much done here for now, and I have a breakfast date with a six-year-old that I'm going to be late for. I'll catch up with you at the office after I drop her off at school."

"Here, take these. I made a copy of my notes for you," Don said, and thrust the pieces of paper into Greg's hand.

Chapter Eight

Excitement greeted Greg as he walked through the door. At least somebody was happy to see him.

"Daddy's home," the little girl squealed. "Where have you been?"

"Hey, Monkey," he said, and kissed the girl on her head. "I know I'm late for breakfast, but at least I'm still here to take you to school. Right?"

"I guess so," she said, and crinkled her nose at him.

"I had to go to work very early this morning, and they wanted me to stay longer, but I told them nope. I've got somewhere very important I have to be," he said to the little girl's delight.

"Daddy? Did somebody die? Is that why you had to go to work?"

"Uh. Well, Hope, honey, I ... uh ..."

"How're you going to answer that one, Greg?" his wife asked, walking into the kitchen.

He always tried to keep the details of his job away from his daughter. He didn't want it to scar her. And if she ever did end up on a shrink's sofa, he didn't want to be the main reason, at least not because of his job, anyway. He was doing a good job of it until two months ago when Hope went into his office. She pulled out crime scene photos from Amanda Cramer's rape and murder. Amanda's case remained unsolved, so he kept the case file on his desk. It was easier to forget the case if they were closed in a dark filing cabinet, but if he had to look at the file every day, it would remind him he didn't always get it right. A lot of sleepless nights were spent in his office pouring over the evidence and witness statements in hopes he would find the missing piece.

He never thought his daughter would go in there when he wasn't home. But she did. She also scattered the pictures everywhere. It looked like she was trying to lay out the photos in order, like she was helping Greg solve the case. His wife, Shelly, was furious. She yelled for a long time. After a while, Greg had to force himself to continue paying attention to what she was saying. She said the pictures had traumatized their daughter for life. Greg thought they had probably messed his wife up far more than his daughter would ever be. Since that day, Hope would ask if somebody died when Greg had to go to work. In the end, Greg installed a lock on the door and didn't tell anybody where he hid the spare key.

"Hope, just because Daddy goes to work doesn't mean that somebody died. Sometimes people just need help."

"If you say so."

"Just go get your stuff for school, so you're not late."

His wife gave him an exasperated look, threw up her hands and walked out of the room to check on their younger son, Jared.

"That's the truth," he yelled after her and laughed. "Well maybe not."

Greg drove to the school with the dispatch radio turned off. They would not like it if they found out he was on duty and had it turned off, but he didn't care. He enjoyed Hope's angelic voice serenading him all the way to school. He didn't know any of the songs she sang, and it didn't matter to him. Shelly made him a CD with all of her favorite songs on it and he played it anytime they were in the car together. The song finished when it was their turn in line for Hope to get out of the car.

"Bye, Daddy."

"Bye, Angel. Remember, don't talk to strangers, say no to drugs and stay in school."

She laughed at him. "Love you."

"Love you too, baby. I'll see you later tonight."

After the early morning wake up call, Greg was tired. He didn't feel like going into the office and dealing with everybody. He decided to go back to his house and work on the case from his home office. His wife and son would be gone for most of the day and wouldn't be back until it was time to pick Hope up from school.

No matter how many times he tried, he was unable to concentrate on his notes. After staring at them for a little while, he got up and walked around the house. Not looking for inspiration, looking for something to distract him long enough to think about the case. He always got antsy when he started a new case like this. He had to get in the right frame of mind so that he could do his best work.

* * *

The ring from an old rotary phone woke him up from his nap. The loud ear-piercing bells almost made him flip over backward in his chair. He was sleeping hard, kicked back in his chair with his feet propped up on the desk.

"Hello. Detective Burns."

"Greg, where have you been all day? I've tried to get you on the radio in your car and called your phone earlier."

"Oh, I have been working from home today."

It was Don Murphy. Greg looked around his office for the alarm clock he set in case he fell asleep. The digital read out blinked 12:00. The power must have gone out at some point. He looked out the window, but it didn't look like it rained, let alone stormed.

"We got the ME's report back. It looks like the cause of death was the blow she took to the back of the head with that ashtray you found. No sign of exhaust in her lungs. She was already dead when the killer started the car."

"Okay. I'm on my way in."

"Nah, don't worry about it. Just go back to sleep," Don said, and hung up the phone.

Greg walked around the house, trying to wake himself up. He didn't know what had come over him. The battery operated clock on the kitchen wall read 6:00. Where were Shelly and the kids? His cell phone rang in his office. It was probably Shelly letting him know they went back to her parent's house. Before he got back to the desk, the phone had stopped ringing. He picked it up and looked at the number. It looked familiar, but he didn't remember where from.

53

While he was looking at the phone, it began to ring again. It was the same number.

"Detective Burns," he answered.

Nobody replied. He could only hear the faint breathing of the person on the other end. This was his work phone. Only people in the department and people from the cases he worked on would have the number. Somebody may be in trouble, he thought.

"Hello. Are you there? Is everything okay?"

"Hello. Is this detective Gregory Burns of the Crystal Valley homicide unit?" the slow drawn out voice asked.

"Yes. Is there something I can help you with?"

"I would like to turn myself in for the murder of Rachel Martin."

Greg calmly grabbed a notebook. There were plenty of times a person tried to turn themselves in for a crime they didn't commit. Most of the time the only thing they knew about the murder was that one had taken place. He wasn't going to get his hopes up, plus how did this guy get his number? It was probably one of the guys at the station messing with him because they found out he was sleeping on the job, again.

"Is this Dave? You guys aren't screwing with me, are you?"

"I assure you that I'm not Dave, nor am I screwing with you."

The guy, who was not Dave, sounded calm and relaxed. It was a bit eerie. A cold chill slithered its way up Greg's spine.

"Okay. First, tell me your name, and then we can meet at the precinct, and we can go from there."

There was a long pause. Greg thought the person hung up. Then he heard a slow guttural laugh that rose in pitch and ferocity burst through the phone. The laugh verged on hysterics.

"Wow. I can't believe you thought I would just turn myself in like that. Are you crazy? Those monsters in prison would kill me. I don't want to die."

The voice changed.

At first, the caller sounded afraid to speak, but he quickly gained the nerve to be assertive when he spoke. He now had the sarcastic, condescending tone of a person attempting to sound like they are from a higher social class. Greg couldn't tell if the guy was trying to sound like that or not. It could still be one of the guys screwing with him or somebody faking, but he didn't think so. He still had to play it like he didn't believe him.

"Yeah, that's a good one, but I have real police work to do now, so—"

"One joke and you're ready to hang up. I thought you'd be a better sport than that."

"Who is this?"

Greg sat down on the edge of his chair. The only way he'd know for certain would be if this guy would tell him something only he and the police knew about the crime.

"I can't just tell you who I am. That would take all the fun out of it for you."

The caller wanted to play games, but Greg thought of every case as a game between him and the killer. Greg was ready to play.

"I don't believe you're who you say you are. I don't want to waste my time with you when I should be looking for the real killer."

"Don't believe me? Okay, let's see, what can I tell you that will change your mind?"

"It'll have to be something good if you want to convince me."

"How about this? She was asleep when I got there."

Greg felt like hanging up. This moron was jerking his chain and wasn't even being creative about it.

"Yeah, it was after two in the morning, so that's a sound guess."

"But Detective, you didn't let me finish. She was asleep, but I got in without it looking like somebody had broken in because she left the door unlocked."

The suspect not entering the house by force hadn't been released, but it was still sketchy. That could be a lucky guess.

"Well, there you have it. I guess it really is you."

"Don't patronize me, Detective. If she hadn't left it unlocked, I would have simply gone somewhere else. Her door was not the first one I checked that night."

"How chivalrous of you."

"There you go with that tone again. How about this? I walked into the house, and then turned on the light in the kitchen. It is the room to the right off the living room. I threw some pots and pans against the wall. Those were no signs of a struggle. The bedrooms are to the left off the living room. Rachel came stumbling out of her room, calling out for her roommate Jessica. She went into the kitchen, and I bashed her in the head with an ashtray I found on the front porch. And, well, you know the rest of the story, Detective."

Greg fell back in his chair. This was the guy they were looking for. They would never release the murder weapon in a briefing. And he knew too much about the crime scene to be one of Greg's friends who weren't on the case. He also knew the layout of the house and the way he described the events made more sense than anything they had come up with so far.

"Detective? Are you there?"

"Yeah, yeah, I'm here. Just going over a few things in my mind."

"Oh, like how did I get your number?"

"For starters, yeah."

"Jessica left your card on the kitchen table. When she left to go to her mother's house, I got it."

He was watching the whole time. Was he in the crowd behind the barriers while he and Don were in the house? Or was he hiding in the woods just waiting for them to leave so he could go back into the house? He could have killed Jessica while she waited on her parents. Why didn't he?

"I also know that guy Mark hates you. It's so easy to tell. And your partner, Don, acts like he's your babysitter, but he also looks like he does most of the work too, so I guess that makes sense."

If he could tell their work dynamic, then he was a lot closer than the street. There was no reason to search pictures of the crowd for his face. He was amongst them in the house. Greg didn't know all the techs well, but he worked with them for years. He didn't think it could be one of them. Certainly not Don. He didn't recognize the voice at all.

"I stumped you on that one, didn't I, Detective?"

"You sure do seem confident with how you think we work with each other. Like you were one of us or something."

Greg didn't think he'd come out and say he worked with them, but it was worth a shot.

"I listen to people and watch how they interact with one another all day long. It's one of the hazards of my job."

"Sounds strenuous. How did you hear us?"

"Oh. I was in the attic. I was right above your heads the entire time. I could hear everything."

The gravity of what the guy on the other end of the phone said settled heavily on Greg's chest. He felt short of breath. This guy could have taken out any number of the people at the house at any time, and they wouldn't have seen him coming. They didn't check the attic. There was no reason to. Most killers don't want to get caught. They get the hell out of the area and avoid cops. They don't call them and have a conversation with them. Greg knew this guy was going to kill again. There was no other reason for him to call and gloat unless he wanted the police to know he was going to kill again, and they couldn't do anything about it. He needed to talk him out of it or get him to slip up and let him know who he was.

"I must confess, Detective. I did not fully think that one through."

"Why's that? Because we could have heard you?"

"No, I wasn't worried about that. The fumes got pretty bad up there too. Apparently, there was an opening to the attic somewhere. Luckily for me, Jessica came home. She kept screaming. I almost yelled for her to turn the damn car off, but she finally did it after she started coughing."

"Yeah, lucky for you she came home."

"Otherwise, you would have found another body when I started to stink."

"Why didn't you kill the roommate?"

"I already accomplished what I went there to do. There was no reason to kill her. But I will say she was much easier on the eyes. I kind of wish she would have been home instead of Rachel. She would have been a nicer vessel."

"What do you mean vessel?"

"Ah, it's nothing. I should really be going now. I'm pretty tired. Don't worry. I will talk to you again soon," he said, and hung up the phone.

Greg sat back in his chair. What did he mean by vessel? He was definitely the guy who killed Rachel Martin, but he didn't say anything that Greg thought was a clue to who he was or why he did it. He didn't block the number he called from, so it was probably somebody else's. The number looked familiar to Greg, and he searched the notes Don had given him before he left this morning. There it was, at the top of the second page of neatly written notes, the phone number and a name. The number belonged to Jessica Duvall. Greg had to get back to that house and make sure the killer was not still there and hadn't done anything to Jessica. He grabbed his keys and ran out the door.

Chapter Nine

Greg pulled into the driveway of the house Rachel Martin and Jessica Duvall once shared. It looked alive in the morning's rising sun. Now the fading sunlight cast a shadow on the front of the house and half of the yard. He walked around to the back of the house. Everything looked normal. He walked back around to the front and saw two neighbors standing at the end of the driveway watching him. He flashed his badge, and they quickly turned like they weren't the least bit interested in what was going on at the house now.

Greg stepped on the front porch and saw a small dustless square on the glass end table. A large X made of police caution tape covered the door. It occurred to him that he came all the way out here and he didn't have the keys. He would need to go downtown and get them. That round trip would take him at least an hour if he didn't get caught in heavy traffic on the streets or in the office. He could ask Don to bring him the keys, but he didn't think he was Don's favorite person right now. Don would also want to know why he wanted to go back over the scene and would want to tag along. Greg didn't want him in the middle of everything. He wanted to do this on his own. He had already screwed up earlier. Plus, he didn't want anybody to know the killer called him. That would start a whole stack of paperwork, and they would interrogate him like any other witness. No, he didn't want to go through all of that. He should probably just come back tomorrow after he went into work. He could grab the keys, and nobody would ever know the difference. If he left now, he might get lucky and Shelly would already have dinner cooking for him. He was about to turn to leave when he tried the knob, and the door squeaked open.

If she hadn't left it unlocked, I would have simply gone somewhere else.

Greg pulled down the tape and walked into the living room. He felt along the wall until he found the light switch. The room looked the same as it did earlier that morning. He walked into the kitchen. Somebody had picked up the pots and pans. They were now in the sink, along with a bowl that still had the last bit of milk in it. The spoon was missing. Did Jessica make some cereal before she left with whoever picked her up? Highly unlikely, she won't be eating regularly for a few days. Someone also tried to clean up the blood on the floor. It looked like they started and gave up when the blood smeared all over the place. That was probably Jessica.

Upset and tired of being idle, Jessica had probably started to clean her friend's blood, but she didn't have enough paper towels or willpower. Instead, she sat against the wall crying until her parents got here.

Was he in the attic the whole time? Did the sick bastard listen while Jessica moved from room to room questioning everything? Did he take a sick satisfaction in hearing her cries?

Greg walked into the garage. The car sat covered in fingerprint dust like an old forgotten relic in a longstanding grimy barn. He turned on the lights and looked for the attic entrance. The pull cord was on the right side of the two-car garage. Nothing would have been in his way to pull down the ladder, but how did he get it to go back up?

Greg dragged the folded ladder down by the cable. He turned on his flashlight and climbed the protesting rungs. He thought about identifying himself before ascending into the attic and thought better of it. There wasn't anybody in the attic, though. There may never have been anybody up here at all. He poked his head through the opening and shined the light around. Old boxes cluttered the attic entrance. They probably belonged to the owners of the house and not the renters. Greg stepped on something soft, and a loud squeak echoed through the empty attic. He jumped back and almost stepped off the platform. One more foot and we would have fallen through the ceiling. It would have been fun explaining that one. He shined the light at his foot and saw what looked like an old dog toy. Beside it lay another stuffed animal; he followed the trail of scattered animals. It looked like the Ark ran aground. Greg avoided cobwebs and ducked below joists to get to the edge of the platform. There, a flattened box hung over the edge and looked like it might be used to extend the floor further over the insulation.

Greg lay down on top of the box and crawled to the edge. Here a lot of the insulation had been pulled out of the way. He shined his light on the area in front of him. There was an air vent with the directional blades removed.

The son of a bitch laid right here and heard everything.

Greg got to his feet and looked across the attic floor. Somebody removed the ductwork from a number of the other vents as well. He bet one was the kitchen and the other was the living room. There was something different about the vent in the garage. There was no ductwork around it. Most garages were not heated or cooled. The killer would have had to cut a hole in the ceiling and put the vent up to make it look like it was real.

Must have been a leak. Yeah, he created the leak.

He let the attic door slam and walked around the car. Everything in the garage looked normal except for the vent. It was right before the door leading into the kitchen. Now that he saw it, he could tell it looked out of place. The corners were not flush against the ceiling. It looked like it was about to fall. If the vent had fallen, this would be over, and Greg would be at home with his family. A broom stood propped against the wall in the corner of the garage. White dust covered the tips of its bristles. Greg moved the broom and behind it was a small pile of white powder from the sheetrock. He cleaned up his mess. If anybody even noticed the broom, they would have thought one of the girls were cleaning recently. Maybe he's not as crazy as he seems. He acts like he is highly functional and is careful not to get caught.

The glass on the counter grabbed his attention when he walked back into the kitchen. He didn't remember it sitting by the sink when he went into the garage. Maybe he overlooked it like the air vent. It was probably there the whole time. He stiffened and listened, but the only thing he heard was the ring of silence. He grabbed the glass and felt the cold water. The condensation covered glass slid through his hand and he drew his weapon. The killer was still in the house. Greg walked into the living room gun first. He looked out both doors, but couldn't see anything now that the sun was down.

Rachel's room was dark and cool. When he was in the attic, it looked like the rooms at this end of the house still had their ductwork attached. The killer only wanted to see the police working in the crime area. Greg and Don hadn't spent a lot of time in either of the girls' room. He flipped on the lights. The room looked the same as it had earlier today—clean and organized. The only thing in disarray was Rachel's bed, but according to the killer, she had been asleep when he came in. This is what her bed looked like the last night she left it. Jessica's room was also clean and in order. Her bed also looked like somebody slept in it, except when Greg made a sweep of the house earlier today, her bed was made. She was at work when the murder occurred. He didn't think that Jessica would have come back here and gone to sleep after the police left. She would have been too scared to close her eyes for any amount of time while her friend's murderer was still running loose.

A door slammed against a wall, and Greg snapped to attention. He pointed his gun at the bedroom door, but nobody came. Slowly, he crept around the corner into the small hallway. He spun into the bathroom, but it was empty. The light was still on in Rachel's room. He lunged through the door with the same results.

The call and response melody of creek frogs greeted him when he walked back into the living room. The back door stood wide open. He hurried to the door, but couldn't see anything in the dark. He made one sweeping pass around the backyard with his flashlight. Whoever was in the house with him had already left. When he closed the back door, a piece of white paper fluttered against the glass. In chaotically scrawled letters, the killer left him a note.

· · ·

"What are you doing?"

The question came from behind him. He dropped the paper and spun with his gun aimed to neutralize the threat.

"Damn it, Don. Are you trying to give me a heart attack or get yourself shot?"

"Why are you here?" Don asked, moving from behind the couch.

"He was here, Don. He was in the house the same time I was. I felt bad about earlier today, so I came by to see if we missed something or if I could get some inspiration on how to catch this guy. Why are you here?"

"Same reason, I guess."

"Here, read this note. He was sleeping in Jessica's bed. I think we need to get a detail on her, just in case he tries to find her."

"Okay, I'll put in the request. He signed it with an N or lightning bolt or whatever it is. Just like the fake suicide note. Oh, look. He likes to take naps too."

It was a cheap shot by Don, but Greg knew he deserved it. He didn't mean to fall asleep, but maybe if he had been awake they would have come back over to the house together earlier and potentially caught the guy. Of course, Greg also knew that the napping on the job was a subtle dig from the killer. He could probably tell from Greg's voice he had been asleep before he called. Greg didn't want anybody to know the killer contacted him, not even Don. It went against all protocol, but he needed to be the one to catch the killer. He had to redeem himself to Don and everybody in the department who thought he was a screw-up, especially Mark Harper.

Chapter Ten

Bobby woke up feeling like he had been asleep for days. He lay in the bed—grateful for finally getting a full night's rest, but he still felt tired and groggy from getting too much sleep. He forced himself to get out of bed and realized he wasn't in his room. The light scent of lilac floated on top of the musty smell of a room that had not been open in a long time. Off white lace covered the lamp on the nightstand beside the bed. The alarm clock sat on a dingy white doily. A picture of him as a child fishing with his grandfather sat on his grandmother's vanity under a thick layer of dust. All of her jewelry was still laid out, waiting for her to return from her last trip.

The ambulance took her to the hospital in the middle of the night. She tried to fight them the whole way out the door. She never left the house without her jewelry, and certainly not without her hair done. Finally, Bobby convinced her to go with the paramedics, and he would bring everything for her. It upset her again when he walked into her room and only had her wedding ring. He squeezed her frail hand and promised her he would return to get everything else, once the doctor came to see her. The doctor made rounds earlier, and Bobby knew she would never return home. She died holding his hand, waiting for the doctor while Bobby waited for the hospice.

Blurry-eyed, he looked around the room and closed the door behind him. Work didn't start for another two hours, but he would need to get ready now since he was moving so slow. He had not been in his grandparent's room since he picked out the clothes to bury his grandmother in. There wasn't enough time to try to figure out how he ended up in their bed last night, but it was disturbing. He stumbled his way to the bathroom.

The vacation was over.

He stood with his face directly in the water, trying to wash the fog and cobwebs out of his head. The alarm on his phone went off. He set it to go off in thirty minutes, so he would not stay in the shower too long. He rushed through washing his body and hair and jumped out to finish getting ready. The shower made him feel better, but his muscles were sore and tired, like he had started a new workout routine. It was going to be hard going back to the Daily Grind. It was the first vacation he had taken since starting there four years ago, and now he wasn't sure if he wanted to go back, but knew he had to.

The humidity hung in the air like used beach towels left outside to air dry. The walk from the front door to the end of the driveway in the heat caused his shirt to stick to him. Exhaustion weighed heavy on his bones, and the heat was not helping anything. He grabbed the door handle of his Bronco, preparing to drive to work today. It was too hot, and he was too tired to be walking. Before he opened the door, a heavier burden fell over him.

Help me, Bobby.

His hand began to shake. She shouldn't still be there ... he already helped her.

Bobby, help me.

Not being able to ignore her cries for help, he decided he would walk to work and check on her, but he couldn't stay. It was too hot out here, and he didn't want to be late on his first day back from vacation.

The temperature had dropped a few degrees when he stepped into the woods, but the humidity was still there. It had only been a week since the path was last used, but the vines started their move to reclaim the open space. The encroachment was minimal, and Bobby walked through it without noticing a difference. Someone yelled up ahead, but he couldn't tell where it was coming from. He needed to get to Emily. She probably heard the voices too, and that's why she called out to him. He needed to get to her and try to misdirect the people in the woods.

It's too late.

It couldn't be too late. He had to help her. She was just scared of being found. She didn't want anybody to take her away from him.

Bobby left his path and pushed into the brush. If he were lucky, all of his noise would frighten away whoever was near Emily. The voices grew louder. There were a lot of them, and they sounded like they were all together. Bobby crashed through the last barrier of foliage between him and Emily.

He broke through the yellow tape like the winner of a cross-country race. The smell overwhelmed him as he crossed the finish line, and he doubled over. He looked up to multiple guns pointed at him and screams for him to 'freeze.' The police found her. Did they do it on their own, or did somebody tell them about her? Somebody had to have called them. There is no reason anybody would be back here.

I couldn't leave. They got to my new place too fast. Don't let them take me away.

Bobby tried to look past the wall of police to see Emily, but they were blocking her. They countered every move he made to look around by stepping into his line of sight.

"I...I don't know what's happening. I'm just trying to get to work," Bobby yelled and put his hands above his head.

A massive man with a bald head walked up to Bobby.

"Son, this is a police investigation. What are you doing here?"

"I'm sorry. I was just trying to get to work. I swear."

"Where do you work?"

Bobby's first reaction was to lie. But that wouldn't help anything. If they checked in on him, it would make him look like he knew something about Emily's death, which he actually had no idea what happened. Also, there weren't too many places within walking distance. There wasn't anything for Bobby to be afraid of. He hadn't done anything. Was that the problem? Bobby wasn't a good liar.

"I work at the Daily Grind. It's the coffee shop by the entrance to the park."

"If you're on your way to work, then why are you walking in the woods?"

"Because...because I live in the subdivision on the top of the hill and I take a shortcut through the woods, and I didn't want to be late for work, so I was running."

Now they knew everything they needed to know about him. He lived and worked too close to where they found her. They would expect him to have found her first. Bobby's arms ached from holding them above his head. Assholes were probably going to make fun of him after he left.

"What's your name?"

"Bobby Cotton."

The man looked him up and down. Bobby hoped he would notice that he was in his work uniform and believe him. The last thing he needed was to get stuck down here with the police asking him questions all day. They would eventually trip him up, and he'd look guilty. He hoped Emily would understand it wasn't his fault they found her. He wasn't ready for her to leave him yet.

"Okay, Bobby. I'm Detective Murphy. Go ahead to work, and I'll probably send somebody by later to ask a few more questions," Don said, and handed him his card.

Bobby didn't reply. He ran, with his hands still above his head, to get away from the area as fast as he could.

Don't worry, Bobby. I won't tell them you were ever here with me. They'll never know.

He stopped at the top of the hill to catch his breath and looked back down to try to get a glimpse of Emily one last time. All he saw was a crowd of uniforms and technicians. The coroner had not shown up yet.

Don Murphy looked up the hill, and he and Bobby made eye contact.

Bobby turned and ran. When he got to the parking lot, there were a few more cops, and they were talking to somebody. He continued on like he didn't see them. He wasn't positive, but he was pretty sure it was Danielle's ex, Mike, standing with the cops beside Emily's car. He stopped at the door breathless and fought to pull the keys out of his pocket. Once inside he sat at a table to catch his breath. He should have driven to work like he planned. Then they wouldn't know anything about him. Now they were sending some-body up here to question him about Emily. Who told them about her? Why was Mike in the parking lot beside Emily's car? There wasn't time to think about that right now. He had to prepare to open the store and prepare for whoever was coming to question him later. He couldn't slip up and let them know he knew anything about the dead girl.

Chapter Eleven

Greg parked in front of the Daily Grind and walked the two blocks to the park. Don called and told him they found another body, but it looked like an actual suicide. He said it looked like an animal was sleeping under the tree beside her at some point. It surprised Greg that whatever it was, hadn't tried to nibble at the corpse. He didn't share that thought with Don, though.

The girl didn't leave a note, and Don didn't find anything that looked suspicious, or out of the ordinary besides the animal bed, so there was no point in him coming to the scene. Don wanted Greg to question the boyfriend and then to go to the coffee shop and question the barista who ran through the crime scene this morning. The only thing noteworthy was that the girl looked a lot like Rachel Martin. The girl's boyfriend called it in when he found her car in the parking lot this morning. Greg stopped at the entrance to the park.

Morgan Cramer already had her voice recorder set up and ready to start rolling on the story. She smiled at Greg as he walked by. She apparently wasn't going to try to talk to him again before he had had a chance to see what was going on. Too bad she didn't say anything. He would have told her this case and the previous murder weren't connected, and she was wasting her time. He just shook his head and kept going.

The boyfriend leaned up against his car with his arms crossed and boot heel on the tire, like he thought he was James Dean. It wouldn't have surprised Greg if he'd had a pack of smokes rolled in his shirt sleeve to complete the look. Police officers surrounded Mike as they searched the girl's car, but he didn't acknowledge their presence; he only stared at the dirt.

"Are you Mike Smith?" Greg asked, looking through his notes.

"I guess so, seeing as I'm the only one that's not a cop around here."

Mike carried himself with what he thought would be an air of importance, and everybody else knew he was a jerk. Greg thought he had the face of a person you just want to punch in the throat just for looking at you. His farmer's tan and faded clothes gave away that he worked outside a lot, probably construction or landscaping. He more than likely thought he deserved more, and it was the world's fault he didn't have it easier. Anybody could tell his car was the most important thing to him, and he used it as a status symbol. But what did his house look like? It agitated him that he had to be at the park instead of anywhere else. Like there was a better place for him to be while his girlfriend lay dead in the woods?

"So it seems, Mikey. You act like you'd rather not be here. Like you don't want to help me find out what happened."

Mike stood up straight and puffed out his chest like a bird, making itself look bigger to stop encroachment on his territory.

"My name is Mike, and yes, I'd rather be somewhere else. I should be at work right now. Instead, I'm standing around waiting on you to show up so you can ask me some questions about my stupid ex. I shouldn't have called. I should have just left her car here."

This guy was a bigger jerk than he appeared to be. He had no respect for Greg or any of the other people out here trying to figure out what happened to somebody he cared for at some point. And worst of all, he had no respect for the girl who was lying in the woods, dead. It wouldn't surprise Greg if it turned out to be a suicide, and he was the reason she decided to end it for good.

"I'm honestly surprised you did call it in, Mikey,"

Being antagonistic toward Mike was not going to help Greg get the answers out of him any faster, but he didn't care. Mike was a piece of shit, and he wanted to get under his skin.

"I said my name is Mike. Call me Mikey again and I'm walking."

"No, Mikey, you're not. You're not going anywhere until I ask you some questions and I am satisfied that you answered them to the best of your abilities. Now, you can keep playing this stupid tough guy routine and piss me off even more, and I'll keep you longer. Or you can chill out and show some fucking respect to the girl you probably drove to this," Greg said, backing Mike up against his car.

The officers going through Emily's car stopped to watch the exchange between the two men.

"You can't talk to me like that."

Greg took another step toward Mike.

"Yeah, I can. Do you really want to try me? Maybe we should just go back to my office so we can talk. I'll give you a ride in the back of my car and when I'm finished with you, you can make arrangements for somebody to pick you up and bring you back to your car. That should only take all morning."

Mike looked to the side and took a deep breath.

"No, there's no need for that. Just ask your questions so I can go. I don't have time for all of this."

"Your compassion is overwhelming. Did you live with...Emily?"

"No, she lived with me. It's my place."

Greg looked up from his notes.

"Right, your place. How long has she been missing?"

"I don't know. A week. Maybe ten days."

"So, she lived with you, and you didn't realize she was gone and you don't know the amount of time she's been missing?"

Mike pushed off the car and slid his boot through the dirt.

"Look, man, she saw me here with another girl last week. She caused a big scene and ran off into the park. I don't know where she went after that because I left."

"She catches you cheating, runs off into the woods and doesn't come home, and you weren't worried about her?"

This guy was in the running for the lowest form of human waste that Greg had come across while he was on the clock or off. But Mike didn't kill Emily. He didn't care enough about her to kill her. If she'd made him that mad, he would have done something psychological to screw her up even more. Murder wasn't his brand of abuse.

"No, I figured she was at her mother's house and would come back when she got over it."

"When she got over it? And you found her car this morning? Why were you here so early?"

"Look, I was meeting somebody here, and I saw her car in the same place that she parked it last week, so I called the cops. That's the entire story. There's not a lot I can tell you."

Meeting somebody else while his girlfriend lay dead in the woods less than two football fields away from him.

"No, you've told me quite a lot. You can go, I'll be in touch if I have any other questions."

"Whatever," Mike said, and jumped in his car.

Greg watched as Mike drove off, spinning his tires in the gravel parking lot. He was an ass, but he didn't kill Emily or Rachel. Don said it looked like the girl killed herself. The questions were only a formality. Now, he had to go to the coffee shop and formally talk to somebody else that didn't know anything about this girl. He was wasting time out here on this call, while Rachel's killer was on the loose plotting his next kill or how to screw with Greg more. Maybe Greg was next. The fact that Emily looks like Rachel could be a coincidence, or maybe he did a better job at covering up Emily's murder. The killer hadn't said anything about it to Greg when he called him. He would have said something. He was too confident and would have used any excuse to rub it in Greg's face that he had killed somebody else that they didn't know about.

When Greg got back to the shopping center, he stopped under the awning. Sweat soaked through his shirt. The conversation with Mike got heated, and the weather didn't help either. He pulled out his phone to give Don an update, but it started ringing before he could click on Don's name.

It was Rachel's number.

"Hello, Detective," the familiar voice said. "You looked hot out there, so I took the liberty of getting you something cold to drink. I left it in your cup holder."

Greg opened the door to his car and got in. A plastic cup covered in condensation sat in the center console. Detective Gregory Burns was written in black marker along the side in the same messy handwriting from the note left for him at the house. The cup had the logo of the coffee shop on it. It read: Daily Grind with a red lightning bolt striking a cup of coffee between the two words. Greg turned quickly to look in the backseat of his car and then at the surrounding area. There was nobody there. A strangled laugh came through the phone.

"I'm not in your backseat, but thank you, Detective. I really needed that. It's been a hell of a day for me so far."

"I'm not much of an iced coffee drinker, but thanks for thinking about me," Greg said.

"No worries. I myself love iced coffee."

"Why don't you come join me in the car and I'll let you have this one? You'd have to sit in the back, of course."

"Aw, Detective, I thought you would have a little more respect for me than that. Has anyone ever fallen for something so lame before?"

"I've never had a killer call me before, but it was worth a shot."

"Oh, I'm you're first. How exciting. It got pretty exciting at Rachel's place too. I honestly didn't expect you to show up that fast. Color me impressed. You almost caught me. I'll have to be more careful from now on."

Greg missed his chance. This guy was there the whole time and was still there when he went back, and he blew it, both times. Now the guy will be more meticulous, making it that much harder to catch him. After almost catching him, Greg didn't expect to hear from him again. He thought the killer would resurface when he found another 'vessel,' as he called them. Greg didn't want to be any part of the killer's sick game.

"This isn't a game."

"But isn't it? I kill. You try to stop me. When you don't, I kill again. It's all one big game."

"What did you mean by calling Rachel a vessel?"

"Oh...don't worry about that. I assure you, it's nothing."

The pause meant it was something. If Greg could keep him talking, he might be able to get something useful out of him. The killer was too calm. Greg wouldn't be able to get under his skin as easily as he had Mike. That definitely ruled Mike out as a suspect. There was nothing calm about that guy.

"Well, since you're assuring me, I guess I'll believe you."

"For some reason, I don't believe you."

He still had the false bravado to his voice, but the more he spoke the more Greg could tell there was something a little off about him today. Maybe almost getting caught had thrown him off more than Greg originally thought.

"Anyway, I was just hanging around and happened to see you in the park. What's going on over there?"

He needed to know why they were there. He wouldn't be curious about another investigation that didn't involve him somehow. They had pretty much determined the girl in the woods was a suicide. Greg didn't see why he would be asking about her unless maybe he knew her.

"Why would you want to know about what we were doing? Did you have something to do with it?"

"I didn't kill her if that's what you are asking."

"Why should I believe you?"

"Because she was dead before our friend Rachel, and I would have already been gloating about how I had killed somebody you didn't know about and probably wouldn't find for a while."

He was definitely telling the truth about that. The playful sound in his voice wavered when he spoke. Either Greg was getting to him, or this girl meant something to him.

"So now you're calling me to get the scoop on the story? Well, I hate to break it to you, but I can't discuss an ongoing investigation with anybody."

"I don't want to know her damn life story. I only want to know how you found out she was there."

"My partner called me and told me, and then I came over to see if it was your handy work or not."

"Detective, you know that's not what I meant."

"Wow, who's tired of playing games now?"

Greg almost had him. A little more pushing and he would be ready to scream at him and hopefully reveal something.

"You really are trying me. I only want to know who called 911 and told them there was a dead girl in the woods of Rusted Lakes Park."

Greg walked around the parking lot trying to see if he could find him by listening for his yelling. He had to be inside one of these buildings or in a car nearby.

"You're not going to find me looking around like that. Quit looking for stupid shit. I'm not an idiot."

"I don't think you're an idiot. Maybe crazy, but not stupid. But I can't have you making me look stupid either because you were behind me the whole time."

"Considering the way some of your coworkers look at you, I can't say that I blame you. How do they feel that you've been talking to a killer on the phone? They probably think you're as crazy as I am."

"Yeah. I guess they think it's weird."

Shit. He hesitated. That's all it would take with this guy, and he'd gain the advantage again.

"They don't know, do they? Don't worry, Detective. I won't tell anybody our little secret. I promise."

A phone rang once in the background, followed by a crash, and everything sounded muffled. He'd covered the receiver to answer another phone. Most people didn't have a landline anymore. He could be at work. Which meant he was stable enough to keep a job where he dealt with the public. A dulled scrape filled the phone like cotton being removed from an infected ear, and Greg could hear again.

"Oh well, I have to go for now, but I will talk to you again soon. Don't worry. My lips are sealed," the killer said, and hung up the phone.

Greg kicked himself for giving the killer leverage over him. He hadn't even told Don. The killer knew he couldn't tell anybody now and could hold it over Greg's head for not telling anybody sooner. Greg could lose his badge if anybody found out. The fate of his job rested in the hands of a killer, like the lives of his victims.

Greg didn't have time to worry about that right now. He still had a pointless interview with the barista that walked through Don's suicide scene. The coffee cup in Greg's car was from that shop. Maybe he remembered the guy who bought it and it wouldn't be as pointless as he thought.

Greg walked into the shop. A customer stood by the end of the counter, waiting for the only barista on duty to make their drink. He went about his job methodically and didn't look up when he addressed Burns.

"Welcome to the Daily Grind. I'll be with you in a minute."

"Are you Bobby Cotton?"

"Or now," he said under his breath. "Yeah, that's me. I guess your boss sent you over to ask me questions about this morning."

Greg watched as Bobby sat the customer's drink on the counter and wiped the condensation on his apron. He put a straw on top, before telling the customer their drink was ready.

"He's not my boss. He's my partner."

"He acted like he was everybody's boss, but whatever you say."

Bobby walked back to the cash register.

"I noticed you didn't write that girl's name or order on her cup. Why's that?"

"Because she's the only one in here. It would be hard to get her order confused with anybody else's."

Greg should have known that, but this guy seemed off and was obviously agitated. Of course, that could be because he has to come to this job every day. Waiting on people who don't care or acknowledge your presence until you screw up their order, then they want to know you and your boss and anybody else's name they may need. People always believe that mistakes happen as long as they are the ones making them. If it's anybody else, then the only logical explanation is incompetence. Greg immediately regretted the way he came at the guy. The killer got him all worked up on the phone and then just left him. He decided to let it go.

"So what happened this morning?"

"Like I told your *partner*, I live in the neighborhood behind the park and I cut through in the mornings on my way to work."

The way he emphasized partner irritated Greg, but he was going to try to get through this as painless as possible, so he could get back to solving an actual homicide. And being antagonistic to the last three people he spoke to didn't bode well for the rest of the day.

"You cut through the woods every day, and you didn't see her or smell her until today?"

A loud crash coming from the front door interrupted their conversation. Greg whirled around, gun drawn.

"Whoa, whoa. Don't shoot," Bobby yelled.

Danielle stopped with the same suddenness that she burst into the store and put her hands up.

"Who are you and why in the hell did you come in here like that?"

"I'm sorry. I'm so sorry. My name is Danielle. I saw all the police in the park and was worried about Bobby. I was coming to check on him."

"Why were you worried about him? What could have happened to him?"

"Hey. I thought you were interrogating me here. She was just worried because of the police, and she knows I walk to work that way."

"Yes. That's all it was," she said, and stepped toward the counter.

Greg watched Danielle for any indication that something else was going on, but he couldn't tell. Maybe she was just worried about Bobby.

"The answer to your question about how I did not see her or *smell* her until today is because I have been on vacation for a week, so I haven't needed to cut through the woods. I just happened to be late for work this morning, and I was running, and I ran into your *partner*," Bobby said.

"Vacation, huh?"

"Yeah, vacation."

"Okay, I have one last question for you, but it's not about that girl. It's about a customer you may have had this morning."

"Besides the girl that was just in here, I have only had one other customer."

"You wouldn't happen to remember what he looked like or have security cameras in here, do you?"

"No cameras, but I remember what he looked like."

Greg's pulse quickened to a deafening pace in his ears. He had to calm down to make sure he got everything that Bobby was about to tell him. This may be the break in the case that he needed. He flipped his notebook to a page in the back. Bobby started sneezing rapidly. Greg tried to be nonchalant and smooth things back over with the two kids.

"Wow. Bless you. Do you always sneeze that many times," he said, his good will a little too forced.

"Yeah," Bobby said. "It's always six times, no matter what. Anyway, he was about 6'2, probably 200 pounds or so. He had black hair, hazel eyes, and a cleft chin. He also had a long scar on his left arm. It went from the inside of his elbow, almost to his wrist."

Greg wrote down every word Bobby said. He sounded like he got a real good look at the man. Too bad he couldn't send a sketch artist down here to talk to him. If he did that there would be too many questions about how he knew this kid would know what the guy looked like. He would just keep this information to himself for now.

"That's all I need to know for now. I'll be in touch if anything else comes up," Greg said, and walked out the door.

Chapter Twelve

Bobby held his breath until Greg got in his car. He knew he was going to have to answer questions about Emily, but he felt like the detective attacked him. He wasn't sure what they could have found down there to make them think that somebody killed her. Maybe they found something where he was sleeping and thought the killer had left it. Bobby didn't have time to worry about any of that. He was on his way to see her this morning before work, and the cops ruined it all. They had her blocked, and he couldn't get one last glimpse of her. He needed to find out who called the police. They were the real criminals here. They were the one who took her away from him for good.

"Bobby ... Bobby. What's wrong with you?" Danielle asked.

"Oh, uh, nothing. I was just lost in thought, I guess."

"I've been worried about you since you disappeared on me the other night."

Bobby didn't have time for this conversation. The more he thought about Emily, the worse it got. He ran to the phone to call Jody. She had to relieve him today and was always looking for extra hours. She wouldn't mind coming in early.

"Jody? It's Bobby. Hey, I haven't been feeling well, and I wanted to know if you would mind coming in earlier. Anytime is fine. The earlier, the better. Okay, thanks. Bye."

Bobby hung up the phone and could feel Danielle looking at him.

He hoped she couldn't see through him. She would never understand. She probably already thought he was crazy and should be
institutionalized. There was no use in trying to explain anything
to her.

"What is wrong with you? You've been acting weird ever since
you found that girl in the woods."

Bobby looked around the coffee shop to make sure Detective
Burns didn't come back inside. Now, he was being paranoid, but
Danielle couldn't be so open about Emily. If the wrong person heard
her, the police might find out he lied.

"I'm fine, I promise. It's been a crazy week, and I haven't been
sleeping, and I've been sick. I'll get over it, and everything will be
back to normal."

"Where did you go the other night when you left my apartment?
Did you go back in the woods with that girl?"

He ducked his head beside the register, grabbed Danielle's arm
and pulled her close.

"Her name is Emily. And no, I didn't. I went home. I didn't want
to be a burden for you, so I left before you woke up."

She calmly pulled her arm from his grip and stood up straight.

"I woke up at midnight, and you were already gone. Why didn't
you wake me and how did you get home?"

"I called a cab."

Bobby looked at the clock on the wall. The ticking did nothing to
sooth him. Now, it sounded like it was mocking him. It was going to
be a long hour before Jody got here if he didn't get rid of Danielle.
She was interrogating him worse than the police. He couldn't tell her
the truth about where he had gone when he left her apartment that
night. She would never understand.

A customer walked in, and Bobby snapped up straight behind the
counter to take their order. He wrote the name and order on the side
of the cup and could see Danielle through the plastic. She was
staring at him with a look in her eye he had never seen before from
anybody. She was trying to rationalize everything. He took his time
while making the drink and taking the payment, hoping she would
decide she needed to get back to work since it wasn't time for her
lunch break yet. She didn't move. She continued to watch every
move he made. Danielle watched so closely, the customer took notice

and moved away from her to the other end of the counter. When he handed her the drink, she pointed her head toward Danielle and rolled her eyes. Bobby only shrugged his shoulders, and the customer left.

"You're freaking the customers and me out with all the staring. Why don't you go back to work before you get in trouble and I'll call you tonight? I'm good. I swear," Bobby said.

"You've had one customer, and you're freaking me out with the way you're acting. I'll go back to work, but you have to promise me you will get some rest and call me later. I don't care what time it is."

"Promise," he said, and gave her the boy scouts salute.

She didn't smile at him, just walked out of the store. Apparently, she hadn't seen the humor in his salute. While waiting for Jody to show up, Bobby tried to distract himself with finishing the prep work for the day. It was not helping. All he could think about was Emily. He pictured her being picked up by two men. They probably would make comments about how she used to be a pretty girl. One would make the joke that she still was a pretty girl, she just smelled a little ripe, as they dropped her into the black body bag.

He felt each tooth of the zipper close. Her face, a washout green and gray color, was the last of her he saw before they sealed her inside. Blood rushed to his face as the anger and rage built. These people didn't care about her. She was a joke for them to talk about so their workday would go by faster.

He threw a stack of cups across the store at the thought of her stretcher being pushed and dragged up the hill by the two clumsy techs. If they let her go, she would go crashing back down, and nobody would care, because to them she was dead. They would just go back down the hill and start again, probably cussing her the whole way because she had to go and kill herself all the way out there. They would never understand. They would take her to the morgue and drop her on a cold steel slab and slide her in a drawer until the family claimed her. Bobby waved as the coroner's car drove around the corner and took Emily away from her favorite place. The place where she felt the safest from the outside world.

"Who ya waving at?"

The voice startled him out of his dream state. It was Jody. He never heard her come in. How long had she been there watching him? She could probably be added to the growing list of people who thought he was losing it.

"Oh, hey. I thought I saw somebody I knew out there. Guess not," he said.

Jody looked outside at the empty street and back to Bobby.

"Thank you for coming in. I thought I was over what I had, but I guess not. And sorry about the mess. I'll clean it up, and then I'll be out of your way."

"Don't worry about it. I'll clean it up. You go ahead and go home. Get some rest. You look like you could use it. Call me later if I need to come in for you tomorrow. I don't mind."

Bobby nodded his thanks and tried not to run out of the store. He turned right, but thought better of it. The cops may still be in the woods, and he didn't want to chance running into them again. He didn't want to have to explain himself anymore to anybody. He would have to take the long way home. It was for the best anyway. He was too mad and didn't want to risk walking past Danielle's office and her coming outside to check on him. If he blew up at her probing questions, it would cause more problems for himself.

He had his own questions.

Who was responsible for taking Emily away from him so soon? They had to pay for what they did. Now she would be alone, and he couldn't help her. Soon they would bury her under piles of dirt and she would fade away. It was his fault for not staying with her and protecting her. He should have done something. The rage built from his stomach and forced its way up his torso and down his arms.

He entered his neighborhood and yanked a yard sign out of the ground. Katherine Myers is graduating; he read and threw the sign like a Frisbee. It landed on the future graduate's roof, and he kept walking. Who ever told the cops would be sorry. At the end of the street, he picked up a rock and threw it through the large front window of the corner house. He searched the windows for signs of life and ran away when he thought he saw movement from an upstairs window.

Getting arrested for vandalism was the last thing he needed right now. He stopped to catch his breath when he got to his street and limped the rest of the way to his house with a stitch in his side. Bobby mounted the steps and turned to face the woods. He didn't think he would be able to hear her, but listened for her anyway. He could hear slight echoes of the police still working in the woods. Bobby stomped up the stairs and surged through the door.

Picture frames fell off the wall. While picking up the fragments of broken glass, he allowed himself to believe what he should have known all along. It was Danielle. She called the police. She was the only other person who knew Emily was there. Why would she do that to him?

Bobby hurled the frame at the wall, and the rest of the casing shattered. He punched the wall, and his fist went through and threatened to come out in the living room wall. He wiped the drywall dust on his pants, walked into his room, and slammed the door.

Chapter Thirteen

He sat in the dark with only his thoughts to keep him company. The droning of the voice in his head sounded like his teachers in school and he nodded off a few times though he was restless. The detective wasn't any closer to catching him than he was the day before. He knew he shouldn't call him, but he had an overwhelming desire to talk to him, to make him understand that he was doing it for her. It was the only way he could help her. She was the only thing that mattered. If his conversations with the detective carried on too much longer, there was always the chance that Burns would figure it out and lead the whole police department to his doorstep.

They would definitely push for the death penalty. He would take his time with every appeal they granted to him. Not because he thought he could win, but because it would be the only way to prolong his life. They would have control over when he slept, when he ate and when he showered, but he would have the ultimate power. They would sentence him to death, but he would only allow them to kill him when he was ready. Not when they broke him, but when he had given up. People who would be anxious to see him ride the lightning and take his last breath would die waiting for the day as he dragged it out for years. He may even die in prison. It would have to be from natural causes or another inmate, perhaps. He would never take the easy way out and kill himself. That would really get to them. They would be glad he was dead, but they didn't get to see it happen. But none of that mattered right now. No need to make plans when he didn't plan on ever being caught.

The detective hadn't told anybody they were talking. Burns must be hard up to prove himself to somebody. All the newspaper articles referencing his last few cases said they were still open. The same journalist, Morgan Cramer, wrote them all. Maybe he should pay her a visit sometime? Burns didn't want to tell anybody about the phone calls because he wanted the arrest all to himself, to vindicate himself for his past failures. A man who needs to justify his actions or past is a dangerous man. His actions would be harder to anticipate and control. But the man with something to prove has a fatal flaw. In their quest for absolution, they are easily manipulated. Detective Burns would play his game and never tell anybody about it until it was too late. Still, he should probably get rid of Rachel's cell phone, just in case the detective had a change of heart. He would get a new one tonight.

This was the longest time he had been able to just sit and think without being interrupted. His mind was much clearer because of it, but there were still many troubling issues he had to figure out. He needed to commit more time to just sitting in the dark alone.

Headlights flooded the living room, and all thought stopped. It was time to concentrate. Looking out the window, he bounced on the couch in anticipation. Why was she taking so long to get out of the car? She swung her legs out of her car and slid to the edge. Of course, she was talking to somebody on her cell phone. That's all anybody ever did anymore. She leaned her head against the headrest and propped her foot on the doorsill. This could be a problem for him. He didn't need any witnesses, even if they couldn't see him stuck in the house, he would get impatient waiting and go get her.

Finally, the girl walked around to the back of her car and pulled two grocery bags out of the trunk. As she walked toward the house, she wrestled with the bags, purse, and keys, all while trying to keep her phone between her shoulder and ear. His heart and breath quickened. She was almost to the door, and he could hear her soft voice as she spoke into the phone. She opened the glass door, and she stopped. His heart stopped with her.

"Shit. I'm trying to get in the house, and I dropped my keys. Let me call you back in a few minutes. Okay, bye," she said, and let the phone slide from her shoulder and into her open purse.

The wait was agonizing. He wanted to open the door, say, 'welcome home,' and pull her in. She stumbled through the front door, dropped her purse on the floor, kicked off her shoes and headed toward the kitchen. He moved to the dining room to wait for the perfect time to pounce on his prey. She put away her groceries and walked back into the living room. This was the first time he stalked anybody from the shadows. It was fun. But he had important business to conduct.

"Hello, Laura," he said, and jumped out of the shadows, trying to grab her.

Laura screamed and swung her fist and barely missed his face. He grabbed her arm and pulled her to him. She drove her knee up, and his groin exploded in pain. His sight faded white, and he dropped to his knees, coughing. Laura moved to try to get to her purse where her phone was, but he leaned to his left, and she lost her nerve.

She ran down the hall and into her bedroom. He stumbled to his feet. The pain was excruciating, but he had to finish what he started. He would not accept failure. Emily needed him. He couldn't come back later because he wasn't wearing a mask. A sketch of his face would be all over the news in an hour if he didn't take care of her now.

His heart raced as he psyched himself back up from the testosterone drain. He took two steps toward her bedroom and heard a loud guttural scream. Laura came charging around the corner with a shotgun in her hand like she was storming an enemy's fortification. She pulled the trigger as she raised it to aim, and the drywall above his head exploded. The sound of the gun going off in the small room was deafening. The force of the gunshot reverberations bouncing off the walls of the small room ran through his body and threw off both of their equilibriums. They shuffled around the room, trying to stand on a sinking ship. His ears rang and he couldn't hear anything, but neither could she.

His hunt suddenly became a fight for survival, and he lunged at Laura. They danced for control of the gun in an unromantic salsa. He led the fight and spun her against the wall, and she lost her grip on the gun. She pushed off the wall and launched herself into him before he could raise the gun.

They fought for the gun above their heads, and his groin exploded with pain again. Flashes of light, followed by tracers of white and green, filled his vision. She pulled the gun from his fingers and fell back into the recliner. He plunged to the floor where the butt of the gun rested.

He lay out on the floor and tried to pull the gun from her grip. She sat in the chair kicking at his hands, trying to fight him off her. With one hand on the gun, he pulled himself to his hands and knees.

She kicked him in the face. When he fell back, his finger got caught in the trigger guard, and the gun went off. He covered his face with his hands to protect it from another blow from her foot. The blast from the gun made his ears ring again even though he still couldn't hear from the first shot. Blood covered his face and hands.

It wasn't the blood from his nose. He already had that cradled in his right hand. Laura had stopped fighting. He looked up, and instead of seeing her pretty face, he saw a bloody mess. What was left of her jaw spasmed and blood poured from her throat. He jumped up from the floor and screamed.

"This isn't how it was supposed to happen. You weren't supposed to go this way. Why did you have to fight me?"

He paced around the room yelling unintelligible words at Laura. He picked up a vase they knocked to the floor in the struggle and threw it against a shelf on the wall. It shattered, and the shelf fell, breaking a goldfish bowl. Two shotgun blasts would not have gone unnoticed in this neighborhood. The houses were right on top of each other. He had to hurry and leave before the police showed up. The goldfish flopped on the floor in a puddle of Laura's blood—his blood, too. He scooped up the fish and carried it to the bathroom.

He dropped the fish in the toilet and grabbed a towel from the cabinet. She shouldn't have died like that. But the way she died did land in his favor. She looked like she killed herself while sitting in her chair after she destroyed the place.

He returned to the living room and wiped the gun clean, so there would be no fingerprints, and carefully placed it back between her knees. Some of the blood on the floor was from his nose, so he sopped up as much of the spots he could find. Hopefully, if he missed any, it was underneath globs of grey matter that littered the floor, walls and ceiling and they'd assume it was all Laura's.

He scribbled his death note on a piece of paper and put it on the table beside Laura. This house didn't have any hiding places. He wanted to stay and see the police when they arrived, and how nervous they were as they checked to make sure he wasn't in any of the rooms. The detective would be expecting that. Burns would search the house and everywhere around it. The house was a mess, so they would be going over all of his mistakes.

He didn't want to see that. Everything had gone wrong tonight. They would make fun of him for not being able to finish the deal without getting his ass kicked. He slammed his fist on the arm of the couch.

She was a lot tougher than he expected her to be. Things could have gone in a different direction. He didn't feel like it right now, but he knew he was lucky she hit him in the nose with her knee. If she hadn't fought back, he wouldn't have accidentally pulled the trigger. She may have ended up winning. He needed to get control of himself before he ended up being the one on the slab.

He walked onto her back porch and heard the sirens headed his way.

Chapter Fourteen

Bobby. Slow down, you're going to wreck. Or worse, you're going to get pulled over by the police. How would you explain yourself? I was sad that you weren't able to make it back to our spot before they took me away. I caught a quick glimpse of your sweet face before that guy you were talking to blocked it.

Don't worry. I kept my promise. I didn't tell them anything about you.

They didn't know that we knew each other and you visited and stayed with me so I wouldn't be lonely. Bobby, you really must calm down. Being this upset is not going to help the situation. I can help you with your problem. Right now you don't know what to do. I'm sure you feel like you are alone and can't count on anybody else, but you're wrong. You can count on me. I will stay with you as long as you allow me to. I think we both know the reason for all of your problems.

It's all her fault.

She has been trying to come between us from the very beginning. She doesn't want us to be together. She doesn't want you to be happy. She wanted to call the police the first time she saw us together. She's jealous of what we have because she knows that you two will never have the same thing we do, no matter what happens between us. You will always be mine, and she can't stand to think about it.

Danielle is the one who called the police and told them where I was. She is the only other person who knew about me. If somebody found me while they were walking in the woods, you would have seen the cops talking to them. But there wasn't anybody else there.

It's her fault I'm gone, and we can't have our spot anymore. She is also the reason you have been distracted tonight, and it almost cost you. If you hadn't been worried about who told on me, then you would never have screwed up and had to change your plans.

You need to go and talk to her. Tell her you don't need her anymore. That I am all you will ever need. She is just getting in the way of your happiness. She thinks she is helping you, but she is only causing you more problems. Go to her house and tell her now.

I'm sure she will be waiting for you.

Chapter Fifteen

The parking lot was full when Bobby pulled into one of the two spaces reserved for Danielle in the Valley Summit apartment complex.

He slid the gear shifter in park and eased his foot off the brake, but left the engine running. She was the one who called the police. There was nobody else that could have done it. He had to figure out a way to bring it up. Busting into her apartment and accusing her wouldn't look good. It would probably scare her, and she would just lie about it. Bobby needed to let her think he was okay with it. The police taking Emily away was the best thing for all of them. Her family could bury her, and he and Danielle could pick up where they left off, and act like none of this ever happened.

But it will never be the same.

What would he do when she admitted to it? He couldn't hurt her. He would tell her he could never see her again. That would break her heart, and she would cry. Bobby didn't know if he could deal with that, but he had to know for sure it was her. He pulled the handle and got out of the vehicle.

A light clicked on and illuminated her dark window. She was still awake. He mounted the stairs, and the first one let out a loud creak, and a bright light washed over Bobby. He dove into the bushes. Squatting behind a bush, he watched as some of Danielle's neighbors exited their car. There was no reason for him to still be worked up about earlier. He'd had plenty of time to calm down. He stayed hidden in the bushes until the neighbors walked past. That would have been awkward to explain if he popped out of the bushes. They stopped at the first-floor door beside the stairs. Bobby grew anxious and sweat formed on his brow as he waited for them to get inside. They were taking far too long. It was like they knew he was there and were playing a game with him.

Let's see how long we can make the weird guy in the bushes wait.

Bobby finally had enough and rose to his feet. He stepped onto the concrete, and their door opened, and they both slipped in, never noticing Bobby behind them. He balled his fists and stomped up the stairs.

His hand hovered inches from Danielle's cold steel door. He still didn't know what to say. There was no reason to try to manipulate her. She was far too smart for that and would see through any crazy story he could come up with. That left the hardest option. The truth.

He was just going to come out and ask her if she was the one who called the police. It would go much smoother that way. He didn't know what he would do when she answered him. There was no way to prepare for her answer. No matter which way it went.

Bobby pulled his hand back to knock, but hesitated again to see if she had locked the door. He turned the knob back and forth, but it didn't give.

She's keeping you out, Bobby. She's trying to hide what she's done from you.

He raised his fist to beat on the door. The apartment across the breezeway had their porch light on. In the dim glow, Bobby caught his reflection in the slick substance on his arm. He stopped himself just before he knocked on her door. Ice filled his veins. The hair on his arms and the back of his neck stood on end, letting him know the potential danger he was in. He walked into the neighbor's light and looked at his clothes. They were still covered in blood. Laura's blood.

He was so upset when he left her house he'd forgotten to clean up before he tried to talk to Danielle. The blood was drying in places, but was still wet in many others. He pulled a clump of hair off his shirt and held it up to the light. It still had a large chunk of scalp attached. There would be no explaining this.

Lucky for him he caught it before he knocked. There wouldn't be a reason to worry about her calling the police because of Emily. She would be calling them on him, causing bigger issues. He would have to come back after he'd had a chance to clean up.

"Bobby? What are you doing?"

Her voice startled him, and he threw the hair over the side of the railing. Bobby never heard the door open. How long had she been standing there watching him? He held his hand out like a crossing guard directing traffic. His mouth ran dry and his tongue stuck to the side of his mouth. Now she would know everything. Escape before she ran inside screaming and called the cops was his only option. She would never understand what he was doing. It was all for Emily. If he didn't do it, she would disappear forever. Danielle would be jealous because of how far he was willing to go for another woman.

"Stop. Stop right there and just go inside, Danielle. I'm leaving."

"Bobby, what is that on your clothes? You're covered in it."

"Please, Danielle, just go back inside."

She walked closer to him and put her hands to her mouth. This wasn't right. She should never see him like this. How could he be so stupid and not pay attention to what he was wearing?

"You need help, Bobby. Let me help you," she said.

Tears ran down her face.

"No. I need to go," he said, and ran down the steps.

He could hear her yelling for him to come back, but it was too late. He had to find a way to get a hold of himself. There had to be a way to get back on top. He would call and talk to the detective. Talking to Burns allowed him to feel in control, like he finally had the upper hand on somebody. He jumped into his Bronco and left, spinning tires through the parking lot.

Chapter Sixteen

The flat, stale smell of drying blood hit Greg before he stepped into Laura Cline's house. The air was stifling inside. The smell combined with the lack of airflow overwhelmed Greg, and he coughed.

"Hey, calm down, rookie," Mark Harper said, walking in from the kitchen. "Take your puke outside. We don't need you contaminating another crime scene."

It was bad enough this guy killed another innocent woman, but he didn't feel like dealing with Harper today. Murphy filled him in on the specifics on the way over. Neighbors heard two gunshots in the middle of the night and called 911. The police showed up and patrolled the area for a while, but never saw or heard anything. The caller couldn't tell where the shots came from, so the police couldn't investigate a particular house. Laura's mother called the police when she found her but couldn't answer any questions. She was hysterical when she found her daughter. They had to sedate her and take her to the hospital. The killer made it look like a self-inflicted gunshot to the face, and he left a note just like the last time.

Greg walked over to the chair where Laura sat. The shotgun was still between her legs, pointed toward the mass of flesh and blood where her face used to be.

"The murder weapon was a shotgun, and it's right here," Greg said, pointing at it for Mark to see. "Oh, did you not need help with this one?"

Mark stuck up his middle finger and walked out of the room.

"You really need to learn to let it go," Don said.

"Hell, he started it."

"He started it? What preschooler did you learn that from?" Don asked. "Here's the letter the killer left. It's just as out there as the last one. I don't know if it's supposed to be from him or how he sees his victims."

Greg snatched the evidence bag containing the letter from Don.

"I got it from my daughter, and she's six and a half."

I've got a job, I own a house, and I'm healthy, not heartbroken. I really have no reason to do all of this. I don't feel any existential pain or agony. I have almost everything that I need. Something is missing. I have no clues. I guess I'll have to go search some other place to find it.

I'll get my coat.

N

"Well, this is definitely a lot more than what he gave us the last time. I still don't think it means anything. I think he wants us to look closer into it, and waste time searching for him."

"Maybe. Or maybe it's a cry for help," Don said.

"I don't think this guy wants any help. He knows what he's doing. I think he's working for a particular goal."

"What makes you think that?"

"Just a feeling, I guess."

The couple times he called Greg, he didn't sound like he was crying out for help. He sounded proud of what he had done, and he didn't care who knew about it. If anything, this note makes him seem content with his life, just bored. Unless the vessel he was talking about before is what's missing, and something keeps driving him to look for one. But why are these women vessels, and what does he want to keep in them? The Martin girl's autopsy didn't show anything abnormal with the body, and this victim doesn't look like he tampered with the body either.

"This one definitely put up a fight," Don said.

"Yeah, I was thinking the same thing. I wonder if she surprised him, or if he just wasn't prepared to take her on, and she kicked his ass before he could shoot her?"

"I hope she kicked his ass. It looks like somebody tried to clean up in a few spots. She may have injured him, and he needed to get rid of the evidence. I've already swabbed for DNA and cleaned under her fingernails. Hopefully we'll get a hit in the system," Mark said.

"Sounds good," Greg said.

Greg never heard Mark walk back into the room. He wasn't trying to sneak up on them. Mark had been civil when speaking, and Greg didn't have anything to quip back with. That bothered him. If they ever said anything to each other, it was never civil. Maybe he and Mark could work together? Or maybe Mark was trying to be professional and wanted to rub it in Greg's face.

Greg's cell phone interrupted his thoughts on Mark's behavior. It was too early for the killer to call him. He wouldn't call him at the crime scene, unless he was here and wanted to see Greg squirm while he talked to him. Greg stepped outside and fished his phone out of his pocket. He looked at the caller ID, but it wasn't from one of the dead girls' numbers. Shelly was calling.

"Hello?" There was an explosion of emotion, and unintelligible words. "Honey, you have to calm down. I can't understand a word you're saying. Calm down and say it slower."

"She's not here," Shelly said.

Her voice was forced and strained.

"Who's not there? Where are you?"

"I'm at the school, Greg. Hope is not here."

Greg went weak in the knees.

"Did you call your mother? Maybe she thought it was her day to pick her up?"

Shelly's mother had mixed her days up before and sat in line two cars behind Shelly for an hour. She caused a scene when she saw Hope get into a stranger's car that turned out to be Shelly.

"I called everybody before I called you, Greg. The teachers can't find her anywhere. They said she came outside when they called her name over the speaker, but nobody remembers seeing her get into a car."

"I'm on my way. I'll get there as fast as I can."

Greg's entire body went numb, and he ran into the house on unsteady legs.

"I have to go to the school, my daughter is missing," he yelled at anybody who would listen.

Don chased him out the door, trying to ask him questions, but Greg didn't hear him. He kept running and jumped into his car and turned on the lights and sirens. Greg's body was full of adrenaline. He no longer felt like he couldn't walk on his own legs. He was in pursuit mode, and his daughter could be in trouble.

Thoughts raced through his mind as he drove. Was she still at the school and somebody made a mistake? Maybe she was hiding in a classroom or the library or some place. There had to be a logical explanation. Kids didn't just disappear at school. Thoughts of her not being at the school, and something happening to her, flooded in. He let off the gas, and the car coasted downhill. Where could she have gone? Why would she get into somebody's car that she didn't know? Why would the teacher put her in somebody's car they didn't know? He snapped out of it and stomped the gas pedal to the floor. He was only a few miles from the school.

The car slid into the parking lot, and he threw it in park. He had to calm down. He needed a clear head. Greg didn't wait for his head to go to analytical detective mode. He was in full daddy panic mode. He ran to the front of the school and found his wife wandering around the front of the school yelling for Hope.

"What are they doing? We have to find her," Greg yelled.

"The teachers are checking all the classrooms for her, and the principal is trying to get in touch with all the buses to make sure she didn't get on one of them."

Greg grabbed Shelly by the shoulders and forced her to look him in the face.

"A car, Shelly. Did somebody say they saw her getting into a car?"

"No, they said she came outside when they called her name."

"Who the hell is watching the kids while they're out here? Do they just let them get into any car?"

It was hard not thinking about the worst-case scenario, but he'd been in law enforcement long enough to see the darker side of

Crystal Valley. And the darker side cast a huge shadow over his thoughts every day.

"Greg, calm down."

He saw it in her eyes. She was on the verge of completely losing it, and he was making it worse by getting as upset as she was. They couldn't both lose it. One of them had to at least act strong for both of them.

"Okay. You keep searching out here. I'll check inside."

Greg ran to the cafeteria. That was where the students waited until their parents pulled up in front of the school and they called their names over the speaker. The room was empty. He ran around looking under all the tables. After he cleared the room, he ran back into the hall and headed for the library. She always said it was her favorite place to go, even more than recess.

Greg rounded the corner and busted through the library door like he was crashing in on a murder suspect. High-pitched screams and cries greeted his intrusion. The after-school program was in the library, and he'd sent all the kids scrambling for cover.

"I'm sorry," he said, and put his hands on his knees. "Has anybody seen Hope Burns?"

After a few stunned seconds, the children and teachers realized he wasn't going to hurt them, and they all told him no. Greg turned and walked slowly out of the library. They couldn't find his daughter anywhere. It wasn't like her to go with anybody she didn't know. The teachers sent her outside when they called on the intercom, and then nobody else saw her after that. The only way they would have called her name is if a car were in the parent pickup area with her name on a sign. Somebody picked her up, and the school sent her out to them. Greg ran to the front of the school where Shelly was talking to the principal.

"Somebody has her," he yelled.

"Mr. Burns, we don't know that. There are still a few buses we haven't been able to get in contact with. She may be with a friend."

"No, she's not. She was in the cafeteria, and they called her name over the intercom. The only reason that would have happened is because a car out here had a sign with her name on it. So, you let her get into the car with a complete stranger."

Shelly burst into tears and dropped to her knees. She looked ashen gray, as if she'd aged twenty years in twenty seconds. The color left the principal's face.

"I have to call this in. I'll have the whole damn department looking for her," he said.

Greg pulled his phone out of his pocket. Before he could dial dispatch, the phone rang and "Home" popped up on the caller ID screen. He looked at the phone like it was an alien tool he had never seen before. The principal and Shelly were watching him, waiting for him to make some sort of sign as to why his ringing phone confused him.

"He...Hello?"

"Hey Daddy, I'm home. Where are you?"

Greg's legs turned to rubber, and he fell on the wood bench outside the principal's office.

"Hope, are you okay?"

Tears ran down his face.

"Of course, I am, silly. I thought you were going to be here when I got home?"

Shelly wrapped her arms around Greg's neck, still crying. Her tears soaked through his shirt.

"How did she get there, Greg? This doesn't make any sense," she cried.

"Hold on, Shelly. I'm trying to find out. Hope, how did you get home?"

Greg pulled away from his wife. It would be hard to find anything out if they were having two conversations.

"The policeman you sent to pick me up brought me home. Tell Mommy I said hey."

"The policeman? Is he still there with you?"

Greg's heart sank, and he jumped from the bench.

"Yes. He's really nice. He said he would stay with me until you got home. I wish he was your partner instead of Mr. Don. He doesn't ever laugh."

"Where is he now?"

"He said he needed to go to the bathroom."

"Don't go anywhere with him. Stay at the house. I am on my way. Try to hide if you can, baby."

Greg was already running out of the school with Shelly chasing after him. He hopped into the car and was about to leave when Shelly started beating on the window.

"Greg, I don't understand. What is going on? Is she okay? Who took her home?"

"She's fine. There is nothing to worry about. I just need to get home and find out what is going on. Just get your car and meet me there. I have to hurry."

Greg sped off toward his house. He'd never sent a cop to Hope's school before. Somebody posing as a cop picked her up from school. There was only one person he could think of who would want to screw with him like this.

A dangerous killer gave his daughter a ride home from school and was now waiting for him to get there. At least, that's what the guy told Hope. He hadn't told anybody the killer was calling him. If something happened to his daughter, it would be his fault. If the guy really was waiting for him, he may be able to arrest him before anybody else got hurt. He was being hopeful, but Greg didn't expect the guy to be there when he got home. If he were already gone, Greg would be okay with it, as long as his daughter was safe.

Greg pulled into his driveway. The few neighbors who were home during the day were looking out their windows at all the commotion. He drew his gun and ran up the steps to his house. Hope sat on the porch swing, kicking her legs.

"Hey, Daddy. Why do you have your gun out?"

"I'm trying to protect you, honey. Where is the man who brought you home?"

Hope jerked her head back and squished up her nose.

"You don't have to protect me from Stephen. He is a police officer, like you."

Hope didn't seem to be in distress, but Greg needed to know everything about 'Stephen' without loosing his temper or scaring his daughter.

"Where is he?"

Greg lowered his gun, but didn't holster it.

"We were sitting on the porch, and when he heard your sirens, he said that you would be home in a minute, so he needed to be going."

Hope's eyes never left his gun.

"Hope, I need you to think very hard about this. What did he look like?"

She closed her eyes and crinkled her nose.

"He ... He was as tall as the hook holding Mommy's summer wreath," she said, and closed her eyes again. "His hair was brown."

"Okay, that's good. Was he young or old? Was he skinny?"

"He was young like Jimmy and was skinny like him too. He wasn't fat like you, Daddy," she said covering her mouth trying to keep her giggles in.

"Hey, I'm not fat. You better watch it," he said.

Greg was able to decipher Hope's description for a decent outline of the guy who picked her up from school. He estimated the guy was the same height as him. If both of their heads came to the bottom of the hook, then the man was about 5'10. Jimmy, who lived down the street, was between twenty and twenty-five years old and probably weighed 170 pounds or so. He cut their grass every week. Hope had a crush on him. She would sit on the porch watching and waiting for him to finish so she could offer him something to drink.

Shelly pulled into the driveway. She left the car running and the door open when she ran and picked Hope up. New tears flowed down her cheeks.

"Why are you crying, Mommy?"

"She's just happy to see you. You two stay outside. I'm going to check the rest of the house."

The door was locked. They had to have gone inside at some point to use the phone. He let her call and came back outside, and he made sure to lock up before he left. Shelly must have left the door unlocked when she went to the school to pick Hope up. Otherwise, he wouldn't have gone inside. He saw it as an invitation and let himself in.

"Greg? Who was it?"

"I don't know."

"You don't know? She says a man in a police car picked her up, and you don't know who it is? You better find out, and it better not be somebody playing a joke on you. That's cruel."

Greg didn't know what to tell Shelly. He couldn't tell her that it was probably a murderer he had been chasing, but they were lucky because he left, and she didn't end up dead in a suicide pose with a note from the killer. He also couldn't let her think that it was an actual cop playing a joke on him. She would burn down city hall until she got to the bottom of it.

"I don't know who it was. I do know it wasn't a cop prank. They don't ever involve the families, and they certainly wouldn't kidnap a child. I want you to take Hope and Jared, and go stay at your mother's for a few days, and I'll have all the locks changed."

"I want a security system with cameras before we come back home."

"I'll call today. Just go get packed."

Shelly picked Hope up and held her tight against her chest.

"Am I going to get to see Stephen again, Daddy? He was nice."

"I sure hope not, baby."

Greg sat on the top step, watching, looking for any sign that the guy who called himself Stephen was still around. He didn't see anything out of the ordinary. There was nothing different about the day. After the sirens were off, and nothing was happening, the neighborhood went back to its normal casual existence. Greg heard the distant ringing of his phone rise to full volume.

"This is Burns," Greg tried to say, but in his distracted state, it came out, "This Burns."

"I'm sure it does, Detective."

Greg jumped to his feet when he heard the killer's voice. He walked around his front yard, looking at all the houses, and in the trees.

"You missed my first two calls. I sure hope that Hope ... Wow, that's a mouthful. I trust that Hope is okay. I would hate to think that I scared her."

"You stay the hell away from my family. They have nothing to do with this."

Greg walked through his side yard. The killer expected Greg to show up with the cavalry and wouldn't wait around for a rookie to get lucky and catch him in a neighbor's yard.

"I was merely trying to help you out. I knew you would be tied up at that bloody crime scene for most of the day. She was definitely a bleeder. Anyway, I thought you might need somebody to pick Hope up, so I helped you out."

"I will kill you if you come near her again."

Greg needed to calm down before he lost it. It wasn't like him to get so emotional when dealing with a killer. But that was before he messed with his family. The coolheaded detective was gone and replaced with a pissed off father who had failed to do his most important job.

"I highly doubt it, and I would never hurt a child."

"Oh, is that beneath you?"

"Yes, of course it is. Detective, I really thought we were starting to become close. You know, friends."

"You're seriously messed up in the head."

Greg walked around the house and down the street past two of his neighbor's houses.

"That's a bit harsh. You seem to be breathing hard. If you're running around trying to find me, you're not going to. I am nowhere near you. I had to return the car that I ... borrowed."

"You expect me to just believe that? You like to hang around and watch."

"I wouldn't lie to you, and as I said, I had to return the car. It all worked out perfectly. I found a decommissioned police cruiser in the Wal-Mart parking lot. I know you guys sell the old cars to make extra money, but do you also sell them because they still look like cop cars, and you want people to think there are more of you on the streets? That's clever. And don't worry. Hope was never in any danger. As luck would have it, this car already had a car seat for her."

"You just took the car back and expected the owner to never know?"

There was a pause followed by a loud thundering laugh. Greg had to pull the phone away from his ear. He put the phone closer but did not put it back to his head until the laughter calmed down.

"You're going to love this story, Detective. I dropped the car off at the Waffle House next door. The owners looked so confused when they came out. They were pushing their buggies around the entire parking lot. I couldn't believe they had been in there the whole time I was gone. And then ... oh, this is the best part, listen. And then when they found it, they loaded up their groceries and came inside and ordered. I sat beside them the whole time. They were confused as hell and blamed each other for moving the car."

"Sounds like you were having a good time, while I was consoling my daughter.”

“More like she was consoling you and your wife. She’s a sweet child.”

Greg’s head ached. The sustained high blood pressure caused a migraine to form behind his eyes.

“Why are you calling me? Just to torment me? To prove you’re smarter than I am?”

“There’s nothing to prove, Detective. I needed to blow off some steam, so I thought I would have a bit of fun. Now it’s all out of my system. I promise.”

“If you come near her again, I will kill you.”

An exaggerated breath of air like a chided teenager blew through the phone.

“Come on, quit with the empty threats. It’s unbecoming a man of your position.”

Greg seethed with anger. His threats were not meaningless or empty. For the first time in his career, he wanted to kill. There was no question that he would break his oath to serve and protect. The guy brought his family into it, and he was laughing about it. Laughing in his face, because he thought he was better than Greg. This was all a sick game to get a rise out of Greg so he would make a mistake and leave another series of unsolved cases. He wanted to destroy Greg.

Greg sat on the top step of his porch and ran his hand through his hair. He was tired.

“How did you pick up my little girl from school and then get into my house?”

“Ah, I thought you’d never ask. But don’t sound so down. You sound like I’ve already beaten you. It was all a bit too easy.”

The complete glee he got from telling Greg what he had done and how he did it infuriated Greg even more. He shouldn’t have given him the satisfaction and hung up on him. But he wanted to know, and he would probably be telling the truth, mostly.

“Finding out where you lived was easy. I’ve known for a while. I followed you home from Rachel’s house when you almost caught me napping. Then I saw the sign in your wife’s car with your daughter’s name on it. I just had to create my own sign, and they pretty much delivered her to me. The car looked like your car, so no questions were asked.”

Greg shook his head. It had been too easy, and he only did it for fun. What would he do if Greg pushed him to react?

"How did you get into my house? My wife wouldn't have just left the house unlocked for you," Greg asked through clenched teeth.

"No worries there. She locked everything up tight. However, I must say, leaving an extra key under the doormat. Come on, Greg. That has got to be the most cliché place to leave a key. Really, you were asking for it. I'm surprised more people haven't invited themselves into your house. Don't worry. I put the key back before I left. However, I would suggest finding a new hiding place."

Greg told Shelly countless times that they needed to move that key. Under the doormat would be the first place somebody would look. He should have moved the key himself, but he assumed it would find its way back under the mat, so he didn't bother with it. Even if he had left the key, Greg was still changing all the locks in the house, while he waited for somebody to install a security system.

Shelly and Hope walked out of the house with their luggage.

"We're about to go and pick up Jared and go to my mother's. I'm serious, Greg. I'm not coming back until we have an alarm on the house," Shelly said.

Greg hesitated at the mention of his son. Until now, he hadn't thought about the killer going after Jared when he left the house.

"I know what you're thinking, Greg. Have no fear. Little Jared is safe and sound. But, it seems like you need to tell your family good-bye, so I'll let you go for now. I'll talk to you later."

There was a click, and then silence. He didn't have time to worry about him. He had to send his family away. Greg loaded the suitcases into the trunk and fastened his daughter into her car seat.

"Love you, Daddy."

"Love you too, Monkey. Take care of your mother and make sure she calls me when you get to Grandma's house."

Greg shut the door and Shelly backed out of the driveway before he could get to the other side and tell her bye. She blamed him for what happened. She would be beyond mad if she found out Greg had been talking to a murderer for days and had not told anybody about it. He could never let her know who gave their daughter a ride home from school. It would be the end of his marriage and the end of his career.

Chapter Seventeen

Bobby thought playing a game with the detective would be fun and get his mind off Danielle. He was right. The entire time spent thinking about how to get Hope Burns away from her school without anybody noticing, and the time he spent looking for a car, he never thought about Danielle—or Emily—for that matter. He poured everything into the game. He couldn't afford not to. One miscalculation, and he'd end up in jail.

But as soon as he hung up the phone with the detective, the game was over. He spent a bit of time gloating and celebrated with an All-Star Special.

Now all the fun was over. When he got in his car, he wanted to go home but drove around aimlessly instead. The windows were down, and the hot breeze blew in, threatening to suffocate him. He fought to push all the thoughts out of his head, but he was fighting a need he could never ignore or sate. He turned the radio on. The deejay's velvet voice swam through the river of humidity, swirling around his head until it whirlpooled into his ear and bore into the abyss of his thoughts.

This is Monica Mayhem on Rock 104.4, the only place for today's new hard rock and the only place to hear the truth. It was her Bobby.

He jerked back to reality and almost jerked the Bronco off the road. He was hiding in a dark and quiet place with no thoughts. Running on basic instinct like people do when they arrive home, but do not remember the route in which they drove. His body went cold with fear.

She is the one who took Emily away. She is the reason you are out here trying to forget everything, but you will never forget Emily. She saw you the other night covered in blood. How long do you think she will keep that secret? She will call the police and tell them about you next. You have to do something, Bobby. You can't wait for her to make the next move.

Bobby pulled the vehicle to the shoulder and slammed on the brakes. He punched the steering wheel, and when it didn't hit back, he punched it again and again, until the skin on his knuckles, now ragged, split and blood ran down his hand.

*You're hitting the wrong thing, Bobby. You should be—*Bobby turned the radio off and put his head on the steering wheel. He tried to calm himself and go to sleep on the side of the road, but he was wide awake. The adrenaline pumping through his system would not let him relax. He pulled the car back onto the road, wanting to drive around until he was calm again. It worked before the radio started talking to him, it should work again now that the radio was off.

It didn't take him too long to find his quiet place again. He drove on autopilot, but when he parked, he was not in his driveway. He was in the extra parking space at the Valley Summit apartment complex. Her car sat in its spot, and the lights were on in her living room window. Bobby stared at the building, not sure of what he was going to do or say to Danielle, but he knew that he needed to find out the truth. Otherwise, he would drive himself crazy.

The radio on his dashboard lit up.

Hey, there metal heads. It's Monica Mayhem, and right now I have a new band for you. Like some of your thoughts, they call themselves Fathoms Deep, and here is their song titled 'The Snitch Must Die.'

The song started with a single bass line, followed by a blast beat from the drums and chugging guitars. A low growl came from the speakers. It wound itself up until it was at such a high pitch that Bobby covered his ears. When the singer reached the top of his register, he screamed, "The snitch must die."

Bobby didn't want to hear any more of the song. He pushed the knob in to turn the radio off, but it didn't work. He continued to push the button, to no avail. The song continued. The lead singer was winding his growl up again to assault Bobby's ears. Bobby grabbed the gun he started carrying with him from the passenger's seat. The gun was brand new and had never been fired. It was only in case things got bad, and that was his only option. He didn't want to take anymore chances after the last girl almost took his head off with her shotgun. He hit the radio with the butt of the gun, but it played on.

Bobby continuously pistol-whipped the radio. The lights went out, but the blows continued. The radio face fell to the floor. He reached for the exposed wires but stopped when he had radio silence. Everything in his head weighted on him. Manning up and confronting her was the only way he'd get any answers. Exiting the vehicle, he reached back in for his gun as an afterthought. Bobby trudged up the stairs, stomping each foot on every step for effect. No wayward neighbors were scaring him to the bushes tonight.

The door slowly swung open. Danielle was still in her pajamas, and she hadn't put on makeup or fixed her hair. Bobby had never seen her like that before. She looked tired, like she hadn't slept in days. She probably hadn't slept since she saw Bobby standing at her neighbor's door covered in blood like some B-horror movie.

"Are you going just to stand there looking at me, or can I come in?" Bobby asked.

Danielle didn't respond. Her eyes grew wide, and she backed away from the door. Charlie sniffed Bobby and growled.

"Hey, Charlie. What's your problem?"

Bobby walked toward the dog. Charlie started barking and ran into the back room. Bobby shrugged and sat down at the bar.

"That's weird. He hasn't ever acted like that toward me before."

"He's not the only one not acting how they used to," Danielle said, and walked behind the counter.

"Yeah. You're right. I've noticed you've been a little crazy too. Everything okay at work?"

"I wasn't talking about me, Bobby. I was talking about you. You're the one who has been acting weird. Ever since you found that girl in the woods, you haven't been the same. I thought with her gone you would go back to being the same Bobby I used to know."

Bobby looked down at the counter.

"So, you are the one who called the police and told them about Emily?"

"No, Bobby. I've tried to tell you over and over it wasn't me. I have no idea who it was."

Bobby jumped up from the bar, knocking over the stool he was sitting on. Danielle jumped and backed against the counter. There was nowhere for her to go. Tears rolled down her weary face.

"Please don't hurt me."

Bobby walked around the counter and Danielle slid further down the cabinets. She stopped suddenly when the handle from one of the drawers jabbed into her side.

"I'm not going to hurt you," Bobby said, cupping her face in his dirty hand.

"Please go. Just go, and we'll talk later."

"I just want to ask one question," he said. "If you didn't call, then who was it?"

He coaxed her face forward with his hand and kissed her lips. Danielle put both of her hands against his chest and pushed him away.

"I already told you. It wasn't me, and I have no idea who it was. But I'm glad they did. I should have done it the first night I saw her, but I didn't. If I had then none of this would have ever happened and we would be like we used to be."

Bobby pushed her hard. She put both hands behind her, bracing herself from the impact of the counter, but it did little to lessen the impact.

"It's your fault she's gone."

"No, it's my fault that you're like this. I should have told the police sooner, but I didn't, and now you need help. Bobby, I loved you. That's why I did what you asked when I knew I shouldn't listen to you."

Bobby's face dropped, and his anger wavered.

"You loved me?"

The question came out as a meek whisper.

"I love who you were before her. I don't love who you have become."

"Don't blame her. It's not her fault. She didn't do anything to you."

"It's not what she did to me. It's what she did to you. Bobby, you're sick and need help that I can't give you. Don't you realize we're arguing over a girl you never met because she is dead?"

Danielle stepped toward Bobby, driving him back.

"Don't blame her," Bobby said, and jumped at her.

He grabbed her shoulder and pulled the gun from his waistband. Danielle screamed, and Bobby moved his hand from her shoulder to cover her mouth. With her arm free, she reached behind her and knocked dirty dishes to the floor. She was searching. Grasping for whatever she could find to stop him. Bobby didn't want to scare her like this, but it had to be this way now.

He pressed his hand firmly against her face, pushing her back onto the counter and put the gun barrel in sight. She screamed louder against his hand and tried to push him off, but his weight was too much for her. Her frantic hand landed on the blade of a knife and sliced her finger.

She lunged again and knocked the knife out of reach. Finally, she stopped fighting him, but she started leaning back toward the knife. This change in momentum threw Bobby's balance off, and Danielle grabbed the knife. She pushed Bobby to get a little separation to move and swung the knife at Bobby.

Bobby stumbled, and the blade plunged into his left shoulder. He screamed and pulled away from Danielle with the knife still firmly buried in his shoulder. He doubled over in pain and yelled to the floor.

Danielle carefully approached Bobby and put her hand on his back.

"Bobby. I'm so sorry. I was scared you were going to hurt me. I—"

Bobby pulled the knife from his shoulder and stood up, driving the knife deep into Danielle's abdomen. His sudden movement cut off her strangled gasp as he knocked all the air out of her. Her eyes were bright with surprise. She stumbled backward, pulling the handle from his hand as she fell to the floor. Blood poured from the wound, bathing her in dark red.

"No. Don't die. I wasn't going to shoot you. I only wanted to scare you." Bobby held his hands on the wound, trying to apply pressure.

A red trail ran from her mouth. Danielle lifted her hand toward his face, but it fell short and landed on his shoulder. Bobby watched the life drain from her eyes. He stayed with his hands on her stomach for a while. She tried to speak between weak coughs, but he shushed her like a child who wouldn't go to sleep. Tears rolled down his face and landed on hers, mixing with the blood. Bobby had seen people die. He'd been the cause of their deaths, but none of them died this slowly. Even his Grandmother's death rattle wasn't so agonizing. As Danielle finally took her last breath, Bobby felt the heavy weight of death drape across his shoulders and settle as a burning fire in his chest. He hadn't experienced the unexpected finality of death since he lost his grandfather. Bobby loved Danielle.

"I believe you. Just come back to me. Please."

Bobby pulled her to him with his good arm and hugged her.

"I'm sorry. I didn't mean it. You caught me off guard when you attacked me, and I reacted without thinking about it. I didn't mean to hurt you."

He sat rocking next to her body, begging for her to come back to him. A growl that sounded like the beginning of the song he heard before coming to talk to Danielle interrupted his pleas. The growl did not begin to rise. Instead, it stayed at the same hateful pitch. Bobby pulled his face from Danielle's hair to see Charlie staring at him. He barked, and Bobby swung the gun, but missed him.

This time Charlie did not run away whimpering. He closed in on his target. Bobby backed away from Danielle, swinging at the encroaching dog. When he got to the door, he turned and ran. He jumped into his Bronco and didn't look back. He threw it into gear and stomped the gas, missing the car behind him by inches.

He didn't want to leave Danielle, but he didn't need to be there if the cops showed up. Somebody had to have heard all the noise they were making. He jerked the wheel before he sideswiped a car and over-corrected, almost sending him straight into another car.

Bobby sped down Red Rock Road. He screamed and punched the seat, the steering wheel and then the dash. The radio light flickered. Why did she attack him? She said she loved him and then stabbed him with a knife. He didn't want to hurt her. He only wanted to scare her with the gun so she would tell him the truth. It was her fault she was dead. If she hadn't attacked him, he never would have stabbed her.

Bobby had trouble keeping the vehicle on the winding road. He punched the dash again, and the radio lit up.

This in Monica Mayhem and I'm out of here for tonight. Don't touch that dial. The Executioner is up next with today's hits from the darker side.

Bobby punched the radio, and the volume went up. The knobs were missing from his assault in the apartment complex, and he could not turn it down. The volume was so loud he couldn't tell if it was music or if the Executioner was on. He punched it two more times, but nothing happened.

He pointed the gun at the radio and pulled the trigger twice. Plastic pieces flew through the air and the radio smoked silently. The recoil from the gun made Bobby swerve off the road. The SUV fishtailed in the loose gravel and he came close to losing control. He turned into the first parking lot he came to and put his head on the wheel and sobbed.

"Are you okay?"

The voice startled Bobby, and he looked up. The man was short, with curly black hair and glasses. He wore a white button-up shirt and khaki pants and possessed an ethereal white glow. Bobby didn't answer the man, only looked at him through wet, squinting eyes. The man moved toward the vehicle and Bobby realized the man was not glowing; he was standing in front of a ten-foot cross, bright enough for heaven to see. He must have pulled into a church parking lot after he shot the radio. How the hell had he missed seeing the cross when he pulled in? Bobby got out of the vehicle.

"Oh wow, that's a lot of blood. Are you hurt?"

Bobby carried his left shoulder lower than the right and shuffled toward the man. His head was foggy about where he had been and what he was doing. He couldn't think straight. Everything flashed in front of him, but it was all a blur. The man wrapped Bobby's unharmed arm around his neck and tried to pull him to his car. Bobby leaned against the car while the man opened the passenger side door.

"Okay, I'm going to ease you into the seat. I'll take you to the hospital. While they're checking you out, I'll call the police."

"No," Bobby whispered.

"We have to call the police. It looks like you've been stabbed, and you're covered in blood."

"No," Bobby yelled this time and pushed the man away from him. The man stumbled back and came after Bobby. Flashbacks of Danielle coming at him with the knife and trying to kill him flooded his mind.

"I didn't mean to kill her."

The man stopped where he was.

"You killed somebody?"

The man backed away from Bobby. He was going to call the police. Bobby lunged at the man, landing on his back and knocking him to the ground. Bobby rolled the man over and punched him.

"No, you can't tell anybody. I didn't mean to kill her. I didn't mean to kill her."

The man tried to roll away, but Bobby straddled him and repeatedly punched him in the face. Blood splashed on Bobby's clothes and face, mixing with his and Danielle's, making a coppery cocktail. Bobby pinned the man's hands down at his side so he couldn't defend himself. He could only move his head from side to side, trying to dodge Bobby's pounding fists.

Rage boiled inside Bobby. He couldn't stop himself. The man stopped moving, and Bobby continued to beat his face. Bones in the man's face splintered beneath his hand. The only thing left of his face was an unrecognizable pulp that looked like a freshly squeezed grapefruit. When Bobby thought the man had had enough and he no longer felt angry with Danielle or himself, he rolled off of him and headed home. He had to work in the morning.

Chapter Eighteen

Emily and Mike met in high school. She was shy and didn't have many friends, but Mike was drawn to her the first time he saw her. When he heard her sweet voice, he knew he was in love and wanted to be with her. It surprised him when she agreed to go out with him. After that first date, they were inseparable. Nothing in the world seemed to matter. Then they graduated. Mike never had a stable home life and found himself looking for a place to live before he had a chance to remove his cap and gown. Emily started at the local State University. She had dreams of being a veterinarian since she was a child. Her plan was to get her core classes at home and transfer to a larger school for the vet program.

After her freshman year, Mike asked her to move in with him. He told her that he was struggling to get by and needed her help. From the first time they met, Emily did everything Mike told her to do. She told him she would get a part-time job to help with bills, but she was going to stay in school. That plan lasted through the first semester of her sophomore year. Mike had always been controlling, but he got worse the more she was away from him. He started fights with her every night when she got home from school. The worst fight happened the final week of classes.

She came home smelling like her favorite perfume. He asked her why she was wearing it but didn't give her time to answer. It didn't matter why she said she was wearing it. To him, the only reason to start wearing perfume to school would be because she met somebody, or worse, she was trying to seduce a professor.

After the fight, he thought everything would blow over like it usually did. The night she came home from her last final, she was in a great mood. She was bubbly and happy, like he hadn't seen in a while. She told him she thought she aced her last test and wanted to celebrate. She went to change clothes, and Mike lost his temper. He didn't plan on going out, so she obviously had plans to meet somebody else. He walked into their room and threw her favorite vase against the wall and told her there would be no more school. He needed more help with the bills and she was going to start looking for a full-time job the next day.

She didn't say anything. She crumbled to the floor and cleaned up the pieces of her vase. That was the first time he realized how afraid of him she was. Quitting school didn't go over well with her family. There were countless fights about her ruining her life. They blamed everything on Mike. He quickly grew tired of all the drama and cut her off from her family. He didn't allow her to call them, and she rarely visited them. Emily found a job working in a doctor's office.

The only males working in the office were the two doctors who owned the practice. They were both pushing sixty, so he didn't worry about them even though she told him she avoided speaking to them as much as possible. There was nothing to worry about and the men coming in were all sick, but he still threw all of her perfume away and told her never to wear it again. She would wake up, go to work, come home and cook for him and any of his friends who happened to be at the house that night. He didn't believe she was completely miserable. To prove it to himself as much as her, he would still take her out. Most of the time they would go to her favorite place.

She liked to go where she ended up killing herself. They would sneak into the park after the sun went down and the park was closed. It was her favorite time because she could see the moon shining down and reflecting across the water's surface. He never cared for it, but it would satisfy her for a little while longer.

He told his friends he would do small things for her so he could keep her around. She was the best maid he'd ever had. Then they'd laugh about it. But he knew she would never leave because she had nowhere to go. Mike loved her, but everything changed the day he met Danielle.

Mike's company was doing the landscaping for a project that Arkwright Construction was working on. When their eyes met, he knew she was different. She was completely professional and ignored his playfully flirting. It took five trips to her office for made up reasons before she finally agreed to go out with him. She was the most interesting person he had ever met. Every time she walked into a room, everybody felt her presence. Whenever she was around, her vitality intoxicated him. She made him feel unlike he had ever felt before. The only problem was Emily still lived with him. She'd been with him for so long he couldn't just drop her. And there wasn't anything he could do to drive her away.

It started with Danielle on the side, but quickly changed to Emily being on the side. Emily didn't suspect he was dating somebody else, and even if she thought there was somebody else, there was no way she'd ever confront him about it. For four months everything went well until he took Emily out to eat for her birthday. Danielle sat two tables away with a few of her friends.

She didn't cause a scene. When he saw the hurt look and tears welling up in her eyes, he thought she would come to their table and blow his cover on everything. Instead, she finished her meal with her friends and left. Mike didn't know how to handle that response. No woman had ever reacted, or not reacted, that way before. It was an open defiance against him and made him want her more. Emily's birthday dinner ended with her crying for some reason, but he couldn't remember what happened.

When he finally got in touch with Danielle three days later, she told him she didn't want to ruin the night for the girl he was with since she looked so happy. He told her they had been together for a long time, but the relationship had been over for a while. He was having trouble trying to tell her that because he didn't want to hurt her. She told him she wasn't going to do it for him and wouldn't be waiting for him on the side until he grew the nerve to tell the poor girl. Then she stopped answering his calls. She wouldn't answer her apartment door, and if he tried to talk to her at work, she would be straight to the point with business matters and ignore any personal conversations he tried to have with her.

He tried to move on, but couldn't stop thinking about her. The situation with Emily only got worse. He didn't tell her about Danielle, but he blamed her for everything and started taking it out on her. Then he met Amy. There was no special connection with her, but she reminded him enough of Danielle that he decided to pursue her, anyway. When Emily caught them together, it lifted a huge weight from his shoulders. He tried to stop Amy from leaving, but didn't try too hard. His heart wasn't in it. The entire time he thought that maybe this would be his chance to get back with Danielle. Emily would leave him as soon as she got home and the problem would be over. It took a lot not to run behind Amy and go straight to Danielle's desk, but he didn't want to seem too eager and held back. When Emily ran off into the woods, he thought she would go to her spot for a while and cry, and be home later to get her stuff. He never thought she would kill herself.

Now, Mike sat in his car outside of Danielle's apartment. She never knew Emily or her name, so she wouldn't know she was dead. He could just tell her there was nothing to worry about. Emily was out of the picture. There was no need to tell her all the details that led to her being gone. He would have to sweet talk her, but he was sure he would be able to at least talk to her now. That would be a start, and then he could work on dating again. The light in her apartment turned on, and he opened his car door.

Before he could take a step, another car door swung open and slammed. The dark figure stalked up the stairs. Mike hit the hood of the car next to him. There wasn't enough light for him to see who was going up the stairs. He didn't even know if they were going to Danielle's apartment. He went to the Bronco the person jumped from. D-7 in faded yellow could barely be made out on the pavement behind the rear tires. The person was either with Danielle right now, or they didn't care whose spot they parked in. Mike kicked the back of the vehicle, putting a small dent in the lift gate. The lights were on in her living room, but no silhouettes moved across the shaded wall. He thought they could be in the kitchen, then the worse thought of them in the bedroom crossed his mind, and he kicked the gate again.

Mike paced between his car and his rival's, trying to decide what he was going to do. He wanted to run up there and beat on the door until somebody answered and then beat on the guy who was in there with her. But, if he busted in and beat up her new boyfriend, he would never get another chance with her. And they may call the cops. The cops were the last thing he needed to deal with now.

A dog's bark echoed into the breezeway and a door slammed. Was that Charlie? Mike had never heard Charlie, bark. He assumed Danielle had one of those bark collars on him. The apartment door swung open, and Mike ducked behind a car. The person ran to the Bronco and jumped inside. Mike stood in time to see Bobby's face as the vehicle sped away. Mike fell back against the car behind him. She was dating the guy from the coffee shop? He couldn't believe she would have anything to do with that guy. He was weird. The few times Mike had been in the coffee shop he could tell there was something off about the guy.

He was running away, so maybe she told him to get lost. Mike looked up the stairs. Light from Danielle's apartment leaked through the open door. He was in such a hurry that he didn't even close the door, but she didn't close it behind him either, and the dog was barking earlier.

Mike crept up the stairs. His boots felt heavier with each step he took. His stomach burned with anticipation with what he would find behind the door. Danielle curled up on the couch crying and just in time for him to swoop in and comfort her. That would be nice. Or Danielle laughing hysterically at that weird guy's advances and ready for a real man to show up. That would be even better. When he pushed the door open, the dog started growling again.

Something dark pooled on the counter and ran red down the side of the cabinets. Mike's body went numb. Charlie ran around the counter. Blood covered his snout and matted the fur around his neck. He walked toward Mike in a crouched position like he was preparing to strike. Mike jumped at the dog and stomped his heavy boots on the floor. The loud echo of the second story floor scared the dog, and he ran out the front door whimpering.

Mike eased around the counter. Danielle lay in a puddle of blood. He froze. His entire body felt like it was full of ice chips being crushed together. Mike stumbled to Danielle and fell to his knees, blood soaking into the worn denim. There was no pulse and her skin felt clammy.

She was already dead. He bowed his head and cried. He reached for her hand and squeezed it. While he was in the parking lot picturing her with another guy, he was up here killing her. People always told him he overreacted to most situations, but the one time he hesitated somebody killed Danielle. If he came up here instead of waiting for the guy to leave, Danielle would still be alive, and it would be the other guy lying dead on the kitchen floor.

Bile rose in his throat, but he forced it back down. Now was not the time to be sick. Through blurry eyes, he pulled out his cell phone and dialed 911. His finger hovered over send. He couldn't do it. He couldn't call 911. Earlier in the week, he led police to the body of his missing girlfriend, and they hounded him over it. They kept asking questions like they thought he killed her when she obviously did it to herself. If he called the police again and told them he found his ex-girlfriend dead in her apartment, they would never believe him. Even if he told them he knew who it was. He would have to prove he was innocent before they would ever listen to him about who it really was. An anonymous phone call, maybe? They would figure out it was him and think he was trying to blame it on the weird barista who worked next door to her and still come after him. Somebody else would have to call, but he couldn't tell anybody. She would have to wait until somebody at work missed her.

Anger soared through Mike's body. The burning sensation melted all the ice. He was ready to take care of the problem himself. Barry. Billy. Bobby? Whatever his name was, the barista needed to pay. He took her away. She couldn't have done anything bad enough to him for him to kill her. The apartment complex didn't have security cameras anywhere. He would get away with it unless Mike stopped him.

Mike didn't know where he lived. The only option would be to wait for him at the coffee shop and follow him home. But first, Mike needed to get out of the apartment complex without anybody seeing him. It wouldn't be good to rush out in a fit looking for retribution, only to be seen by the old cat lady, and end up in jail. He looked down at Danielle's face one last time and brushed her hair from her face. He fought the urge to look toward her blood-covered stomach and the gaping hole that monster put in her. The last glimpse of her needed to be how she actually looked before the mortician created a caricature out of her.

Mike slipped out the door, quietly shutting it behind him. He walked down the stairs on the tips of his toes and tried to look as natural as possible walking across the parking lot to his car. Bobby wouldn't be at work until morning at the earliest. He pulled out of the parking lot but didn't go home. Instead, he drove around Crystal Valley most of the night in hopes that he might pass Bobby's Bronco by chance. After four hours he gave up and went home, but didn't go to sleep. He lay staring at the ceiling, thinking of all the different ways he wanted to kill Bobby. None of his ideas seemed brutal enough to fit his crime.

Mike wanted to be at the coffee shop as soon as it opened. Being there that early, waiting for Bobby to show up was not a good idea. If he saw him, he may not be able to hold himself back and end up attacking him right there in front of anybody who happened to be around. He'd end up in jail. Worse still, he could survive and point the finger at Mike for Danielle's death. There was a good chance Mike left more incriminating evidence at the scene if Bobby went over there planning to kill Danielle. On the other hand, if nobody was around, he could grab him and dispose of him before Emily's funeral that afternoon.

Options weighed, Mike stayed at his house, pacing from the living room to his bedroom. He didn't need to call his boss and fake sick. He'd already given Mike a couple of weeks off when the police found Emily. His boss told him to take all the time he needed while he grieved. He wondered if it would have been better if he were still working. He could go in and distract himself from Bobby and leave early for the funeral.

By eleven o'clock Mike could no longer stand being cooped up inside his house. He dressed in the black suit he last wore two summers ago to his mother's funeral. While looking for his left shoe, he took notice of Emily's clothes hanging in the closet. Her side of the closet was full of the summer dresses she was fond of wearing when she wasn't clad in the pink and gray uniform scrubs she wore to work. His first thought was that he needed to get rid of her stuff. Her parents weren't coming near him, so he would probably end up donating everything to charity. His thoughts drifted back to her parents. He never really cared for them, but that was mostly because they didn't like him and tried to get Emily to leave him. Now, he thought about them buying new clothes for her. The clothes would be the first things they bought for their daughter since they stopped talking to each other, and they would be burying her in them. That is, unless they picked out her casket first. He pushed Emily's parents from his mind. They were the last people he needed to be thinking about while Danielle's killer was loose. He would be busy trying to avoid them soon enough.

He left his house with the intention of driving around town looking for Bobby's Bronco on the chance he was off of work or called in sick after what he'd done last night. How could anybody go to work after slaughtering such a beautiful person? With no destination set, Mike drove straight to the coffee shop and parked across the street. He had trouble seeing through the tinted glass, but after a few minutes, he made out Bobby's face beside the window, wiping down the tables. He didn't even pause at Danielle's table.

Mike gripped the steering wheel tight. Last night, he stabbed Danielle and left her dead on the kitchen floor like she was nothing to him. And today, he's back at work. Acting like nothing happened. Just a normal day making coffee and cleaning the table the woman he killed sat at every day. Mike's clenched teeth throbbed. The pain pulled him out of the death stare he gave Bobby, and he reached for the handle. He pulled himself out of his car and walked across the street. He was going to throw him through that window and cut his throat with one of the pieces of broken glass, so he could see what it felt like to be left dying on the ground with nobody to help him.

Mike burst into the coffee shop. The bell above the door swung up on the length of its rope and hit the wall behind it. The girl behind the counter jumped, dropping the customer's drink she was making. Foam shot into the air followed by hot coffee. The frothy liquid splashed onto the counter and the employee's apron, shielding her from the scalding hot liquid. The customer gasped and shook her head in his direction. Mike focused on his mission to find Bobby and hardly noticed any of the commotion in the shop.

He charged into the men's restroom, kicking in the one stall. He pushed into the woman's restroom and kicked in the stall doors as well. Fortunately, they were empty of customers. He would have a hell of a time explaining the situation that led to his mania to the police and him kicking in the door on some little old lady or somebody's child. He went back to the front of the shop. The employee had the phone in her hand, preparing to dial.

"No, no, no. Don't call the police. I'm just looking for somebody."

"You scared the hell out of us. You should have asked, instead of running through here like you're insane. I think I'm still going to call," she said.

"Please, don't do that. I'm sorry. Here let me pay for this woman's drink and the one that I made you spill. I'm very sorry. I just need to find Bobby."

Mike pulled a wad of crumbled bills and threw it on the counter. He wasn't sure how much money he threw on the counter, but knew there was plenty enough to pay for the drinks and leave a nice tip for the barista.

A concerned look crossed the girl's face. She looked at the customer who now seemed calm and willing to take his apology and allow him to buy her drink.

"You just missed him. He said he had somewhere to be and asked if I would come in early."

Mike's drive left him in his next breath of air. It felt like a gut-punch. He had just missed Bobby, again. It was for the best, but now he would have to come back and hope he was at work tomorrow. He thought about asking the barista if she knew where Bobby went. That would be a bad idea. It already looked bad enough that he burst in on her looking for him like a madman on a rampage. When Bobby turned up dead, the only thing this girl would remember, beside Bobby leaving earlier, was Mike tearing through the store looking for him.

He didn't want to push his luck with her. Besides, the look on her face told him she had given him all the information he was going to get. Hopefully, she wouldn't warn Bobby about this incident and spook him. Mike looked at the clock on the wall. He didn't have time to think about any of that. He didn't want to be late to Emily's funeral.

* * *

Mike pulled into Pine Grove Cemetery and gunned the throttle. He wasn't sure where her grave would be. The funeral directors tried to give him directions when he called, but the only thing he understood was that it was somewhere in the back, in a newly cleared area. The small roads twisted their way through the property. There were places the roadway was just wide enough for one car to go through at a time. These small areas seemed to be all the places that people decided to park and walk to their family member's graves. Mike used it as an excuse to rev his engine as he passed these cars. The low rumble and then growl of his flat black Chevelle scattered the birds in the low-hanging trees. Mourners snapped their heads up like a herd of gazelle finally noticing a predator was near. Their glassy-eyed stares were lost on Mike. They were in his way. Keeping him from getting to a funeral. So was he really the asshole in the situation? They had lost their loved one in the past, but everybody trying to drive to the back of the cemetery was experiencing new loss.

Mike found the small gathering of cars and parked on the edge with his car pointing toward the exit so he could make a quick escape. All the people attending the funeral heard his arrival at the front gate. He received dirty looks from faces with running mascara. The fact that his entrance and loud engine revving was considered rude didn't bother him. Emily's parents had no doubt told everybody salacious lies about him. Not wanting to give them the satisfaction of blaming him, Mike stayed back from the small crowd and stood on the opposite end from Emily's parents.

When the preacher began his service, Mike tuned out. He did rejoin the service a few times to see if it sounded like it was winding down. The preacher shared a lot of stories given to him by her family and a few friends. They were all old stories, from a time before she ever met Mike. The few he heard were all new to him. The preacher seemed to draw these stories out longer than needed, and there were a few more songs played than Mike remembered hearing at past funerals.

It had to be hard for the preacher to give a message full of hope and promise of redemption to the family of a girl who committed suicide, when he expected she was more apt to be tanning by the lake of fire than in the loving embrace of her savior. Mike didn't believe either one of those scenarios was possible and decided it would be best to ignore it, considering the only thing currently on his mind was revenge and murder and both of those would put him on the same beach as Emily if he were inclined to believe in any of that.

The final song ended and the loud sobs of Emily's mother roared over the preacher's final prayer. A comforting arm went around her shoulder and pulled her closer. Mike wasn't able to tell who the person was, but the shaggy black hair was not her father's strawberry blonde. It had been years since Mike had seen anybody from Emily's family, so not recognizing somebody when he couldn't see their face didn't surprise him.

Still, there was something familiar about the person, and it made Mike uneasy, and he started shifting his position to see who was comforting Emily's mother. He leaned forward as far as he could without sticking out too bad. Other faceless family members blocked his view, and Mike leaned back on his heels for another angle. The mystery person's face almost came into view a few times. Every time he thought they were about to turn his way, they would move away again. It was like the person knew he was watching and was playing a game with him to see how long he would continue to bend and twist to see their face. Mike's face flushed with irritation and exertion. He was about to give up and hope to catch a glimpse of the person before he lost them amongst the other people. Emily's mother shifted in her seat, and Mike saw the face of the comforter.

It was Bobby. Mike's legs weakened, and he stumbled back into the person behind him. He threw up his hands in a mock apology and focused on his target. There was no way Bobby and Emily would have ever been friends. She only had a couple, and they were all female. Mike wouldn't have allowed her to have a friend who was a guy. Bobby may have made her drink a couple of times when she went into the coffee shop, but that wouldn't explain why he was at her funeral. Her mother seemed comfortable enough with him, though. Maybe he knew her, but that didn't feel right either.

The funeral ended, and Bobby said his goodbyes, giving Emily's mother a long embrace. Emily's parents saw Mike, and he could feel the hatred radiating off them.

"You have no right to be here. This is all your fault," her father said.

Mike backed away and headed to his car. Her father didn't intimidate him, but he didn't want to cause a scene and let Bobby see him or give him the chance to escape, again.

"Raymond, just let him go. Don't cause a scene here. He's done enough to this family," her mother said.

The Bronco with the dented lift gate rolled past Mike. How had he missed it? He practically parked beside him and never paid attention to it. Mike revved his engine and threw some rocks in the air for her dad's sake as he drove off in pursuit of Bobby.

He drove through the cemetery like one of the ghosts wandering the grounds, looking for a way out had possessed him. The dam holding a small pond from flooding the creek running out the back of the property barely held onto the speeding car. He ran onto the grass to pass a car that pulled out in front of him. Bobby was at the exit preparing to turn right onto the main road, and Mike let off the gas, coasting a little ways so he wouldn't get on his bumper and let him know he was there.

At the exit, he pulled out and gunned the engine to catch up with Bobby and then kept a safe distance. The Bronco pulled into a gas station, and Mike followed. He waited patiently until Bobby pulled out. Now that he was so close, it was hard not to run across the parking lot and deck him, but he held himself back.

Further down the road Bobby pulled into a bank and went inside. Mike felt a slight irritation because he would not just go home. After a few minutes, Bobby walked outside of the bank. He never looked in Mike's direction. He pulled out of the parking lot headed for his next stop at the grocery store. Mike cursed his luck. Who runs errands after a funeral? After thirty minutes, his patience began to wear thin. The air conditioner in his car was not the strongest, and he kept wiping sweat from his face. After forty-five minutes, Mike was livid. He was ready to go into the store and pull him out, when Bobby emerged from the store with only a few bags. The rest of their ride was uneventful. Mike followed Bobby to the entrance of his subdivision and kept on driving when Bobby turned. He would drive around the neighborhood later until he found his car.

He just hoped he didn't have a garage.

Chapter Nineteen

The old Chevelle rumbled through the neighborhood at a crawl. After driving around for thirty minutes, he found his target. Mike circled around the block and parked three houses down from Bobby and backtracked through the neighbor's yard, trying to avoid the streetlamps. The vehicle was there, but he needed to make sure it was the right one. He crept across the yard to the back of the SUV and shined the flashlight from his cellphone on the lift gate. The two dents bumped under his hand. The original plan was to walk up the front stairs and kick in the door. But now that he was at the house, he thought better of it. He didn't know if Bobby would be alone or have a gun on him. It would be best to look around and find a quieter way to get inside.

Mike stalked up the steps, trying not to make any noise. Sweat poured down his face and stung his eyes. He knelt beside the one window with the light on. It opened up into the dining room. Other than a place setting for one at the table, the room was empty. Mike stood to walk away, and Bobby entered the room.

Startled, Mike crouched down. His heart felt like it was about to beat out of his chest and fall beside him on the porch. His head pounded with the pressure, and he braced himself against the windowsill. He looked back through the window, and Bobby sat at the table facing him. Mike ducked back, and when he didn't hear any movement, he dared to take another look. Bobby was still in his chair eating dinner and reading a book.

Mike's blood pressure rose again. Bobby killed a woman and left her body for anybody to find, and here he was, calmly eating liver and reading *Portnoy's Complaint*. He wasn't looking out the windows paranoid or packing his bags, preparing to leave town. It was just another day to him. He wasn't acting like anything even happened. Mike walked off the porch and headed around the house.

The side of the house faced an open lot going into the empty cul-de-sac. There were no neighbors to light up the area, and everything was cast in total darkness. It would be easy to hide in the shadows. Only the soft glow coming from Bobby's dining room emitted any light, and that didn't leave the porch. Mike walked across a retaining wall and held his arms out for balance. The blinds on the side window were only open a crack, but he could still see Bobby sitting at the table. He hadn't left his meal or his book.

A rusted chain-link fence surrounded the backyard. Mike tried the latch, but a decades old padlock protected it. The key probably wouldn't even open it. The fence wobbled back and forth as he used the links as footholds to climb over. It protested his weight, but he didn't worry about the squeaking of rusted steel on steel alerting Bobby. He swung his leg over the top and missed his next foothold. He swung his arms wildly, trying to grab onto to anything that would stop his momentum. The ground didn't break his fall. The inside seam of his jeans caught on the sharp barb at the top of the fence. The rusted barb cut into the soft flesh of his inner leg and scraped down the length of his thigh. The pants held and swung him back into the fence. After a few swings, the denim ripped, and he landed hard on his shoulder.

Mike lay in the tall grass, too scared to breathe. He put pressure on his thigh to stop the blood and ease the pain. He expected Bobby to come flying out the door, shotgun in hand. The cops would believe he shot a burglar, and he'd end up getting away with another murder. But Bobby never came. The crickets were the only creatures to greet Mike. Maybe he hadn't been as loud as he thought. When you're sneaking around and trying to be quiet, every sound you make echoes like a jackhammer breaking up concrete that nobody can hear but you.

Mike picked himself up and limped to the back door. There was no window for him to see where Bobby was in the house. An old wooden crate sat beneath one of the back windows. It came up to Mike's knee. It might have been used to store lawn tools, but from how high the grass felt, they hadn't been used in a long time. Mike pushed down on the wood to test the strength of the box and see if it would support his weight and still climbed on hesitantly with one foot cocked in the air ready for it to cave in.

He peered into the window, but the room was too dark. The lights were off, and the door was closed. Mike pulled out his pocketknife and cut through the mesh screen covering the window. He hoped the window wasn't painted shut or very loud. Since there was a screen on this window, he thought there was a good chance that Bobby regularly opened it to let a breeze into the house. Just to be safe, he slid the knife blade where the window met the sill to clean out anything that might have been there. He placed a hand on each end of the window and pushed up at the same time so that both sides would move simultaneously, hopefully making no noise. A crooked window would screech loud enough to alert the neighbors one street over.

Mike paused at every slight squeak, but managed to get the window open enough to climb in. He leaped off of the box and his chest hit the windowsill, causing a muffled cough to escape his lips. He froze and listened for any footsteps that may be coming his way. When he was sure nobody was coming, he pushed himself through the window. The exertion burned through his thighs and his wound ripped open wider as he slid to the floor. Mike lay panting in the dark, pulling the flap of his ripped jeans tightly around his thigh to try to stop the new bleeding. Fresh blood on the windowsill wiped away like it'd never been there. He would have to check the side of the house when he left. It might be harder to clean, be he didn't want to leave any evidence behind for the cops to find.

Mike sat against the wall and tried to look around the room. It was pitch black, and there was no light in the backyard to help him see where the door was. He pulled his phone out of his pocket and only used the home screen for light. The flashlight would give off too much light. The dull glow only lit up a few inches of the ground in front of him as he crawled his way around the room so he wouldn't trip over anything. Sweat ran into his eyes, blurring the light and making it more difficult to see. He bumped his head against a chest of drawers. The impact was solid but did not seem to make too much noise. He felt his way to the edge of the furniture and found the wall. From there, he worked his way around until he found the door.

Mike eased the door open and stepped into the hallway. No lights were on in the hall, but the lights were on in the two front rooms and provided enough light for him to see where things were located. He ducked into a dark doorway that must have been the living room. Through the darkness, Mike could see the dining room where Bobby had been eating at the table.

He was no longer there, but his book and dishes were. Mike looked around the house and down at the plate again. It still had a lot of food on it, like he hadn't finished eating yet. Mike realized how quiet the house had been the entire time he'd been inside. Even if you live alone, you make noise. You probably make even more because you're not worried about disturbing anybody else.

Mike walked out of the dining room and peeked into the kitchen. It was empty. He mounted the stairs and took one step at a time, moving as softly as he could, in hopes of catching any squeaks before they became too loud. A thick blanket of dust covered the handrail. The rest of the house seemed relatively clean. The dust build-up probably came from lack of use. Bobby was young and needed no help climbing the stairs at night; he also didn't need to put any weight on it trying to lighten the load on the stairs. The final step up onto the platform of the second story was the loudest. Mike had not expected that part of the floor to make a noise and landed with his full weight.

He froze as the sound echoed through the house and his head. Most of the volume had probably been in his head. He stayed in the same position, balancing his body on one foot while his right hand barely touched the rail behind him. The wait to tell if he had broadcasted to anybody in the house, and possibly the neighbors that he was there felt like an eternity. When he was sure nobody was going to come rushing from one of the rooms or up the stairs behind him, Mike continued down the hall. There were four doors on this level. All the doors were closed except for the last one on the right. The door stood ajar. Mike walked toward that door, thinking it may be his bedroom and he had gone to sleep. That would be a lucky break if he were asleep. It would be much easier to grab him without so much of a struggle.

He pushed the door open with the palm of his right hand, his left balled up ready to pound anything or anybody that may jump out at him. The room was dark except for a lamp beside the bed that gave off a sickly yellow glow. The bed and the rest of the room looked to be empty. Mike stepped in, looking for a door to a possible bathroom, but there was none. The room looked too small to be the master bedroom. Bobby's work clothes were draped over a chair sitting in the far corner. His hat hung from the post on the bed. Pieces of paper littered the dresser. Some of the paper was balled up while others lay randomly on the glass top.

Mike shuffled through the papers. A large N with the vertical lines extended in each direction in blue ink covered the first page. It was surrounded by hundreds of smaller versions. Some ran off the page. The same symbol covered the rest of the papers as well, except each page was in a different color ink. Mike threw the papers down and went to the bed. The right half of the bed had been made, while the twisted sheets at the foot of the left side looked like it had rarely been made.

Mike looked around the room in amazement. It appeared as if two very different people lived in this one tiny room. Half of it was neat and clean. He bet nothing was ever left out of place on that side of the room. The other half of the room was the exact opposite. A mentally disturbed person inhabited this area was the only opinion Mike had. Ripped books and paper scattered across the floor. The furniture was upside down and covered with the same N as the paper. The darkness looked like it clung to everything a little longer and didn't want to let any light in.

Mike picked up a red notebook with a large white N rubbed onto the cover. It looked like he had taken a pencil eraser and erased the color on the cover. Mike remembered doing the same thing in middle school, except his notebooks usually had band names and that block S everybody used to draw on the cover. He fanned through the book, but it was more of the same nonsense letter over and over again. Something in the middle of the book caught his attention, and he flipped back to it. It was a sketch of a girl in black ink. The girl leaned against a fallen tree in the forest. She held her hand out like she was beckoning for the artist to save her. The vines of the surrounding forest pointed toward her. Dark rivers of thick ink ran from her wrists and formed a puddle on the ground. Mike recognized the scene from the picture. It was Emily. Bobby knew she was there the whole time and never told anybody. Anger reignited in his body and flowed through his veins. Bobby was crazier than he thought. Killing Danielle was bad enough, but knowing about Emily and drawing her picture was on a different level. And why was she reaching out for him? He threw the notebook on the bed and backed into the hallway.

Bobby had to be in one of these rooms. But was he hiding or going about his business while Mike stalked through his house? Mike walked back to the first door beside the stairs and pushed his way in. The air in the room was still and tasted stale, like the room had been kept closed up for a long time. The room was as outdated as the rest of the house, maybe more so. It looked like an old person's room. The house probably belonged to his grandparents. Were they the ones who raised him? Was it their fault he became a murderer or was it his parents who originally screwed him up and the grandparents did the best that they could before they died? These questions ran through Mike's head as he searched the room, but he didn't really care what the answers were. Bobby deserved to be dead for what he did, and it didn't matter why he was messed up, he had to pay.

Dust covered everything in the room. Mike wiped the grime from a frame hanging on the wall. *The Lord is greater than the giants you face* was crocheted in red on the ivory fabric behind the glass. Stitched under the epigraph were the names Nicholas and Hazel Cotton, June 16th, 1951. Below the first frame was a blank area of wallpaper that looked brighter than all the rest. It looked like there was a missing frame that had been there for many years. Mike looked around the room. There wasn't a frame that looked out of place on any of the furniture or other walls. Mike touched the bare place on the wall and looked down at the floor. He could just make out the silhouette of a frame leaning against the wall behind the nightstand. A thick sheet of dust covered this frame as well. Mike wiped it away. It was an old faded letter. Mike held his cell phone light closer to the glass, so he could make out the words.

My dearest Hazel. I hate to think that you will be the one to find me here. Know that I have held out as long as I can. The bad days are starting to outnumber the good ones, and I don't want to cause you any more pain. I can see it in your eyes every time you look at me, and it kills me that I can't do anything about it. The only way I know how to help you is to end everything on my own. Know that I have always loved you, even when I couldn't remember. I love you and hope to see you again someday. Don't worry about me. Take care of Bobby, I'm afraid he won't understand why it had to end this way. Love, N

The first vertical line of the N was longer than the other lines of the letter. It was wavy, unlike the rest of the neat handwriting, and did not end; instead, it only faded from the paper. Mike guessed Nicholas had died while signing the letter. Who would frame a suicide letter and keep it beside their bed? That was sick. He placed the frame back on its nail in the wall. The hair on the back of Mike's neck and arms stood on end, and his entire body felt electric, like a dog who knew he was about to get beat for leaving the yard.

Bobby's face illuminated the doorway as he stepped into the room holding a baseball bat. He swung, striking Mike's thigh. There wasn't much room, but the blow was strong enough, and Mike hit the floor.

"Damn. I was aiming for your knee. Guess that's why I never played baseball."

Mike rolled on the floor, holding his leg. Bobby lifted the bat above his head and chopped down at Mike, but he rolled out of the way. The reverberations from striking the floor ran up Bobby's arms, and he released the bat and shook his wrists.

Mike saw it as his chance and kicked the bat, throwing Bobby off balance as he reached for it. He then kicked Bobby's knee and sent him to the floor. Mike jumped up and lunged for the bat.

Grappling for it, they smashed heads, dazing both. Bobby swung at Mike's face but missed wide right. Mike countered, connecting with Bobby's jaw. He punched Bobby in the face again and knocked him to the floor. He grabbed Bobby by the shirt and pulled him closer, punching him over and over.

Bobby spit blood in his face, and Mike released his hold on him. Lightning bolts of pain shot through Mike's injured thigh when Bobby kicked him. Mike bent over and pushed himself up off the ground.

When he turned to face Bobby, he was gone. He sensed Bobby

behind him, but too late. Pieces of glass bounced off the wood floor, and Mike fell to the ground. The thick base from a vase fell in front of his eyes and was the last thing he saw before everything went black.

* * *

When Mike came to, the back of his head throbbed, and his vision was blurry. The last thing he remembered was Bobby punching him. The realization of where he was snapped his fuzzy head in focus and caused him to panic. He tried to move but was unable.

Mike bounced up and down trying to set himself free, but he was sitting in a chair and couldn't get up. He looked down and tried to focus on what kept him to the chair. His vision swirled and finally sharpened enough for him to tell his forearms were duct taped to the arms of the chair. Duct tape wrapped around his ankles cut the circulation off to his feet, and they tingled with tiny pinpricks. Thick bands of tape wrapped around his chest, holding him to the back of the chair.

Mike struggled against the tape, but couldn't move. There must have been a full roll used on his chest. He was only wearing his boxers, but it surprised him that Bobby left his mouth uncovered. Either he wasn't afraid of anybody hearing him yell or he wanted to talk.

"Hey. Hey, you son of a bitch. Let me out of here. Where are my clothes?"

Bobby walked into the room from behind him and laid his hand on Mike's shoulder.

"You're finally awake. I dozed off on the couch waiting for you. I wasn't sure you were ever going to wake up. I hit you pretty hard. And then," Bobby laughed. "And then I dropped you when I was trying to get you downstairs. You must have hit your head on every stair on the way down. Definitely could have been a funny home video moment. I should have just left you upstairs and brought the chair to you. I'll remember that for next time."

"You're sick," Mike said.

"Weird. I don't feel sick. Anyway, why were you following me?"

This guy thought he was cute. Mike hated people like him. They

133

always thought they were so smart. If he weren't taped to the chair, Bobby wouldn't think he was so smart.

"You knew I was following you?"

"Of course I did. That's why I made so many stops on the way home. I thought it would be funny to make you wait around for me. Your car isn't exactly inconspicuous either."

Mike fought to free himself from the tape.

"I'm going to kill you," Mike said through clenched teeth.

"That's highly unlikely," Bobby said, and laughed. "I can see my fence attacked you. Really got a hold of your jeans. Seriously though, you didn't have to cut my screen. I left the front door unlocked so you could just come in without all the sneaking around. I bet you didn't even try the door."

This guy was getting off on playing games with people's lives, and Mike wasn't going to let Bobby use him for his amusement.

"Why were you at Emily's funeral?"

"To console the family and pay my respects. Why else would one go to a funeral?"

"You didn't even know her or her mother. You were there to mock them."

Bobby stepped back and gave Mike a tisk, tisk shake of his head. Mike hated him even more.

"Judging from her stories, I wouldn't think you'd care why I was there. They were all surprised you even had the nerve to show up. I'm done listening to this. You're the one tied to the chair. I'll ask the questions. Why were you following me?"

Mike tried to thrust himself forward but barely moved. Bobby picked up a knife from the table and walked to Mike. He put the blade on the back of Mike's wrist and with a quick slash cut him. Blood rushed to the top of the cut and flooded the sides. Mike gritted his teeth. He wouldn't give this sick fuck the satisfaction of screaming. Bobby moved to the other wrist and did the same thing.

"That all you got? You're hardly cutting me. It's more like a scratch."

"It's not wise to provoke me. Now tell me what I want to know."

Bobby stuck the tip of the knife into the wound and slowly pushed it deeper into his arm. Mike strangled the scream and bit his lip. His head swirled, and he felt lightheaded when the blade finally hit bone. Bobby worked the knife slowly across the bone while looking Mike in the eyes.

"I saw. I saw what you did."

"Well, that's a start. I thought you were going to pass out on me. That looked like it really hurt," he said, and removed the knife from Mike's arm. "I know you're not talking about the funeral again, so what did you see me do?"

"I saw you kill ... Danielle."

Bobby slashed both of Mike's legs below the tape line and backed away. His face darkened.

"Nobody was in the apartment. How did you see me?" Bobby asked and put the blade back to Mike's arm.

"I was in the parking lot. I saw what you did after you left."

Mike didn't want to tell him anything. He felt like he was betraying Danielle, and he needed to remain silent. But Bobby wouldn't allow that to happen.

"Oh. So you didn't actually see me do it," Bobby walked a circle around the chair. "For all you know, I found her first and ran out and then you found her. Hey, are you the little bastard that put the dents in my truck?"

"Yeah, that was me."

Mike smiled.

Bobby backhanded Mike and slashed him across the shoulder.

"Ahhh. Why do you keep cutting me like that?"

"You'll find out soon enough."

Mike tried to stand up again.

"I know you killed her."

"I didn't want to kill her. She made me do it. She told me she wouldn't tell the police about Emily's body in the woods. Then she did, and they took her away from me."

"You sick fuck. Danielle didn't call the police. I did." It was Mike's turn to laugh. "It was me."

Bobby stepped back and dropped the knife on the table. Mike twisted his wrist, and the tape gave a little. If he kept him off balance talking about Danielle, he could get free and finish the job he came here to do.

"No. It had to be Danielle. She was the only other person who knew where she was."

Mike leaned as far forward as the tape would allow.

"I was dating Emily, you idiot. When she didn't come home, I went looking for her and found her car at the park. I called the police. They searched the woods and found her. You killed Danielle for no reason."

"No," Bobby screamed and picked up the knife. He stomped to Mike and slashed his other shoulder. "You're lying to me. It was her."

"No ... It wasn't her. You killed her for no reason. She didn't deserve to die."

Bobby slashed Mike right above the hip on both sides of his abdomen and plunged the blade into the arm of the chair. He ran out of the room and down the hallway, out the back door. If Bobby kept cutting him, Mike would pass out from the pain and loss of blood. It would be all over if he passed out again.

Mike twisted his arms and fingers, trying to reach the knife, but it was too far from his fingertips. He wiggled back and forth and tried to loosen the tape enough for him to lean over and grab the handle between his teeth.

The tape stretched and gave him a little more room to lean forward. He almost had the handle in his mouth when back door slammed shut and Bobby stomped down the hallway. There was a loud vibrating noise that he knew he'd heard before, but couldn't place quite place it.

"I hope you didn't think you got to me and I was going to run out and leave you here to figure out how to escape," Bobby said.

"I didn't think I'd be that lucky. Why don't you come around here and face me?"

Mike said it, but he didn't want to see what Bobby went outside to get.

"Gladly. Earlier you asked why I was cutting you. I know you asked in jest, but I'll tell you. All of those cuts represent where I'm going to cut your body into pieces. I thought you'd like to know in case you faint from the pain."

Bobby stepped in front of Mike and revved the small motor of the reciprocating saw. The last thing Mike felt before he passed out was the saw cutting into the bone of his right ankle.

Chapter Twenty

The plastic bag plopped in the soft mud beside the lake and sucked back in when Bobby picked it up. He worked through the night and pushed his muscles as they protested each trip. The sun started to rise behind him and exhaustion from no sleep and his fight with Mike, while he was both living and dead, was setting in. Five bags and four trips later, all of Mike sat beside the shore. Thirteen-gallon kitchen trash bags were not the optimal bag for carrying body parts. Next time he was at the store, he would be sure to pick up a box of lawn bags, in case this situation arose again.

The final trip was the worst. He cursed himself for saving the heaviest bag for last as he slid and tripped his way down the hill while Mike's torso bounced and slammed off of his back. Triple bagging all the parts to keep the bag from ripping on a tree branch and spilling Mike's organs all over the forest floor was the best decision he made through this entire process. That would be a big mess to clean up before he could go to sleep. Waste disposal was not his strong suit.

Now, he sat on Emily's tree, watching geese glide across the water for their first swim of the day. He tried to force his eyelids from closing, but only managed to move them halfway. The trash bags piled at his swinging feet needed to be disposed of before somebody happened to walk through the woods and find him asleep on a tree surrounded by enough evidence to put him away for life. That would be hard to explain.

He jumped off the tree and stumbled to the trash bags. The first one he picked up was the last one he brought down. There was no way he'd save it until the end again. Bobby swung the bag back and forth to get enough momentum to carry the bag far enough into the water. He leaned back and propelled himself and the bag at the lake. Momentum from the release carried him forward, and he almost followed the bag into the muddy water.

Thank you for taking care of him for me. I was hoping karma would come back around and take him out.

He bent over and put his hands on his knees. Water bugs skated across the surface of the lake. Ripples from the splash only rocked them faster toward their destination. Bobby spit into the water to divert them, but they altered their course and skirted around it.

He closed his eyes and rocked back and forth on his heels.

I don't want to sound completely ungrateful, but why did you bring him back to my tree? At least he didn't die here too, I guess.

The limit of what his body would do before resting rapidly approached. There was only one thing that would get him going enough to finish the job. He kicked the bags around until he found the one containing Mike's feet and jeans. He untied the knot, reached inside and pulled out the jeans and fished around in both pockets until he found Mike's cell phone.

Why are you calling somebody else? I am here with you. I should be enough to keep you company. You don't need anybody else.

He dialed a number he now knew by heart.

"Burns."

"Hello, Detective. I hope all is well. I haven't talked to you since I helped you out the other day."

Bobby put the phone between his ear and shoulder and leaned against the tree for leverage to retie the garbage bag.

"You kidnapped my daughter. That's not helping me out. Now, I've had to send my family away until I catch you, so you don't harm them again."

"Harm is a bit of an overstatement, I think," Bobby said, and threw the bag he was holding into the lake.

"I'm not going to waste my time talking to you when I should be looking for you."

Detective Burns answered the phone, pissed. Either Bobby was getting to him or something else was going on. Bobby doubted the alone time at home would agitate him so much.

"I would think that talking to me is the best and only way you have of finding me, but I'm not the detective. I'm only the bad guy."

"You're calling from a different number. Does that mean I'll be getting a call about another dead girl soon?"

And he refocused. Talking to the Detective Burns rejuvenated Bobby. He felt like he was talking to a best friend he never had. He picked up the bag containing Mike's arms and threw it into the lake.

"No. No body today. I've hit a bit of a rough patch lately."

"What's that noise? What are you doing?"

"Oh, just taking out the trash," Bobby said, and threw another bag into the lake.

"If you haven't killed anybody, why are you calling me?"

"I never said I hadn't killed anybody. Just that you wouldn't get called about another body soon. Like I was saying, it's been a little rough lately. A lot of stuff on my mind."

Bobby hopped back on the fallen tree and swung his legs.

"Excuse me if I don't give a shit about your rough patch or what's on your mind."

"I've missed this. This banter between us. I know you care. It makes me feel better."

Two bags remained on the bank, but he wasn't in as big of a hurry as earlier. Nobody would walk down here, and the police finished their investigation. Not much to investigate with a suicide. The 'why' is only important to the family and friends left behind.

"Well, tell me where you are. I'll come over, and we can talk in person. Maybe that will make both of us feel better."

"I'm where it all began," Bobby said.

"So you're at the Martin house?"

Bobby pulled a piece of bark from the tree and threw it at the lake, but it fell short of the water. Of course, he would think of Rachel first. That was where he and Bobby didn't properly meet, but first learned of each other's existence. It was a nice thought, but brought up memories of what he lost with Emily. Burns and his partner took her away from him. Maybe Burns wasn't much of a best friend. He wasn't even a fair-weather friend.

"No. I'm where I first met her. You know, everything was going great, and then you had to find her and take her away from me."

"Take who away from you? I don't know what you're talking about."

Bobby jumped off the tree and landed in Emily's spot.

"Emily," Bobby yelled. "She was mine, and then somebody told you where she was and I had to take care of them."

"Did you hurt them? I know you want to tell me. Go ahead. You'll feel better once you have it off your chest."

This phone call started off the right way, but Burns turned it around and had Bobby furious enough to lose his cool. He needed to calm himself before he let out something he couldn't take back.

"Your empathy is overwhelming, Detective. But I'm too smart to fall for that. I took care of the person I thought it was. I killed somebody who meant a lot to me, but she didn't deserve it. Then I took it out on some guy in a parking lot. Then somebody broke into my house and tried to kill me. So, you can see why I've had a lot on my mind."

"Sounds like a tremendous burden you're shouldering there. Why do you think she didn't deserve to die, but all of these other women did?"

Logic. He wanted to use logic to confuse Bobby, but Detective Burns would never understand. No amount of logic that Burns could comprehend would ever be enough to grasp what Danielle meant to him. Even after her perceived betrayal. People don't come by something so pure and emotional every day. Their connection wasn't easily severed. But then, Emily came into his life and changed everything. The bond between him and Emily transcended what most people thought a relationship could be. The two could never coexist.

"They were chosen. She was not. She was pure and not meant for the burden of being Emily's vessel." Bobby took a deep breath. "If I didn't know any better, I would think you were starting to like our conversations too."

"Hardly. The only reason I put up with it is because I'm hoping you will give me something I can use to catch you. What do you mean by vessels for Emily? That doesn't make sense."

"I see. Well, if that's how you truly feel, I'll leave you with one last question to think about until we speak again. If you're not enjoying this just a little bit, why haven't you told anybody that I've been calling you?"

Bobby ended the phone call and started to put the phone in his pocket, but thought better of it. He leaned back and threw it into the middle of the lake. As an afterthought, he tossed the remaining bags into the water.

He turned and looked toward the peak of the daunting hill. Under normal circumstances it would be a relatively easy hike to the top, but after the night he just had, he would have to fight his way to the top. His muscles protested as he forced himself to move. He bent toward the top to add any momentum he could. Each tree he came to, he used like a walking stick and pulled himself up.

Halfway up the hill he stopped and leaned against the trunk of a large pine. The woods were thinner here, and he could feel a slight breeze. He closed his eyes and leaned into the wind. After a few minutes, he had to start moving again or if he continued to rest like this, he would end up asleep on the forest floor.

When he reached the top of the hill, he stumbled to his Bronco and fell into the front seat. Originally, he loaded up the bags containing Mike into his vehicle and drove them to the end of the cul-de-sac so nobody would see him walking back and forth to the house for more pieces. Now, he was glad he drove down the steep hill because he was afraid he would not be able to make it back to his house at this point.

The last burst of energy flowed through his body as he climbed the steps to his house. He walked with heavy feet into the dining room, mindful enough to step around the puddles of Mike's blood that ran off the sheets of plastic he put on the floor. He grabbed his dishes from the table and took them to the kitchen sink. Cleaning up after Mike would have to wait until he woke up. The walk up the stairs felt like the hill all over again. He collapsed on his bed.

When he stirred awake, the sun slipped below the last blade on his blinds. Light from the ceiling fan attacked his eyes, and he looked out the window expecting to see the sun beating down on his backyard, but only saw a darkening landscape. The alarm clock read 7:30.

It was going to be another long night. He ran down the stairs and grabbed a sandwich on his way out the door.

He hadn't had the time to process what Mike told him while he was interrogating him, but now sitting in his truck, the implications of what he said poured in on Bobby and threatened to drown him. Mike said he had been the one to call the cops when Emily went missing. If he was telling the truth, then Bobby accused Danielle of something she didn't do, and she died because he didn't believe her. He killed her because he thought she took Emily away from him, but it wasn't her. He closed his eyes, leaned against the headrest and thought back to the day he saw the cops in the woods.

After he talked to them, he ran the rest of the way to work. He didn't see anybody at the tree that wasn't a police officer, but he did remember running past another group of them at the entrance to the park. They gathered around Emily's car. He squeezed his eyes tighter as he tried to concentrate on the group of people. Faces blurred behind scrunched eyes. There was somebody there who wasn't in a uniform and didn't look like a detective. Bobby never saw his face, but he remembered there being another car parked beside Emily's.

Bobby's eyes snapped open. It was a black car that could have been Mike's. He wasn't positive, but the more he thought about it, the more he realized it had to be his. So, Mike had been at the park that day, and he was talking to the cops. He was telling the truth.

It was him, and Danielle died for no reason. She should still be alive, and it was Bobby's fault that she was dead. If he had listened to her, it wouldn't have gone that far. He could have explained away his behavior, and they could have worked it out. Why didn't he believe her? Now, Danielle was lying dead in her apartment waiting for somebody to find her. She didn't deserve anybody treating her that way. Tears ran down Bobby's face as he put the car in gear and headed to Danielle's place.

He drove slowly into the parking lot. There were no emergency vehicles loading her body up or waiting for him to return. He pulled into another apartment's empty space so nobody would see him parked in one of her spots. There were no outside lights on, and he moved easily through the complex and up the stairs to Danielle's apartment door.

No police tape barred entrance to the apartment, so there was a good chance nobody had done a welfare check on her yet. He remembered leaving the door open when he ran out. Mike must have closed it behind him when he left. Luckily, he didn't think to lock the door, and Bobby walked in with no issues. The entire apartment smelled like old copper. He could taste it in the air. As he approached the kitchen counter, he hoped Mike hadn't closed Charlie up in here with Danielle. Seeing what the dog hadn't eaten for a meal was not how he'd like to remember her. He came around the counter and saw no dog. Only Danielle covered in blood. He dropped to his knees at her side and wept openly. There was no comfort in her lifeless hand as he pulled it to his face and wiped the tears away.

Her green eyes looked darker than he remembered. They gazed out at him, no longer trusting. Accusing him of killing her and leaving her alone on the dirty floor, waiting for somebody to come and find her. No longer able to hold eye contact, he looked away, ashamed. He ran his hand through her hair and down her face, closing her eyes so she could no longer judge him. Held back tears fell, and he kissed her forehead and gently laid her back on the linoleum floor. On his way over, he zoned out and wasn't sure what he was going to do once he got to her apartment. Now that he was here, he realized he couldn't just leave her on the floor to rot like a swatted fly left for the broom and dustpan.

He paced around the room. Getting her out of the building without being seen wouldn't be easy. Reverberations of the reciprocating saw lying on his kitchen table buzzed through his head. She didn't deserve to have her body desecrated like that. She deserved to have a proper burial. A proper, but secret burial. He grabbed the red sheets out of the closet at the end of the hallway and laid them on the kitchen floor. The red ones would help in case somebody saw him loading her up. No way a nosey neighbor would catch him with a giant red stain spreading across white sheets. The king sized sheets swallowed her small frame as he placed her in the middle. He positioned her legs straight, and her hands resting comfortably on her chest, and wrapped the sheets tightly around her body and tucked it under the other side. Bobby picked her up and walked to the front door, taking care not to hit her head on anything as he maneuvered through the apartment. He adjusted her legs and grabbed the knob, and the doorbell rang.

Bobby panicked and looked through the peephole, expecting to see the police outside, but only saw an older woman with a blonde bob haircut. There wasn't anywhere in the living room to hide Danielle until he could get rid of the woman. He shuffled down the hallway and put Danielle on the floor between the bed and the wall. The kitchen was still a bloody mess and needed cleaning. He grabbed a towel and mopped up the blood on the floor. It smeared, and he had to grab another towel. The doorbell rang again. Apparently, this woman was not going to give up and leave him alone. He ran to the door and paused to gather himself before opening the door.

"Danielle, honey, we're wor—never mind your door is opening. Well, hello," the woman said, closing her cell phone.

She walked into the apartment uninvited and took a quick look around. Bright pink and green gym clothes created tracers as she inspected the living room while acting like everything was normal. The woman looked old enough to be Danielle's mother. That was the last thing he needed right now. If she was her mother, she would want to see her, and would not leave until she saw her daughter.

"Where has Danielle been hiding you? We didn't know Dani was seeing anybody."

"Hello. She didn't tell me she had a sister," Bobby said, extending his hand. "My name is Stephen."

The woman laughed like an aging valley girl who had never seen the west coast and placed her hand in his.

"Oh, heavens, no honey. You are too sweet though. I am her Aunt Susan."

"Pleased to meet you. Do you live around here?"

"No. I live in Atlanta. I'm just passing through on my way to Florida, and her parents asked me to stop by and check on her. They haven't heard from her in a few days and were starting to worry. But now that I'm here, I can see why it may have slipped her mind to call home," she said, and rubbed her hand up and down Bobby's arm.

"So where is Ms. Danielle at?"

"She's running by a friend's house and then to the grocery store before she comes home."

The woman paused. She didn't seem to care that her inspection would be obvious to anybody.

"Oh, I could have sworn that I saw her car outside," Susan said.

Susan didn't believe him. She was flirty, but after years of living with that façade, it would be hard to hide. Bobby's attempt at charm was a good start, but he had to be smart. This woman was air-headed enough to not take no for an answer long enough to figure everything out.

"She took my car. She likes to drive it."

"I bet she does. You must have a sports car of some type."

"Red Mustang convertible. She likes to drive around with the top off."

Bobby was glad he decided to park in another space. It would have been hard to explain why two cars were parked outside and Danielle was not at home.

"You know what? I have not seen her place since she moved here. I think I'll take a self-guided tour. She wouldn't mind."

Self-guided? She didn't want Bobby around to lead her to what he wanted her to see, or not see. Either she was telling the truth and had not seen the place and wanted to waste time until Danielle arrived home or she didn't believe Bobby and wanted to check the place out for herself. He wasn't sure which one it was, but he couldn't deny her and had to hope she would not find her niece wrapped up in sheets against the wall.

"Be my guest," Bobby said, stepping aside with his hands extended like a butler announcing a new arrival.

Susan walked into the small dining room and wiped her finger across the table, inspecting for dust. She looked at herself in one of the mirrors that lined the back wall of the apartment and flipped her bangs back out of the way. She looked over her shoulder at Bobby and smiled. Was this her being flirty again or checking to see how closely he would follow her? Susan turned and did a quick walk-through of the living room and down the hall to the bathroom.

Bobby released an audible sigh when she skipped the kitchen. The woman probably ate out every night and wasn't interested. Or was it a more calculated search? Paranoia buzzed through his body. It would be so easy to slip up behind her and drag a knife across her throat. It would be easier to kill her than the clean up.

Susan walked into Danielle's bedroom and flipped the master bathroom light on. She checked herself in the mirror again and opened cabinets and looked into the shower.

"This is a nice size shower for an apartment," she said.

"Sure is," was all Bobby could muster.

Susan walked out of the bathroom, past Bobby, lightly brushing against his shoulder. She walked to the edge of the bed with her back to Bobby. Her foot inches from Danielle's head. He stalked up behind her, preparing to jump on her if she discovered the body. Sweat ran down Bobby's face. The thought of potentially having to kill her didn't bother him, but he didn't want to have more people snooping around looking for another missing family member when she didn't arrive in Florida. This situation could spiral out of control and lead back to him. As unlikely as it seemed, somebody could be waiting in the car for her. Though an uncle would want to see his niece as well, and Susan would want to show off any boyfriend she had, especially if he were younger. She turned suddenly and sat down on the bed.

"Quite comfy," she said, and ran her hand across the comforter.

"I wouldn't know ma'am," Bobby said.

Susan was making him feel uncomfortable. It wasn't the flirting, but was it her plan to make him feel awkward? If so, she was succeeding.

"You don't have to be like that with me. I'm no prude."

Bobby's face flushed, and he turned away from her. She stood up and walked into the spare bedroom. Bobby checked on Danielle while Susan quickly explored on her own. He ran his hand across the bed and smoothed out Susan's indention and bloused the bed skirt out toward the wall to block the view, but not on top of Danielle's head. Susan was back in the hallway.

"You know what? I didn't check out the kitchen," she called from outside the door.

When Bobby walked into the dining room, Susan was looking in the pantry. She closed the door and looked closely at the floor beside the sink.

"What is that?" she asked, scrunching her nose.

She bent down and wiped the red substance off the floor.

"Is that blood?"

Bobby tripped over his feet trying to get into the kitchen.

"Yes, it is. I was washing the dishes in the sink, and I cut my finger on this knife," he said, picking the butcher knife out of the sink and holding the blade toward her.

She jumped at the sudden movement, and let out a nervous laugh.

"I was cleaning up the blood when you knocked on the door. I guess I missed a spot."

"Always nice to have a man who helps around the house, but you should be more careful," she said, and walked around him.

She leaned toward the door as she went around him. She was no longer using the flirty tone she had before. In the dining room, she put the counter between Bobby and herself.

"Well, I should probably be going. It's getting late, and I have a long drive ahead of me."

Did she suspect something? Pros and cons of taking out dear Aunt Susan ran through his head. There were too many. Indecision would not help in this situation.

"No need to rush off. Danielle should be back soon. I'm sure she would love to see you," Bobby said, trying not to sound forced.

"I would love to stay, but if I don't get there soon, they may send a search party out for me," she said. "Just tell her to call her parents. And me, we have a lot of things to discuss, like her new beau."

Bobby opened the door for her, and she walked out. He started to close the door behind her when she stuck her head back in the opening.

"Stephen? Where is Charlie?"

"He went with her. He likes the convertible too."

"She took the dog to the grocery store?"

The look on her face said she didn't believe him, but would give him the benefit of the doubt if the answer sounded plausible with no hesitation.

"People take their dogs with them everywhere nowadays."

"Yeah, I guess so," she said. She paused with her hand on the doorframe. "Okay, well I'm going to go now. Tell her I loved her apartment."

"Will do. Have a safe trip," Bobby said, and closed the door before she came back with another question.

Bobby fell back against the door and blew his hair out of his face. He had no idea where the dog ran off to, but he hoped he didn't return and meet Susan at her car. There would be no explaining that. The only recourse would be to kill her. That is, if she didn't call the police before she knocked on the door with the dog in tow.

The few spots of blood he missed on the floor cleaned up easily. The bleach wasn't really needed, but he used it anyway. He scrubbed the floor where he remembered the blood being. The goal wasn't to clean it all up and conceal what happened, but he didn't want to make it easy for the forensic techs if they ever considered the apartment a crime scene.

He placed Danielle's body on the couch, walked out of the apartment, and stood on the landing. Aside from the ticking of a few cooling engines, the parking lot remained quiet and deserted. Would Susan wait in her car to see what he did once she left? He took his time cleaning up inside so Susan would have plenty of time to leave, but he didn't know what kind of car she drove.

A gentleman would have walked her to her car. You never knew if a crazy murderer lay in wait for an unsuspecting person to walk by. Knowing what kind of car she drove would be nice, but she struck Bobby as the type to pull into a person's driveway even if they weren't home, so the homeowner would have to move their car before she left.

Danielle's car sat alone in her parking spots, but he couldn't be sure. After a few minutes of pacing the breezeway, he walked through the parking lot to check as many cars as he could. A small puddle of water stood in the empty space beside Danielle's car. Susan probably sat in her car with the air conditioner running, trying to decide if she should trust the man she just met in her niece's apartment. She left, so she believed him, and headed to Florida expecting a call from Danielle later, or she went to get help. At this point, it didn't matter anymore. Bobby needed to move hastily to get out of the apartment before somebody else showed up.

He ran up the stairs and grabbed Danielle, gave one last look around the apartment complex for cameras and nosey neighbors, and went to his waiting Bronco. The lift gate slammed down on its hinges as he fought for the handle while holding Danielle. He gently laid her in the back, made sure she was comfortable, and shut the gate like a glass lid coffin.

Now that he was out of immediate danger, the tears returned. While cleaning the apartment and figuring out how to get Danielle's body out, he was able to distance himself from the situation. He tried to see her as any of the other women that had walked into his coffee shop or ended up on the wrong side of his issues with Emily. Trying to read and manipulate her Aunt Susan had been a large distraction as well, but he had to do that for survival. There was no telling if any of it actually worked, but he'd have to be careful because she might not have raised an alarm tonight, but when nobody received a phone call, they would send all sirens for him. Well, send them for Stephen, anyway.

Rough cotton burned the corners of his eyes as he wiped the tears away. The ten-foot illuminated cross where his emotions last took over, taunted him as he drove past. It did not accept the bloody sacrifice left on the pavement. The quick look he gave the church did not reveal itself as a scene of violence. Maybe the Good Samaritan survived? Bobby beat him severely. He didn't think the man was breathing when he left, but he didn't check either.

Bobby pushed the man from his mind. He had more important things to worry about now. Like deciding where to take Danielle. Of all the places he knew in the Crystal Valley area, there was only one place that made sense to him. It was a place that meant a lot to Bobby. She would be close to him, so he could go and visit her whenever he wanted to, and nobody would interrupt them. There were only two issues he saw with the place. It was the site of where he and Danielle first started having problems with one another and the second was Emily would not be happy sharing their place with the other woman in his life. It was their spot as well, but he wasn't hearing from her as much anymore. Her essence may have left the area by now.

Bobby pulled up to the edge of the woods at the bottom of the cul-de-sac and killed the lights and waited, watching and listening for any joggers or neighbors following behind him. The only sounds he heard were the crickets and a lone bullfrog from down in the valley below. Carrying Danielle, he stepped through the wooded threshold.

He took the same path he took with Mike's trash bags. That trip, he had been exhausted and just wanted to finish. He bumped and bounced his way down the hill. There were a few extra slams against trees with the bag containing Mike's head. He wanted to be gentle and delicate on this occasion. He pulled her head to his chest and ducked under branches, never allowing her burial shroud to touch the ground. It was one of the coolest summer nights they had had in a while, but sweat still poured down Bobby's face. The scent of approaching rain glided on the slight breeze that penetrated the curtained forest. He would have to work fast before the rain came in. That would be a mess he didn't want to deal with. He picked up the pace but continued with the same reverence as before. At the bottom of the hill, he placed Danielle under the tree where she found him, and ran back up to his house to get a shovel. Encroaching thunder rumbled in the distance.

The shovel pierced the soft red clay. It was in a floodplain, but it had been years since any of the rusty lakes had breached its banks, and had never happened in Bobby's lifetime. Most years the banks seemed to grow. He dug a hole two feet deep and five and a half foot long and pushed his hair from his eyes. Sweat soaked through his shirt and pasted it to his body. He pealed it off and threw it. The shirt made a sick plopping sound as it landed on the trunk of Emily's fallen tree. It reminded Bobby of the sound Mike's intestines made when they fell from his belly and landed on the plastic-covered floor. He stared at the tree, lost in thoughts of the previous night. Mike wasn't his typical subject, but he knew Bobby had killed Danielle and was a threat. It was obvious he hadn't told anybody what he knew because he tried to kill Bobby. Mike was dangerous. The only option for dealing with him was death. Mike may not have been the norm for Bobby, but he definitely enjoyed dissecting him.

A bolt of lightning shook Bobby from his trance. The hole needed to at least be another foot deep. He would need to double his pace to finish before the rain came in. The clay became harder and more compact the deeper he dug. The blade of the shovel glanced off the side of a rock.

Bobby picked it up and held it to the sky. In the pale moonlight, he could barely see the color of the rock. He washed it in the water on the banks of the lake and looked at it under the flashlight of his cell phone. It looked like a rose quartz rock the size of a worry stone found in any store that sold polished stones. The only blemishes on the pallid rose color of the stone were the veins of a mineral Bobby didn't know that ran across parts of its surface. He pocketed the stone and continued to dig.

He gently placed Danielle in the hole and uncovered her face. He brushed the back of his hand across her face and pushed her hair behind her ear. Then he kissed his hand and pushed it to her forehead.

A harsh voice floated across the lake.

Bobby...what are you doing?

He looked across the lake, and in the middle saw a ghostly figure in white. Her hair blew in an invisible wind, floating around her stark white face. The white gown she wore fluttered in the same indiscernible wind. Large black orbs stared at him. Her mouth moved, and she reached her hand out toward Bobby. Her shimmer transfixed him.

Bobbbby,,,what are you doing to our place?

Bobby shook his head, and the figure faded. He covered Danielle's face and jumped out of the hole. Raindrops fought through the forest shroud and plopped on his head. He wanted to hurry up and leave before the woman on the lake came back. The figure was Emily, but she didn't look the way he remembered. Wrinkles covered her face and arms, like she had aged fifty years since he last saw her as she sat against the tree. The memory of her and her hold on Bobby was starting to fade. He dropped the last shovel full of clay on Danielle's resting place and drug the shovel across the top to smooth it out.

Before he went back home, he carved Danielle's initials into the tree beside the destroyed heart that once symbolized Emily and Mike's love.

Chapter Twenty-One

Why? Why did you have to bring her here, Bobby?

This was supposed to be our place where we could be together no matter what was going on outside. She is the reason they took me away from you. It was all her fault, and now you bring her to our spot and bury her where we first met.

I thought I meant more to you than that. How could you violate our spot, and me? It is now forever tainted with her disgusting, rotting body, while my body lies in the ground, surrounded by people I don't even know. I don't know where I am right now.

I feel lost without you. Sometimes I can see and talk to you, and other times I'm confused by what I see, even though it is familiar. It looks like the lake where you found me, but it is so much darker and colder here. I can barely move any part of my body. It doesn't sound like the beautiful forest I once loved. The only thing I can hear is the water rushing around me. Sometimes I think it is rising and will even- tually pull me under and take me away to a place that is always quiet and dark. It scares me to be in this place.

Am I here because I killed myself? Is this my hell? Destined to be alone while the man I love ignores me and acts like I'm not there while he is with his new woman. I bet she won't ever come to see you and take care of you. It doesn't matter that you've hidden her. She will never come to you. She is probably with somebody else right now.

I know you saw me tonight. You could only see me for a short time before I disappeared again. I felt it when you looked at me. There was hate and contempt in your eyes, and I don't know why. All I have ever done is to be there for you. We still have the same connection as before. I can feel it. We can still be together, but you have to help me again. I'm feeling weak. I don't want to leave forever. I will need somebody else soon. You act like you are trying to forget about me and what you need to do.

Now, I think the only thing you enjoy is killing. But you need me, Bobby. Without me, you're nothing. Nobody will want you. You're damaged goods, just like me. I am the only one who can help you. Soon you will see how much you need me.

Bobby rocked in his grandfather's chair on the porch, staring off into the woods.

"You're wrong, Emily. I don't need you anymore, and I never did. I now know who I am, and it's time that I did stuff for me. You were right about one thing. I do enjoy killing. You have led me astray from what I have to do. I have killed three people because of your lie. Mike deserved to die, and his death doesn't bother me. The man in the parking lot? Wrong place, wrong time. But Danielle never should have died. She is gone because of you. She didn't tell the police anything. It was Mike. I am done with you. Do not try to contact me again."

Chapter Twenty-Two

Morgan woke to a light clinking noise that sounded like somebody was about to make a toast at an important dinner. It was three in the morning. Most of the time, she slept like death, nothing could wake her, but now her house seemed quieter than normal. The stillness in the air made her uneasy. Her heart started beating fast as adrenaline poured into her system. She didn't want to move or make any sound by rustling her comforter. Instead, she strained her ears to try to focus them on any sounds in the house, but heard nothing. She lay back on her pillow and forced her head deeper, covering her ears with a soft fluffy shell to protect them from any other outside disturbance.

As a child, she was scared of the dark. Any sound the old, creaky house they lived in made would wake her up. Some nights she would lie in bed staring at the ceiling, covering her ears and telling herself there wasn't anything to be afraid of. On other occasions, her fearful whimpers would wake her twin sister Amanda, who she shared a room with. Amanda was not afraid of anything and would walk around the room and down the hallway and back to show there was nothing to be scared of. She would then climb into bed with Morgan and stay with her until morning. Having her sister with her always calmed her down. As she thought about her sister, her heart rate slowed. Then the toastmaster dropped the spoon.

Morgan bolted upright in bed with her arms down at her side like a vampire rising from a coffin, ready to feed. She listened again but heard no sounds. She wished Amanda were here to walk through the house and check it for bad guys and come back and tell her everything was okay, that she was imagining things again. But she wasn't here. A bad guy took Amanda away from her. Morgan would have to do it on her own.

Quietly as she could, she slipped out of bed and grabbed the baseball bat leaning against the wall beside her nightstand. She pulled her bedroom door open as far as she could before it would make that horribly loud squeaking noise. She cursed herself for not putting WD-40 on the hinges yet as she sucked her body close to the frame and stepped out into the hallway on tiptoes. In the open hall, she froze. What in the hell was she doing? It was never a good idea to go check strange noises in the dark.

She hadn't been this scared in years. Flipping on the light in this situation would be bad, but not knowing what awaited her felt worse. She walked on the balls of her feet to make less noise. The bat rested on her right shoulder. The voice of her old softball coach yelling at her to get the bat off her shoulder, she wasn't going to hit anything standing like that thundered through her head. She adjusted her grip on the bat and carried it with both hands together, extended out in front of her. The kitchen light beckoned her. She didn't leave the light on, did she?

A strong whiff of coffee hit her nose. The aroma confused her. Nobody would break into her house and make coffee. The coffeemaker started brewing at the wrong time. She probably bumped it getting one of yesterday's cups and changed the timer. Her grip on the bat relaxed and she walked into the kitchen.

"Ah. I was about to come and wake you, but I didn't want to scare you to death. Here, I made you some coffee. This may take a while."

Morgan's body stiffened, and her breath caught in her throat. She felt like she had a giant bubble trapped in her airway, and she would suffocate. The man dressed in all black and wore a black mask over his face.

"Just sit down and relax. I'm not going to hurt you. I don't need you stroking out on me," he said. "Oh, go ahead and leave that bat against the wall. I wouldn't want you to get any crazy ideas and end up getting one of us hurt."

She leaned the bat against the wall. She wobbled to the kitchen table on rubber legs. With shaky hands, she pulled a chair out from under the table. The wooden legs jumped and scraped across the tile floor. She fell into the chair, never taking her eyes from the man. He pushed the coffee mug toward her.

"Really, there's nothing to be frightened of. I'm going to need you to get over the shock factor here so we can proceed."

She reached out for the mug and brought it to her lips. She wanted to show him she would comply with what he wanted so he wouldn't hurt her, but she stopped when she thought about what he may have put in the drink.

"You think I did something to the coffee, don't you?" He grabbed the mug and took a sip. "There, nothing in the cup beside the horrible house blend dreck that you bought. And you do that to yourself."

He walked to the kitchen sink and poured his coffee down the drain.

"I think I'll just have water for now."

"Wha ... what are you going to do to me?" she asked.

"Do to you? Why I'm not going to do anything to you. I promise. I need you to do something for me."

She shifted in the chair. If he thought she would do anything sexual for him without a fight, he made a mistake approaching her like this. The bat wasn't too far. If her legs would stop bouncing, she could reach it before he made it to the table.

"What do you want?"

"I want you to interview me. It seems like nobody has really been paying attention to me, and I think it's time that this town had something to fear."

"What if I refuse?"

The question came out before she had time to think about it. She didn't want to do anything to provoke him. Typically, she was only brash when she knew she had the upper hand. Perhaps she was responding to his promise of not hurting her. Who did he think he was for people to be afraid of him? This guy obviously had a screw loose with visions of grandeur, but an interview wouldn't provide that. But he would let her live, as long as she went along with his ploy. She didn't even know who he was yet. He could just be a nut who has nothing better to do than frighten people in the middle of the night, or he could be serious with his threat of terrifying the entire city. Now was not the time to be calling him out to see which one he was.

"Refuse? I don't know why you would want to refuse an exclusive interview with me. That's just crazy. However, I did plan for this, and if you refuse or renege, then I will kill your mother. I would say that I'd kill your sister too, but it looks like somebody beat me to that one."

"You asshole," she yelled and jumped up from the table and took a tentative step toward the baseball bat.

"Sit down," he pleaded, but she acted as if she didn't hear him. "I said sit down!" he yelled and slammed his hand on the counter.

The anger and rage she felt quickly dissipated. The red color faded to a pale white, and she sat at the table once again. Maybe he was crazy, but he also sounded dangerous. Threatening her mother, she expected, but bringing up her sister meant he knew her or did his research.

"Now, you've made me lose my temper once. That's all you get. The next time I will go straight to your mother's house at 7799 Pine Crest Court, slit her throat and bring you her head on the end of that baseball bat. Do you understand me? Say yes."

"I'm sorry. Don't hurt her. I'll do whatever you want."

"I said, say yes."

"Yes," she said, and looked down at the table.

"Now," he said, wiping imaginary lint from his clothes. "Now that we know your sister is a sore subject and that I'm serious about your mother, we can move on. Here, take this notebook."

Morgan knew the only thing she would be able to do at this point is whatever he told her to. She didn't want to risk her mother's life by angering this guy anymore.

"What do you want me to interview you about?"

"See. This is my point. You don't even know who I am, and you write the news. I am the one who killed those two girls using the suicide tableaus."

Morgan opened the notebook. It was brand new, but the black cover had a large white N scratched or rubbed into it.

"Yes. I know about them, but the cops are being really secretive with any details on those cases. That's why there has been little press about them. So far there have only been two murders, and they didn't want to tell the city prematurely that there was a serial killer and cause panic."

"Only two? I guess I have to knock off a few more before I get a higher distinction," he said, and playfully threw his hands in the air. "Of course, I've only killed two like that."

"How many people have you killed total?"

"Five."

Morgan could feel herself falling into the story. She had to be careful. This guy wasn't like the law enforcement and victim families she usually dealt with. This could be a career-defining article for her. That is, if she lived through it. Why did he pick her? She wrote this question down and circled it to remember to come back around and ask. Right now she was going to let him lead the interview in whatever direction he wanted.

"Why do you kill? Are you angry at them or somebody else for some reason?"

"No. I've only killed once out of anger," he said.

He looked her directly in the eyes when he said this, and a cold chill ran down Morgan's spine. The brown irises darkened as he spoke. Out of all the murders he committed, the one who enraged him enough to kill seemed to bother him the most. She didn't know if it was because of the life that he took or the reasoning behind why he was mad that bothered him the most. She sat back in the chair and wrote her notes closer to her, so he could not see them unless he really tried. She didn't immediately ask a follow-up question to see if he would continue talking about the subject.

"It wasn't his fault. He just caught me at a moment of weakness. But the other guy, he deserved it."

"What other guy? I thought you only killed out of anger once? Why do you think he deserved it?"

He hesitated and looked her up and down, assessing her.

"Yes, that is what I said. I guess I'll need to clarify. Anger has only been the cause for me to murder an innocent person one time. The other guy who pissed me off broke into my house and tried to kill me first, but he was a lowlife who didn't deserve to live anyway."

"Sounds like he knew you and had a reason for trying to kill you. Did he see something he shouldn't have?"

Morgan thought she saw his eyes flicker and give him away. Now she was beginning to feel like herself, in control of the situation and the interview. She didn't let him answer the question; his eyes already gave her the answer she was looking for.

"So, you've killed more without your signature or tableau, as you call them. Why's that?"

"Look at you getting all psychological on me with these questions. The simple answer is because I haven't had enough time. I've been busy dealing with other issues. But now that I am free from those obligations, there will be more."

"Why do you like to kill?"

"I'm sure you want something grisly, but the truth is it has never been about the killing. It's always been about the possession. They have been used as vessels of possession in this life from the next. I'm not sure all of that is mine, but I doubt anybody will sue for plagiarism."

"Rachel Martin and Laura Cline were both young, pretty blondes. Is that the type you like to use as vessels?"

Morgan attempted to throw him off by mentioning the girls by name. She wanted him to see them as people, not just vessels for whatever sick game he thought he was playing. He only smiled.

"That certainly helps, but really it was because they left their doors unlocked. It was like they invited me in. Like they wanted to die, and only I could provide an out for them. They could not do it themselves. They just needed a little assistance. If those *women* locked their doors, I would have gone somewhere else."

Morgan hadn't done extensive research on either of the victims yet, but there were no signs that either one was depressed or unhappy with her life.

"Or they just forgot to lock up."

"Perhaps. Speaking of which, you did not leave your door unlocked, so I did have to break in. And for that, I am sorry. This is a first for me. It goes against my morals, but you're the only one I could talk to about my problem. However, I'll make a deal with you. If you do a good job with the article, I promise I will have the window and screen replaced for you."

"Don't worry about it. I'll have somebody take care of it."

The words rolled around in Morgan's mouth. They tasted acrid, like she hadn't brushed her teeth in days. They sounded too nonchalant, as if she were having a conversation with a friend and they offered to do something for her as a way of being polite, and she was returning the politeness with a "hey, don't worry about it, pal." She didn't want to give the impression that she was getting comfortable with the guy. She was tired and trying to show this man that she was not as terrified and shaking as she was on the inside.

He walked to the counter, put a bagel in the toaster and stood above the appliance like he wanted to intimidate it to cook faster. The stare down made Morgan feel uncomfortable, and she adjusted herself in the seat. His head snapped up, and he looked at her over his shoulder from the corner of his eye. When he was satisfied she hadn't moved in a threatening motion toward him, he looked back to the toaster in time for it to pop up the browned bread. He threw the two halves on a plate and sat down at the table and spread cream cheese on both sides. He took a bite from his half and slid the other across the table to Morgan. She didn't pay attention to the bagel. All she could focus on was the knife lying on the table less than a foot away from her.

"It's the least I can do really," he said, finally breaking the silence.

His smile swam behind the mouth opening of the mask he wore. He wanted to continue the guise of a friendly conversation, and it disgusted her even more. She needed to bring the conversation back to him so she could hurry up and hopefully, he would leave, but he didn't seem to be in too big of a hurry.

"You said they wanted to die, and you were assisting them. Does that mean you see yourself as some new age Kevorkian? Is that why you leave a fake suicide note?

"Yes, thank you for bringing us back on topic. Definitely don't see myself as a Kevorkian rip-off, but he did do good work. The notes are just a signature."

"Why sign them with an N or is it a lightning bolt?" she asked and held the notebook for him to see.

"So you have heard about the case? Guess even the Crystal Valley police department has its leaks. As for the signature, my fans are going to be a little disappointed. It doesn't mean anything. I saw it drawn somewhere, or it is on a logo or something."

"Your fans? Why do you think you would have any fans for killing innocent women?"

She asked it, but she knew it was a stupid question. All of these insane people develop a following, but it's usually after they are caught and paraded on the TV and make outlandish claims while on trial. Once in prison, the groupies come out, some people even end up getting married while incarcerated. It made her sick every time she saw a story like that. But this guy was different. He wanted the adoring fans now. He sounded arrogant enough to believe they would never catch him.

"Every serial killer gets a fan club. Well, at least the charismatic and good-looking ones do. And they all have books written about them. Even the ugly ones. The books about me will be different because I will never be caught. I'll have rows of them like the Zodiac killer. All of those books written about him are all just speculation. One of the authors got caught making shit up about who he thought it was, and his books still sell. Hell, I've read them."

"That doesn't bother you to think if you were never caught your whole story would never be told? That everything written about you could be a lie. That would kind of tarnish your legacy, right?"

He draped his arm on the top of the chair to his left and put his foot in the chair to his right. He was comfortable around her. She wanted to use it against him, but there wasn't anything she could say or do to him to worry him.

"I see what you're saying, in a sense. But all of that true crime stuff is bullshit to a certain extent. Even the ones interviewed for the books probably made most of it up. It's part of the game of infamy. On the other hand, it is also the story that they want to be told about them. There is a dichotomy in everybody. Even people who society would label as normal have a separation between what is perceived and what is. To answer your question though, if a writer made up stuff like giving the credit of everything I did to some loser who he thought was the perfect suspect, I would have no choice but to kill the writer. Probably after I killed his suspect, though. So that he would feel a little humiliation before I killed him. I almost wish that would happen just so I can do it."

Morgan sat back and let his words sink in. She agreed that everybody had an internal contradiction that they lived with every day.

Everybody thought they were more than who they actually were. Especially this guy. Too many times this paradox creates a sense of entitlement within the person. She didn't think people should accept their lot in life. They should try to achieve as much success as they want, but they should also know where they are so they can make their situation better. Not assume somebody should give it to them because they want it. His words were starting to seep into her mind, and she hated herself for allowing it to happen. She wished he would finish spewing his garbage and leave her alone.

"That's one way of looking at it," she said.

"It's a pretty accurate picture, and I think you know it too."

"There is one thing that those serial killers have that you don't."

"Oh, really? And what's that?"

He sat up in a fast, fluid motion. Not as a threat to her, but as if he was genuinely interested in what she had to say. She kept her hands together on the table. The knife still lay inches away from her fingertips. Since he left it on the table, she tried to not look at it so he wouldn't catch her and move it. But now, it looked like the blade was reflecting all the light from the room toward her, mocking her. She stretched her fingers out and retracted them.

"A name. All of them have a name. The media usually gives it to them, so I guess you'll be getting yours later. Once they know you exist. Too bad you won't have one for the article title."

"Scary," he said, and laughed. "I was just thinking the exact same thing. Great minds and all."

"I'm nothing like you."

He slid up in the chair and rested his face on his hands.

"You never know, someday, maybe. Anyway, I was thinking about that, and I didn't want to leave it up to the media to use some generic name. I mean, come on, how many Rippers and Butchers and Stranglers do we need, really?"

"So what do you want to call yourself then?"

He paused and seemed to be thinking it over, but she knew he had a name in mind already.

"I was thinking about The Suicide Killer. It has a nice ring to it, don't you think?"

"It sounds oxymoronic to me."

"Hmm. I guess it does. But I still like the sound of it," he said, looking off like he was lost in thought. "Tell me something. Have you ever wanted to kill anybody? I don't mean the way everybody says that they would so they can to prove how mad they are at somebody. No, I mean really want to take somebody's life."

The Suicide Killer had a ring to it and all the news outlets would eat it up. Given his M.O., it made sense, but it was enough of a contradiction to make people pay attention and want to read or hear more about him. Almost like a marketing ploy. Maybe he had marketing in his background.

"No."

"Seriously? You wouldn't like to find that miserable piece of trash who took your sister away from you and jab a knife through his heart or perhaps something a bit more creative?

"No. That's what the police and judicial system are for."

"Wow, that is without a doubt the lamest answer you could have given me. The 'police and judicial system' you believe in has let you down. They still haven't found her killer. I bet I could find him and take him out before Detective Burns even looks at the case again."

Morgan looked past him and stared at the wall. She knew her answer was a horrible lie. She would love nothing more than to see the man responsible for her sister's horrific death suffer. But this guy didn't need to believe she was anything like him. If he was feeling like an outsider, and she made him believe they were on the same wavelength, it would help him justify his actions. She hated the way he was making her feel. She wanted to grab the knife and jump across the table and take him out for all the people he killed or would potentially kill.

"You look like you're thinking about it," he said. Morgan only shook her head. "I would do that for you. If you'd like."

She looked directly at his lonely dark eyes. "No," she said, and sat back in her chair.

He threw his hands up in mock surrender.

"Okay, no worries. I thought I felt a connection and was trying to take our relationship to the next level," he said, and laughed.

She gave a tip-lipped smile and scrunched her eyes. He looked at her for a beat, pushed away from the table, and swept his crumbs from the surface onto his plate, then grabbed hers. Morgan watched the knife, hoping he wasn't going to pick it up next. When he started to turn his back without it, she relaxed. He stopped midway to the sink. She knew he was going to turn around and grab the knife, but he hesitated and launched into a sneezing fit. She counted six sneezes in a row before he finally stopped.

"Excuse me. This damn mask is driving me crazy," he said.

"You could take it off."

"Nah, you wouldn't want me to do that."

"Why? Are you disfigured or something? Scared I'll turn away and reject you?"

He let out a booming laugh she had not expected.

"Now, that's funny. But you watch too many movies. If you saw my face, I'd have to kill you. And that would be no good. Cause then who would write my story? I picked you because you were damaged, that way I could try to help you. But, if you want to write that I threatened to slice your face off and use it as a mask like they did in those movies, be my guest. That would sell some papers, I guarantee."

He scraped her uneaten bagel into the trashcan, and the thought of him peeling her face from her skull and parading around the house flashed in her mind. She shivered as he walked to the kitchen sink. He was talking to her, but she had turned her focus back to the knife and what she could do with it. The words sounded fuzzy and far away.

She leaned forward, and her hand hovered above the handle. He still had his back to her, while he rinsed the dishes off. Morgan had to react now or risk doing nothing. Keeping the mask on made her feel safe, although he might kill her after his story runs.

Her chair screeched on the floor as she went to stand, but he didn't seem to notice over the sound of the running water. She walked on the balls of her feet with the knife poised above her head, ready to strike. She quickly closed the gap between her and the killer and plunged the knife down as he turned to face her.

Everything moved in slow motion. She could see the fear in his eyes when he turned, and she was on top of him. The fear changed to something like anger or hatred as he threw his left arm up, hitting her descending forearm, the knife inches away from the soft spot on this collarbone.

Morgan was focused on the near miss and tried to force her arm down further. She did not see his right fist cross toward her face. Blue spots with white tracers filled her eyesight, and the knife fell from her hands. The clanking sounded louder than it should have when it hit the floor. It sounded like failure and certain death. She stumbled back, falling hard on the tile floor.

He grabbed her by her hair and slid her against the cabinets. A new spark of color flooded her eyes as the back of her head hit the dense wood. He scraped the knife's blade across the tile as he picked it up and pressed the point of the blade at her throat.

"And you said you never thought of killing anybody before. Sure as hell didn't stop you from taking a swipe at me. I guess you need the anger there to feed that instinct. I'm sorry I had to mangle that pretty face of yours, but you did try to kill me."

"Don't kill me, please," was all she could muster.

Tears ran down her face. She wasn't crying at the thought of death. She was crying because her one chance to save herself went wrong and now she was waiting for him to end her life. Memories of her sister's funeral came to mind. There must have been over three-hundred people who showed up, all dressed in black. There wouldn't be near that many people show up to hers. Amanda had always been the outgoing one. Morgan was the quiet introvert who everybody treated differently because she was a journalist. It was like they thought she would write something about their mundane lives or maybe overhear their salacious secrets and print those. People were so self-centered, like anything they did would be newsworthy to other people.

"Aw, don't worry. I'm not going to kill you. You still have to write that piece on me. It's getting late, so I should probably be going. Don't worry. I know it won't be in tomorrow's issue, but I fully expect to see it in the next days or else, you know?" He made a sweeping motion across his throat, using his thumb as the blade and made a sickening ripping sound with his mouth. "With your mother, and all that." Then he laughed.

Morgan tried not to look in his direction as he spoke. He walked to the back door and stepped outside. The breath she held for too long burst from her mouth. He stuck his head back through the door, and her breath caught again.

"You know, earlier I had you pegged as a runner, not a fighter. I left the door unlocked to see if you would try. You surprised me tonight. I didn't think you had it in you. Thanks for the hospitality. I'm leaving now. Good night and sweet dreams," he said, and closed the door.

Morgan slid to the floor. The pent-up tears flowed. She could no longer stop them, nor did she want to. She lay on the floor until she finally fell asleep. Dark and twisted nightmares awaited her.

Chapter Twenty-Three

Greg woke up alone. These last few days were the longest he had slept without his wife since before they got married twelve years ago. The first couple of nights hadn't been so hard, but now, waking up without her by his side and one or both of the kids already awake and running around the house or terrorizing the cat, left him feeling empty and alone. His muscles ached as he rolled out of bed. He checked his cell phone for any calls he may have missed and then stumbled into the shower. The direct blast of cold water shocked his senses before it warmed and relaxed him. Stress and tension from the cases piling up on him were starting to take their toll as well, but the largest burden came from being in contact with the killer.

Not that the conversations were especially trying, but he had not told anybody about the phone calls, not even Don knew about them. He should have told everybody after the first call. There was a part of him that wanted to and then another part of him that wanted to keep it a secret so he could use it to catch the guy and then he could take the credit. It wasn't an ego trip; he needed to prove to himself that he could still do it. When he was unable to solve Amanda Cramer's murder, his ego did take a hit, but the perp didn't leave any incriminating evidence and as far as anybody knew, never committed another crime. Greg would still pull out the case from time to time and look over it to see if he had missed anything. He never found anything new. Neither did any of the other detectives who he asked to look at it.

The Cramer case started a three-year trend of backed up case logs. A lot of those remained unsolved. They say everything comes in threes. There were more than three cases, but Greg hoped his bad streak would end after three years, and he needed this case to be the one to end it all. If anybody found out about the phone calls, at the least they would suspend him for a while and possibly demote him, and at worst they would fire him. He would never be able to work in law enforcement again if that happened. Nobody would want to hire a washed up detective who hid potential evidence from the department. He dressed and contemplated all of his decisions. If he called Don and confessed all of his sins, maybe they could still work everything out and catch the guy. Maybe he wouldn't lose his badge in the process. Risks weighed, he went with option one and put the phone in his pocket.

Shelly cooked breakfast for him every morning before he went to work. She would cook bacon and eggs with a side of toast, and on special occasions, she would make him waffles or French toast. He thought about his morning rituals as he stirred his lumpy oatmeal. He missed his family and their routine. Tomorrow he would switch to cereal. The cold breakfast congealed around his spoon, and he picked the entire bowl up with his spoon. He walked to the sink and washed what he could down the sink. Water ran down the drain, and he flipped the switch to turn on the disposal. The whirling blades cut up his gelatinous meal and pushed it on down the line. The sound of the spinning knives caused a moment of clarity in the hazy mood he found himself in.

The last time he spoke to the killer, he said he was where it all began. Greg thought he was talking about Rachel Martin's house. But he wasn't. He was where the police found Emily. Greg reached for the notebook he kept in the inside pocket of his jacket, but it wasn't there. Thoughts of the killer breaking into his house and walking around while Greg slept ran through his mind. The alarm keypad beside the door still read armed. He ran up the stairs to his office and found the notebook lying open on his desk. He must have left it in there last night when he was going over everything for the thousandth time before he finally forced himself to go to bed.

By now Greg had memorized all of his notes on the killer, but the dead girl in the woods had never been part of the case. He flipped through the book and found the girl's name. It was Emily. When the killer said he wasn't at the Martin house, Greg hadn't given much thought about who Emily was. The day in Rusted Lakes Park came back to him now. Police found the missing girl with slit wrists deep in the park woods. The boyfriend made the call about her disappearance when he found her abandoned car. He was an asshole, but he couldn't be the killer, he was too emotional and stupid to stage a scene like that. Anything would push that guy over the edge. If he were mad enough to kill, they would be looking at a bloody crime of passion. For the most part, the guy Greg was looking for remained calm and restrained.

The only other notes from that day were from a short interview he did with a barista named Bobby Cotton. He was the one who ran through the scene on his way to work. So far he was the only one to see the killer and give a description of him, but Greg had to keep that bit to himself. Greg wanted to go back to where they found Emily and see if he could kick anything up. The coffee shop was on the way and he could see if his guy had been back to the store since that day.

* * *

Greg sat in his car outside of the coffee shop. A steady stream of people, looking like they rolled out of bed and managed to get dressed somehow, dragged themselves through the swinging glass door. Greg wanted to get to the lake, but he wasn't too excited to go stomping through the woods for what may turn out to be a waste of time. He patiently waited inside his car for the half dead traffic to slow down before he went inside. Bobby walked past the large open window, taking and making orders, so he knew he wasn't wasting his time waiting for the morning rush to calm down.

It amazed him how many people came to this small shop in the morning to get their fix. He liked his coffee as much as the next person, but he preferred to have it before he left his house. That way he would be awake while driving. Leaving the house before he had his morning coffee could be dangerous for anybody who happened to be sharing the road with him. Also, it was cheaper that way. He supposed it had become part of their morning rituals, much like he had his own.

Once the horde subsided, Greg stepped from his car and stretched his stiff legs. Maybe he would go ahead and order a coffee while he was here. The small bell chimed as he walked through the door.

A disjointed voice greeted him.

"Welcome to the Daily Grind."

Greg walked to the counter where Bobby stood, but he seemed like he didn't recognize Greg from the previous encounter.

"Yeah, can I get a medium coffee. Black."

"Name?" Bobby asked without looking up.

"Greg. My name is Detective Greg Burns."

This time the barista looked up and locked eyes with Greg.

"I'm just going to put Greg on here. I think we'll figure the rest out."

Bobby carefully wrote Greg's name on the side of the cup. Greg couldn't tell if he was concentrating and trying to write it neat or if he was just tired. He didn't seem to remember that Greg had been in the store and talked to him.

"I was just in here last week."

"I get a lot of customers. They all run together after a while," Bobby said, and poured the coffee.

"Yeah, except when I was in here, I was questioning you about a potential suicide in the park."

"Okay," was the only reply Bobby gave.

"I also asked you about a customer who you had earlier that day," Greg said, and pulled his notebook from his pocket. "You said he was about 6'2, two-hundred pounds, and had black hair and hazel eyes with a cleft chin."

"Okay."

Complete apathy radiated off the barista and permeated through the store. Customer service wasn't the reason for the amount of customers he served. The coffee wasn't that great either. It wasn't any better than what Shelly bought at the store. If not for the hospitality or coffee, it had to be ritualistic or for the convenience.

"You also said he had a long scar down the inside of his arm. Do you remember that guy?"

"Yeah, vaguely. The scar sticks out in my mind, though."

"Well, have you seen that scar again since the last time we spoke?"

"No, I haven't seen him since that day, but I don't work every day either, so he may have come in on my day off."

Bobby secured the lid on Greg's coffee and slid it across the counter to him.

"Okay, thanks. I thought I would just stop by and check. Maybe I'll stop by sometime when somebody else is here. They may remember him."

"Maybe so. Have a good day."

Greg walked back to his car and fell into the driver's seat. Bobby stood at the counter, looking out the window, but not in Greg's direction. Greg watched as he helped another customer who walked in. He wasn't sure why, but he felt like Bobby was acting too disinterested. Almost to the point, he was trying to act that way to throw any suspicion off him. Maybe he was just a weird guy, and Greg was grasping for any semblance of a lead. He backed the car out of the parking lot and turned onto Park Road, leading to the entrance of Rusted Lakes Park.

The same group of moms sat on the park benches flanking the playground, watching their young children eat sand and throw sticks at each other. They turned their heads in unison as Greg's car crushed the gneiss gravel. He stepped from the car and their passing interested faded. The Stepfordwifeness of the scene squirmed through Greg's thoughts as he moved past them, avoiding eye contact. No longer seen as a threat, they stopped paying attention to him like he was part of the green park backdrop.

Greg walked down a path leading into the woods. The path was well traveled and clear from most brush. He didn't remember the trail being so easily maneuverable. After the trail cut to the right and started up the steep hill, he realized he took the wrong path. He turned in the direction he thought the lakes should be and could barely make out the rust colored water through gaps in the tree canopy below him. The hill looked steep, but he could manage the incline if he was careful. It would be faster than turning around in hopes that he'd get lucky and find the right path.

He stepped off the trail, and his dress shoe slipped on loose rocks, forcing him a few feet down the side of the hill. Too late to turn back now. He pushed off with his right leg and threw his hands in the air for balance. The slippery rocks became a jagged skating rink, and he slid down the hill. He propelled his body forward and backward to accommodate his motion so he would not fall as he skated down the hill. Sweat beaded on his brow. The forest floor appeared through the brush with the chance that he might make it to the bottom without falling.

The toe of his shoe slid across a hole and wedged in the opening. The momentum of his upper body continued downhill while his lower half stayed with the hole. Greg put his hands in front of him to brace for the inevitable collision with the ground.

Rocks cut deep gashes in his palms when he landed and ripped them as he slid to base of the hill. Greg lay at the bottom, not wanting to move. Fire burned down his wrists and shot from his fingertips. Birds that weren't there before jumped through tree branches and chirped at once like they all released a collectively held breath.

Greg finally pushed himself up on the base of his wrists. The sun filtered through the tree branches made him feel like an ant under a magnifying glass. He attempted to brush the red dirt from his suit, but it only smeared, leaving a hazy red mark on his arms and legs. The house would be his first stop after he left the park.

He pushed his way in the direction of the lakes, not caring at this point if he was going to the right spot. Limbs and briars pulled at his red dusted charcoal gray suit while he kicked his feet free from the vines and thorns that littered the forest floor. Greg decided he had gone the wrong way and was about to turn in another direction when he heard the soft sound of water lapping at its banks. With a final heave, he pushed into the small clearing he was looking for. Cloudy water enveloped his hands when he crouched beside the lake to wash them. The clay from his hands mixed seamlessly with the water, only the ripples from his hands proof that he was ever in the water.

He looked out over the lake. A cold chill ran down his back, and the hairs on his arms and neck stood on end. This was the place the monster had been standing when he talked to him. It would have been nice, and easy, if the guy had been here when Greg bounded through the foliage. Maybe he was, and Greg scared him off when he came crashing down the hill. Either way, Greg cursed his luck as he looked at the muddy bank, but only saw indiscernible shoe prints, now trampled by his own. Knowing the killer had recently been here, Greg could not shake the feeling that he was being watched.

He turned and faced the fallen tree where Emily took her life. Greg had seen her driver's license picture, and she had been a pretty girl. She had a big, friendly smile that welcomed all who crossed her path. There was a sadness in her picture as well. She may have looked happy and bubbly on the outside, but her eyes gave her away like they do for everybody. The mouth always lied. Cover the mouth on a picture and the eyes speak louder. Her eyes told the story of a haunted girl. It wouldn't have surprised anybody who noticed the look in her eyes that she would end up the way she did. After talking to her boyfriend, Mike, he knew he was partly, if not completely, to blame for her taking her life. It was a sad situation, and Greg couldn't help but think about his daughter and what she had been through or would go through in her life. Tears formed in his eyes for what had happened to this girl, for her to end up alone at the bottom of a hill beside a dirty lake and for the imagined suffering of his daughter.

Through blurry eyes, he could see a discoloration and the damage to the tree Emily chose as her final headboard. He wiped the tears from his eyes and ran his hands across the chopped and scarred tree. Mike told them that he had carved a heart with their initials in it on a previous trip and that she was probably trying to destroy it because they were about to break up. Beside the old heart, there was another carving. The hastily carved initials D.I. stood in stark contrast, like a new lover taking the place of the previous one.

Greg hadn't heard of there being another carving in the tree. When was it cut and who did it? Maybe it was his guy trying to tell him something, or just a game he wanted to play. It could also be some completely random person walking through the woods or somebody wanting to see where the body was found, but Greg didn't think so. He had a feeling the killer put it there. But why?

He pulled the battered notepad from his pocket and wrote the letters down so he wouldn't forget to remember them later. While writing, he noticed the dirt around his feet looked darker and turned over. He finished his reminder and put the notebook up. All the dirt in the surrounding area was dark brown with hints of red Georgia clay swirled in except for a large square patch in front of the tree.

The dirt had been turned over recently, and black topsoil covered the space. Greg stepped back to get a better view of the area. He bit his top lip as he considered his options. He could call it in and get a crew in here to dig up the area and see if there was a body buried here and then come up with an excuse as to why he was down here in the first place. Or, he could try to dig up some of it himself and explain everything later. There may not be anything in the ground at all. The techs could have moved the dirt around when they first found Emily. But Greg thought there was a good chance somebody was under there and the carving in the tree was their headstone.

He draped his jacket over one of the branches of the fallen tree and loosened his tie. Excavation was not on his list of things to do this morning and nothing in the vicinity looked like anything he could use as a tool to dig. He walked around the area, but only came back with a few big sticks and his bare hands. The patch of Earth closer to the lake looked softer than the rest of the area.

Using his hands, he scrapped away dirt and flung it into the water behind him. Dirt pushed under his nails and into the cuts on his palms. Within a few minutes, sweat soaked through his shirt and coated his body as the hot sun attacked him from the other side of the lake. He wiped sweat from his brow and left a long smear of dirt across his face. The thought of finding a body drove him harder. Dirt flew in all directions. The deeper he dug, the more he had to use the sticks to stab at hard packed earth.

After breaking two sticks, he went back to using his hands. Over his loud breathing, he heard his cell phone ring. It was in his jacket pocket, hanging on the tree. He decided to ignore it and continue digging. The phone went silent for a moment and rang again. Greg stopped and looked at the surrounding area. The thought of the killer watching him and trying to call him was terrifying. He was an easy target in an open area surrounded by woods that could easily conceal somebody sneaking up on him. He forced himself onto his feet, leaned over to his jacket and pulled his phone out. The missed calls were from Don. This is the last thing he needed. Don would think he was sleeping on the job again. Greg prayed there wasn't another murder. Before he could click on Don's name, the phone lit up and rang again.

"This is Burns."

"Greg, where the hell are you? I've been trying to get in touch with you for an hour."

Greg rolled his eyes. Always the dramatics with Don. And theatrics with the killer. Greg wasn't sure which was worse.

"I guess I have a bad signal here. I'm just following up a few leads. What happened?"

"Have you read the paper? Your girl Morgan apparently thought it would be a good idea to get an interview with the guy we've been trying to catch. She even gave him a cute nickname. The Suicide Killer."

Dramatics won this round.

"Shit. I don't know what she was thinking."

"I had planned on asking her that, but she hasn't shown up at work for two days. I was about to go by her house."

Greg stepped out of the hole. It definitely felt deeper while digging it.

"No. Don't do that, Don. Let me do it. I'll handle her. The whole town is going to be in a panic."

"They already are. There have been forty-seven calls in the last hour about strange men in people's neighborhoods. They've been calling about the damn lawn guys, Greg. You better get over to her house and handle this. Find out where this information came from and make sure she doesn't print another interview whether it was him or not."

Don hung up the phone before Greg had a chance to respond. He looked at the hole in the ground and felt foolish now that real issues were threatening again. Irrational or not, he would return later with a shovel to finish digging up whoever was buried in the ground or finish digging his grave, whichever it came to. But first, he had to go and find out who Morgan had spoken with.

Chapter Twenty-Four

After getting off the phone with Don, Greg went home to change clothes and read Morgan's article. Now, he sat in her driveway with the newspaper riding shotgun. He wasn't sure how he was going to approach the situation. The article had caused a minor panic. The police station and 911 were fielding calls of suspicious people. There were also calls from people stating they had seen a dark figure walking through their yard late at night, they said they hadn't thought of calling the police until they read the paper and thought it might be the killer checking to see if they had left their doors unlocked. There were also the calls of 'concerned' citizens who were up in arms because the police did not warn the public earlier about the danger they were in. It was still early. As soon as the story made its way around social media, the Internet, and the networks picked it up for their leading story at midday, there would be too many calls for a regular shift to handle.

Greg decided to knock on the door and see what her reaction to him would be. She would know why he was here. If she acted apologetically and realized the issue, then he would be nicer about it. However, if she yelled and used the tired excuse that she was just doing her job, then he wouldn't be as nice. He thought the front curtains fluttered as he stepped on the front porch, but the door didn't open. Greg knocked on the door like a cop preparing to issue a warrant with the paper held up in hand. He was already starting to lose his temper. So much for the nice guy routine. The door finally swung open.

"What the h—"

He was unable to finish his question before the person behind the door turned and walked away. Anger rose as he stepped into the dark house and slammed the door behind him. Morgan stopped and shuddered at the sound, and then continued to the couch, dragging her baseball bat. She curled up with her legs underneath her and laid the bat beside her on the cushion.

"What the hell is this, Morgan? Do you know what kind of panic you've caused?"

She looked up at him, and his anger faltered. This wasn't the same strong, fearless and annoyingly assertive woman he usually dealt with at crime scenes. She looked frail, like she hadn't eaten or slept in days. Her hair a tangle of fine black threads. It was obvious that she hadn't planned on going to work today either. Greg looked around the house, but it didn't seem as disheveled as its owner. It looked like she may have been camping out on the couch.

"I had to," she finally said.

"You had to do an interview with somebody who claimed they killed two women and three unknown cases?"

Greg shifted his weight to his front foot, giving the impression of a questioning father. The 'it's my job' argument was just getting started, and he wanted to shut it down before it went too far.

"He said he would kill my mother if I didn't publish the article. He said he would have threatened to kill my sister too, but somebody got to her first," she yelled.

Tears streamed down her pale face. She brushed her hair away and revealed her bruised face.

"Damn. Did he hit you because you refused?"

Greg felt like an ass for the way that question came out and walked to the kitchen. He came back with ice wrapped in a rag.

"Here, put this on it. Your face is still pretty swollen."

She took the rag from him and gently put it on the bruise.

"No, I didn't refuse. I tried to stab him when he wasn't looking, and he hit me. It pissed him off and then he left."

Morgan stared at the wall when she spoke, like she didn't know or care who she was talking to in the room. Greg turned his head and looked at her sideways.

"It'd piss me off too if you tried to kill me."

She looked at him through squinted eyes, and he threw his hands up in surrender and moved out of her way.

"How did you know you were talking to the real killer and not somebody looking to make a name for themselves?"

"I didn't."

An over-exaggerated sigh escaped his lips.

"Then why did you write an article telling people to lock their doors because The Suicide Killer is watching them? It could have been anybody. Even somebody you know."

Morgan's head jerked toward him. He had her full attention now.

"If I had to write it, I wanted people to be safe. He said he only went in houses with the doors left unlocked. I didn't want anybody else to get hurt."

Greg felt like the air had been kicked from his lungs. The killer told him on the phone if the doors had been locked he would have gone somewhere else, but he couldn't share that information with anybody. The man who told Morgan that he would kill her mother if she didn't run the story was actually the killer. Greg sat down in a soft armchair and pulled out his notebook.

"Okay. I need you to tell me everything you remember about that night."

"Oh, now you believe it was him?"

"I have to be thorough, just in case."

Greg paused. He had to be careful. Morgan was in a state of shock and not herself, but she was smart. He couldn't underestimate her current ability to see through his bullshit. One wrong word and she'd turn it around on him.

"How did you find him?"

"I didn't track him down for an interview. That's your job. He broke into my house in the middle of the night and woke me up."

She was getting aggravated with him. That was not his intention. Some of it came from their history together and the rest was because it's awkward interviewing somebody you know. He knew all of her pressure points and what would set her off, but he also needed some answers so he could catch the guy. It caused a bigger problem when the interviewer didn't want to upset the interviewee. Greg had seen too many of Morgan's tears from her sister's death, through the investigation and then not being able to solve the case.

"Okay, okay. Don't get upset. Did he do or say anything that might make you think that you knew who he was?"

"I'm not getting upset. A serial killer broke into my house and threatened to kill who's left of my family and me if I didn't write something to inflate his ego and make the city afraid of him, because the cops weren't doing a good enough job of keeping the citizens informed. I haven't slept since he left. Every time I close my eyes, I hear noises around the house, and I think it's him again. And no, he didn't act or say anything familiar to me."

"I'm sorry, Morgan. I'm doing my best to catch him. Did you leave your door unlocked that night?"

"No. He cut the screen on one of my back windows and broke the glass."

Greg walked through the kitchen and into the room the killer crawled through. Morgan used the room as an office. Pictures of her with various local celebrities lined one wall. He looked closely at a picture of her and Heath Clement, a homegrown kid from Crystal Valley who was out in Colorado playing Major League Baseball. Morgan looked younger, and Heath was wearing his college uniform. Morgan was more casual in this picture than the others. They looked like they were dating. Greg wondered if he left her behind when he made it to the majors or if she wanted to stay close to home. Greg's phone rang.

"This is Burns."

"Have you talked to her yet?"

It was Don calling to check on him. The only caller that could have been worse at this point was the killer.

"Yeah, Don. I'm with her now."

A diploma hung on the wall behind her desk beside a large bay window. The desk had normal paperwork scattered across it. The only picture on her desk was of her and her sister taken when they graduated from college. Both girls wore their cap and gowns and smiled like they were ready to take on the whole world. The sisters in the picture did not know two years later one would be dead and the other one destroyed by it.

"Did you tell her about the shit storm she has created?"

"Yeah, she knows. She hasn't been to work because she's scared to death of this guy."

There was a blank spot in the middle of the desk where her computer usually sat. He turned to the window, and the drapes were pulled tight, not letting any light or prying eyes into the room. The window had a cardboard vodka box taped across the broken area.

"Then why in the hell did she interview him? Why didn't she call us?"

Greg looked through the doorway to make sure Morgan had not walked up on his conversation.

"She didn't have a choice, Don. He broke into her house in the middle of the night and forced her to do it. Threatened to kill her family if she didn't. I'm sure I don't have to remind you of her family history to explain why she would believe him, do I?"

An irritated breath blew directly into the speaker. Don did it on purpose. It was his way of letting Greg know he wasn't happy, but he knew there was nothing he could do about it anymore.

"No, I know. Can she at least give you anything we can use to catch him?"

"Not yet. But I'm not finished talking to her."

"Okay. Keep me posted," Don said, and hung up the phone.

Greg shook his head and walked back into the kitchen. Morgan's computer sat on the table positioned so her back would be to the wall. She could see the entrance to her office and have a good view of the front door. He didn't blame her for setting up shop in here. There's no way he would have sat with his back to that window, waiting for somebody to reach in and grab him when he wasn't expecting it either. She would never use her office desk again. He walked back into the living room, and Morgan sat in the same spot he left her. She didn't stir when he walked into the room.

"Is there—?" Greg started, but the doorbell cut him off. "Are you expecting anybody?"

"It's either somebody to fix the window, or he's being polite and ringing the bell before he kills me. He said if I did a good job with the article, he'd send somebody to fix the window. If I did a bad job, he would fix me."

Greg drew his gun and walked to the front door. Through the

peephole he saw a man wearing a Valley Glass uniform. He cracked the door but kept his gun at his side.

"Good afternoon. I'm Roy with Valley Glass. We got a call about a broken window."

Greg leaned back inside.

"Looks like he liked your article. It's the glass guy. Do you want me to let him in?"

"Might as well," she said.

He moved out of the way and showed Roy to the office with the broken window.

"Hey, Roy. My name is Greg Burns. I'm a detective with the Crystal Valley Police Department," he said, showing him his badge.

"Oh. It was a break-in."

"Yeah, something like that. But let me ask you, did you talk to the person who ordered the repair?"

Roy paused. People didn't like being questioned by the police, even if they didn't have anything to do with the situation. Greg always attributed it to an innate issue with authority. But it might be self-preservation. There had been enough shows with dirty cops to scare anybody into thinking they were being hemmed up for something they didn't know anything about. The actual dirty cops in the news didn't do anything to help matters either.

"No, sir. They do all of that in the office. They give me the work order, and then I do the job and return it to them. I only deal with the customers at the residence or their business, whichever the case may be."

"Do you mind if I look at that work order?"

"Not at all. Somebody has to sign it when I'm finished anyway," Roy said, handing over the clipboard.

Roy started removing the packing tape from the vodka box while Greg looked over the carbon copy. An S. Killer placed the order yesterday afternoon and paid in cash this morning. Mr. Killer left the money in an envelope in the mailbox, paid in full. Great, that meant there would be nobody to question at the office. But they did have a phone number to call when the job was complete. Greg wrote the number down, hoping it wasn't fake. He also hoped it wasn't the number of another victim.

"I guess the window is one less thing you have to worry about," Greg said, returning to the living room.

"Yeah, unless he wants another article from me. What's he going to do next time?"

"I don't know," was all Greg could say. He sat watching her. She wasn't going to be okay until he caught the guy. And the sooner the better, for her sake and for the city. Crystal Valley's two hundred thousand residents woke up to find out they weren't as safe as they thought. It was one thing to know that faceless crime happened and they should be vigilant, but it was a whole different feeling when crime formally introduced itself. The gravity of the situation weighed on him. He typically dealt with the aftermath of a killer's work, not the present fear they instilled. He almost forgot he was there to question her and not stand guard in case he came back.

"Is there anything you can tell me about the man who broke in here? Anything could help me to catch him, like what he looked like or if he had any visible scars or tattoos."

Morgan readjusted herself on the couch.

"Not really. He wore all black with long sleeves and had a black ski mask on. The only thing I could tell was that he was white and had dark eyes. They looked black but were probably brown. That's all I could tell."

Morgan's description wouldn't help much. But it was a good sign for her that the killer didn't want to hurt her. If he planned to kill her, he wouldn't have bothered covering anything. Still, he needed to have surveillance around the clock set up for her.

"What about the way he walked? Did he have a limp or anything like that?"

"No. He moved and spoke like a normal person. No limp or lisp or anything. He was normal, besides the psycho killer part."

"Naturally."

The phone number was burning a hole in Greg's pocket. He wanted to get outside so he could call it. Maybe the killer would answer. Sitting back and waiting for the killer to contact him was tiresome. The number was more information that he knew he should tell everybody. They could find out whose number it was, but that was a crapshoot. The system would only give them a name and address if the phone was connected to a utility bill and the phone company would more than likely want a warrant for the information, and that could take a few days. Greg didn't have a few days. With this stunt, the killer was escalating. If Greg didn't find him now, it would be too late for another young woman.

It was probably a burner phone if the number was even real in the first place. Unless the killer already found his next victim. Greg could call the number, and if it was bogus or somebody else picked up the phone, he could send it in for evidence and let them track down the dead end. But if it was his number, maybe Greg could throw him off because he called him and catch him off guard. Greg could have an arrest by the end of the day, and his family could come home, and the rule of three would be off his back, and he could move on. Maybe solve a cold case or two.

"I guess I'll be going now if you think you'll be okay with ole Roy in the house with you. If not, I can hang around until he's finished."

"No, I'll be fine, but thank you anyway."

"Okay. I'm going to call and have a car outside your house until we catch this guy. If you think of anything out of the blue, give me a call whenever. I haven't been sleeping much either. You still have my number, right?"

Morgan seemed to relax enough to breathe. Hopefully having a cop car outside the house would allow her to get a little sleep.

"Thank you. And yes, I have your number."

Greg opened the door and started to walk out.

"Greg, there was one thing that just came to me that was kind of strange."

"Oh? What's that?"

"At one point he started sneezing. He sneezed like five or six times in a row. It probably won't help, but I thought it was weird at the time."

"Yeah, that's a weird one. I'll be on the look-out for a serial sneezer as well," he said with a laugh that said he knew it was an inappropriate joke at the time, but he couldn't help himself and walked out the door.

Chapter Twenty-Five

Greg sat in Morgan's driveway with his phone in his hand. He wanted to see the situation as a moment of crisis, and he couldn't figure out what to do, but he had already made up his mind, he just needed to force himself to dial the number. He put the car in reverse and left Morgan behind with Roy. He would call her later tonight and make sure she was doing okay and not still sitting on the couch, jumping at every sound she heard.

A car behind him at the stop sign honked its horn. He waved his hand out the window and drove off. Huge moths bounced off the walls of his stomach and threatened to flutter up his esophagus in search of light. It had been a long time since he'd been this rattled about making a phone call. It was like the first time he called a girl in middle school, praying that her dad wouldn't pick up. He dialed the number and hit the call button before he had time to back out. It wasn't a little girl's father who answered the phone on the second ring.

"Hello, Detective. I must say I am surprised to hear from you. It usually doesn't work this way."

"I got your number from a mutual friend."

"Ah. I see the repairman got to Ms. Cramer's house. I was going to use a fake number, but decided that I wanted to know when the repairs were complete."

Greg second-guessed himself about leaving Morgan alone. He

should have waited for a patrol car to get to her house before he left, but he was in too big a hurry to leave that he hadn't even called in for the car yet. She was with a stranger who, for all Greg knew, could be working with the killer. He turned into a subdivision, preparing to turn around.

"Detective, are you there? I sense you are thinking about Morgan's wellbeing. I can assure you that I have no ill intentions toward her. She is perfectly safe. I think she and I had a real connection the other night."

"Forgive me if I don't believe a murderer who broke into her house, held her hostage, and then beat her before he left."

Greg turned back onto the main road and headed back to Morgan's house.

"Now that is an entirely false accusation."

Greg could hear the anger in his voice. Somehow, he convinced himself he did nothing wrong.

"You broke her window and climbed in and would not let her leave until you were finished with her. Her face is swollen and black and blue. Sounds dead on to me."

"Okay, yes, I did technically break in. But I am having the window replaced. She wasn't a hostage. She could have left or refused, but if she had, then her family would have paid the price. She wasn't a hostage, but she would have had to deal with the consequences of her actions. That is everyday life. And as far as beating her, I did no such thing. She attacked me with a knife, and I defended myself. I never went there with the intention of hurting her."

Greg turned back onto Morgan's street and rolled to a stop in front of her neighbor's house. Roy was still working. Everything looked the same as he left it moments ago, but he still couldn't shake the feeling the rest of the killer's plan was about to drop.

"That's a pretty twisted way of looking at things," Greg said.

"Twisted in all the right ways, Detective. I'm quite found of her now. So you haven't told me. How did you like the article about me? I thought she did a lovely job. I have been all over town today, and people are talking about The Suicide Killer everywhere."

"She definitely nailed you as the sick, insane bastard you are."

Greg was trying to get him to lose his temper again.

"I'm not that bad. I have friends who believe I'm sane. Even you like me to a certain extent. There are always going to be people who don't understand, no matter what you're doing. The main reason I wanted the piece written is because the cops have failed to warn the public about me. And by cops, namely, I mean you. They didn't even know that I existed, and that hurts. But now they all know who I am. Some will be frightened, but others will be asking for my help to alleviate their pain."

"Leaving the door unlocked is not an invitation to come in."

"Isn't it, though?"

Roy walked out of Morgan's house and loaded his tools into the back of his truck. Morgan appeared in the doorway and signed the work order on his clipboard. With a tip of his hat, Roy got in his truck and drove away. She watched as his truck passed Greg's car. At some point, she had changed clothes since he left. She waved to Greg and closed the door. A few moments later, she opened her blinds. Greg assumed she was trying to act a little normal again or wanted to see anything coming after her. He put his car in gear and drove off. He would still be checking in on her later. The banter with the killer was going nowhere, but he didn't believe he was anywhere near Morgan. Greg probably caught him on a smoke break or something.

"Sounds like you're driving again. Did the repairman finish up? Oh, hold on, Detective. I have a beep," he said, and clicked to the other call.

Greg was getting irritated. The killer was playing games with him, and he didn't have the time for it anymore. He needed to find the guy instead of having a phone conversation with him like they were friends. If he wasn't afraid it would set him off and make him hurt somebody, Greg would hang up the phone and worry with another way to catch him.

"Are you there? Sorry about that. It was Roy from Crystal Valley Glass. He wanted to let me know that he completed the job. Very nice guy. If their work is anything like their customer service, I highly recommended them, Detective."

"I'll keep that in mind. Look, I—"

"You can't go yet. Don't you want to know what I have been up to?"

Greg didn't know where to go, but found himself on Morgan's street again.

"Yeah, I do, but I didn't think you would be that forthcoming about it."

"All you had to do was ask. When you first called me, I was sitting in the grocery store parking lot."

The closest grocery store was two miles away. Greg punched the gas and hoped he wasn't too late.

"What were you doing there?"

"I was waiting for somebody."

Greg's stomach turned and soured. He didn't call him while he was on a smoke break. He called him while he was stalking his next victim. But he didn't typically follow his victims first. Or did he? The only information he ever had on how he selected his victims came directly from him, and he could have been lying.

"Imagine my surprise when I happened to be getting gas, and she pulled up."

Horns blared as Greg ran a four-way stop sign.

"When who pulled up?"

He didn't acknowledge Greg and continued talking.

"We exchanged pleasantries at the pump and then she went to a yoga studio down the street. It took an hour, but she finally came out."

The woman sounded familiar to Greg, but it couldn't be her. She should have been at her mother's. His foot hesitated on the gas.

"What have you done, you son of a bitch?"

"Whoa, Detective. I haven't done anything. She was in the grocery store while we were talking. I was surprised she was back in town."

"Leave her out of this," Greg yelled into the phone.

He pushed the gas pedal to the floor and headed to his house.

"That's too late. I'm at her house now, watching her walk back and forth from her car to the house unloading the groceries. Everybody eats well in this house. I thought about getting out and asking if she needed any help, but it's hot out here. I think I'll wait until she's finished. Do you think she'll leave the door unlocked for me, Detective?"

"If you hurt her, I will hunt you down, and I will kill you," Greg said between clenched teeth.

"It's touching that you care about your partner that much."

"Go to hell," Greg said, and threw the phone into the floorboard.

It seemed like everybody in town was out today, and they all wanted to drive as slow as they could. He swerved into the oncoming lane of traffic to pass the cars going below the speed limit. Why was she back in town? She shouldn't have come home until he told her it was safe. It didn't make any sense for her to be home and go to yoga. He understood the grocery shopping. There hadn't been food in the house in days. The killer didn't say anything about the kids. Were they with her or did she leave them at her mother's house? He hadn't been hostile toward his kids before, but he never knew what could change his mind.

Greg tucked back into his lane, and the car in front of him pulled over and stopped their car. He blew through two red lights without slowing down to check for traffic crossing from the side roads. He prayed he wasn't too late as he fishtailed onto his road.

The engine revved, and he pushed the pedal to the floor again. He slammed on breaks in front of his neighbor's house and jumped the curb, landing in his front yard. The tires hit the soft grass and ripped it from its roots. When the car finally came to a stop, two deep moats ran across his front yard.

Chapter Twenty-Six

"That was a little rude," Bobby said to himself and put his phone in the center console. "Time to go to work."

He looked around the neighborhood and pulled his mask down over his face. It was hot outside, and the sweat formed before he stepped outside of his vehicle. The only other time he had worn a mask was when he was at Morgan's house for the interview. He didn't want to wear it now, but this was the first time he'd attempted anything during the middle of the day. He checked the streets again and slipped out of his car. Two doors down, he doubled back, crossed the street and ducked behind the minivan. He picked up the newspaper behind the rear tire and skipped up to the house. The doorknob turned freely in his hand. It was unlocked.

"I guess you do need my help."

A rush of cold air blew through the holes in his mask as he entered the house. He pulled the mask off and checked himself in the mirror. Cabinet doors slammed in the back of the house. Bobby walked into the living room. A TV hung above the fireplace, flanked on both sides by built-in bookcases full of picture frames. Wedding and vacation pictures of the happy wife and tolerating husband lined the shelves. A dust-covered piano sat in front of French doors that looked out over the well-manicured backyard. Bobby ran his fingers across the keys and wished he could at least play the famous part of Beethoven's fifth. That would make an excellent entrance in the middle of the night. Dun, dun, duh dun sounded like Death creeping through the house and announcing you're, go—ing, to die. Dun, dun, duh dun. He would have to look into that later.

Bobby stopped at the foot of the stairs and propped his foot on the edge of the banister. The cabinets continued to open and close; he still had time. He ran up the stairs and opened the first door he came to. It was the master bedroom with a king size bed in the middle of the wall, making it look smaller than it actually was. Bobby fell onto the comforter and looked at the crowded walls. Paintings of flowers hung on each wall, accompanied by more photos of the detective and his wife. He went back into the hall and opened the next door. It was an office containing two small desks. One was messy, littered with papers, and a row of used coffee cups. The other neat. Paper sat stacked with the edges squared, and a cup full of pens organized by color sat at the right corner. Bobby didn't need to guess which desk belonged to whom.

He closed the door and walked to the last room on the floor. The door stuck in the jamb and Bobby had to use a little more force to open it. Dusty air hit him as he stepped in. Nobody had been in this room for a long time. Two of the walls were painted a pastoral green, and the opposite two were painted a pale yellow. Bobby twirled the safari animal mobile that hung above the white crib. A stuffed lion ready to pounce on a giraffe sat on the dresser. The only other furniture was a changing table and rocking chair. Bobby picked up a small frame on the dresser and wiped away the dust concealing the printout of an ultrasound. He put the frame down and walked out. Apparently, he wasn't the only person with a closed off vault in his house.

In the hallway, he could smell food, but couldn't tell what she was making for him. He followed the scent and light humming into the kitchen. She stood at the stove with her back to him. Bobby didn't know the song she hummed, but he had heard it many times on the horrible pop radio station they have to play at all times in the coffee shop.

"I brought the paper in for you," Bobby said, throwing it high in the air so it would make a loud snap when it landed on the table.

Her body went rigid at the sound of his voice. She turned around and backed up against the stove, burning her hand on the red eye.

Shock from the burn outweighed the intruder long enough for her to grab the nearest towel and wrap it around the scorched hand.

"Who ... who are you? What do you want from muh, muh ... me?" she asked, her voice trembling.

"Damn, that had to hurt. I'm Stephen, and I think it is what you need from me, not what I want from you."

Fear flashed in her eyes. He knew thoughts of his intentions must have flashed through her head. It would be interesting to know which she landed on.

"My ... my husband is a cop and is on his way home. You better leave before he gets here," she yelled and moved to keep the rolling island between them.

"I know who and what he is. I also know he's not on his way home."

She began to cry and tried to outmaneuver him. Bobby stopped the island with one hand and rolled it across the kitchen. The island hit the wall and left a large gash in the drywall.

"Stay away from me," she yelled.

She grabbed the pot on the stove and threw it at him. Bobby dove out of the way, and it hit the floor. Boiling spaghetti sauce spattered the wall and kitchen table. She jumped in the hallway and headed for the front door, but Bobby circled around through the dining room and blocked her exit. Like the agile prey of a lion, she turned and headed up the stairs. Bobby shook his head and stomped on each stair.

"You're just prolonging the inevitable by hiding up here. I will find you. It's too late to change your mind. You should have locked the door."

Bobby stalked down the hall and threw open the doors to all the rooms.

"Come on, let's make this easier for both of us."

He walked to the window at the end of the hallway and looked out. A child ran down the road after his friend, riding a bike, who left him behind, or maybe it was an older brother leaving the younger one behind because he wasn't cool enough to play with the big kids. Bobby waited to see if the situation would play itself out.

The pattering of small feet running toward him interrupted his observations. He turned in time to see the woman running in his direction with a pair of scissors in her hand. She raised them above her head as she barreled into him.

The domestic daggers missed his head by inches and buried the blades in the wall. The weight of her body pushed Bobby into the window and shattered the glass. She backed up and drove her shoulder into his chest, trying to push him out the window. He buckled from the blow but managed to keep his balance.

Time was running out for her, and she must have realized he would get the upper hand because she abruptly stopped fighting and turned to run away. Bobby leaped and grabbed her ankle and she stretched her arms out toward a small table, but could not reach it.

He released her leg to readjust his grip, giving her the amount of space to reach the table. She picked up the vase sitting on the surface and swung it by the neck at his head. Bobby twisted to the side, and the vase struck his arm with a glancing blow and shattered on the floor. The drawer slid from the table, and she swung it, connecting with the side of his head. Starbursts of blue and green filled his vision. In an attempt to stop the spinning, he held the side of his head. Blood trickled down his temple and ran between his fingers.

She ran down the stairs and collapsed against the front door, breathing hard. When she looked back, he was not at the top of the stairs. She twisted and fought with the doorknob, but it fought back, locked.

"Unlike you, I always lock the door," he said from the bottom of the stairs.

She screamed and twisted the button to unlock the door. The lock clicked, but the door did not budge when she pulled it. He grabbed her by the hair and threw her to the floor against the foot of the stairs.

"I lock the deadbolt too," he said with a laugh.

Bobby jumped on top of her, straddling her legs and holding her arms down. He pulled a small rope he made by tying two shoelaces together and tied her hands above her head to the banister. The pressure on her wrists caused her to scream, and she tried to wiggle loose. He lifted his shirt and pulled a knife from a sheath on his belt, and she stopped struggling.

"Please. You don't have to do this. Leave now and I won't tell anybody you were here."

"Now we both know that's not going to happen. You say it like you have the upper hand, and clearly ..." he looked at her hands tie about her head, "it is I who has the upper hand."

The knife sliding against the leather sheath wasn't quite as loud as the movies, but the sound still excited him. He slid the edge of the blade across her red face, and she squeezed her eyes tight. He moved the knife down, tracing her neck and the curve of her breasts. When he reached her waist, her eyes shot open.

"No. No. Please don't rape me. Please, I'm begging you. Don't rape me," she pleaded and burst into fresh tears.

What kind of world was this lady living in? To think he would do something so vile and disgusting. There was a special place in hell for men like that, and Bobby hoped it was nowhere near his.

"Shh. Be quiet now. Honey, I'm not going to rape you. I'm not a fucking monster."

Slight relief flashed in her eyes, and it perplexed him, again. How could he threaten this woman with a knife and rape still be her main fear?

"Then what are you going to do to me?"

"Oh, I'm going to kill you. But even I have some morals."

She screamed, and Bobby turned his knife sideways, plunging it between her ribs. All of his weight fell onto the knife and drove it in until her ribs stopped the handle. She gasped, and blood ran from her mouth as he felt her last heartbeats through the pulse of his knife.

When she stopped breathing, he carried her up the stairs to the final door on the second floor. He sat her in the wicker rocking chair and placed her right hand on the handle of the knife. He placed his note on the changing table and left, locking the front door behind him.

Chapter Twenty-Seven

Greg spilled out of his car and closed the door softly. It wasn't lost on him that his dramatic entrance alerted everybody in the neighborhood, not to mention anybody who may be in his house. Being quiet was a moot point now. He drew his gun and tripped his way across the gorges left by his lawn darting sedan and crashed into the railing of the front porch. Pain shot from his hip, up his spine.

At the top of the stairs, he turned and watched for movement in the streets. Harold and Janice from two doors down watched him with the rapt attention of a couple watching their favorite detective show. Nothing happened in the subdivision without those two noticing. They even employed the neighborhood kids to ride their bikes and come back with recon. Aside from the two snoops, there was nothing else.

An eerie lukewarm feeling wormed its way down his spine and unnerved Greg. There were no cars parked on the road that could be the killer's, and worst of all, Shelly's van was not in the driveway. He could have left his car down the road and taken her car with him. Did he take Shelly with him, or was Greg too late with Shelly inside with a mocking note? Why would she have come home? She didn't say anything about coming home early when he talked to her last night.

Greg pushed all thoughts from his head and opened the screen door. The keys to the house hung from the key ring in the car's ignition. He held his breath and tried the door. It pushed open. A new surge of adrenaline poured through his body, and he ran into the house, preparing to shoot the first person he did not recognize. He wouldn't give the son of a bitch the time to make any smart quips or talk to him long enough to distract him. Just pull the trigger and call it in, after he made sure the guy was no longer breathing.

The house was quiet. Footsteps echoed through the house as Greg ran through all the rooms on the ground level; everything looked exactly as he left it this morning. He went upstairs, but nobody was there either. Greg was too late. The killer had taken her somewhere else. Maybe she was still alive. The killer took his daughter and brought her home safely. This was another scheme to scare the hell out of Greg. He walked out on the front porch and contemplated calling him and trying to reason with him. The killer never said anything about the kids. Greg needed to call their grand-mother and make sure they were with her, and everything was all right.

Harold and Janice stood beside the mailbox at the end of the driveway. They didn't say anything to Greg. They only stared. Harold's face looked like he wanted to find the right words, but ended up with a generic question.

"Eva'thing 'ight, Mr. Burns?"

Greg's anger flared, and he prepared to unleash his wrath upon this nosy old man. They always knew what was going on and what didn't look right. Why hadn't they called the police? Greg attempted to calm himself enough to try and sound polite enough to get some information out of him.

"No, Harold. It's not 'ight."

"If there's something me and Janice can do for ya, alls ya gotta do is ask and we'd be happy to help."

Greg wanted to shoot Harold. What could they possibly do to help him catch a serial killer? Harold stood with his hands interlaced on his protruding stomach, while Janice tried to figure out what to do with her hands. Instead, she resided to straightening the nightgown that she wore for the majority of every day. Greg walked to his car and looked for his cell phone in the floorboard.

"Have you happened to see any cars today that you didn't recog-nize? Anything out of the ordinary?" Greg asked.

"Naw, sir. Day's been mighty quiet 'round heuh. The Smith's

down thar got uh delivery 'bout an hour ago. It was a couch. Ugly thang, mustard yella wid white polka dots. Janice here loved it. Said we should get one too. Told her not in my house."

"Okay. Thank you, Harold," Greg said, and walked back to the front door.

"It was an ugly thang. You should a seen it."

"Okay. Thanks, Harold."

Greg walked back into the house, and the old couple started down the road, probably so Janice could check out how the Smith's new couch looked through the living room window. They hadn't seen anything. If an unknown car had been sitting outside of anybody's house in the middle of the day or Shelly had come home early, they would have seen the cars. And they definitely would have seen a struggle if one took place. Greg pulled out his phone and called his wife.

"Hello?"

Greg choked.

"Shell? Shell, baby, are you okay?"

Tears ran down his face.

"Of course I am. What's happened? Are you okay, Greg? It sounds like you're crying."

He wiped the tears from his face to conceal them from his wife on the other end of the phone.

"I thought. I thought you came home and something happened to you."

"Why would you think that? I'm still at Mom's. What happened?"

All the deadly possibilities of what could have happened ran through his head.

"Nothing. I just had a bad feeling, and I guess the more I thought about it, the realer it seemed. I love you. I've gotta go. Call you later."

"Okay, but I'm still worried about you."

"I'll be fine. I promise. Bye."

Fresh tears flooded his eyes before he hung up the phone. He wanted nothing more than to get in his car and drive to his mother-in-law's house and hold his wife and kids, but he couldn't. If Shelly wasn't the target, then who was? Was the killer just screwing with

Greg while he sat with his feet kicked up in his living room some-where or was he talking about somebody else and Greg missed it?

Greg tried to remember what he could from his last conversation. They spoke about Morgan, but Greg had been in front of the house when he was watching the woman on the phone and Morgan hadn't left her house in days. Roy left, and he was never on a phone while at the house. Then he talked about running into the woman at the gas station. He knew she had been out of town. When Greg told him he would kill him if he hurt her, the killer said it was touching that he cared about his partner that much.

The killer had already convinced Greg that his target was Shelly, and she was the partner he was talking about, but he was wrong. The killer was talking about his work partner, Don. Don's wife, Mary, had just gotten back from a cruise with her sisters. Greg's stomach sank. He ran out of the house and got in his car. Muddy grass flew behind the rear tires and covered the neighbor's yard. The rear tires spun, couldn't find traction.

Greg let off the gas pedal, jammed it down again, and the tires bit. The car bounced over the curb, throwing dirt in all directions, in front of Harold and Janice. They turned and headed back to the Smith's house as Greg spun tires out of the subdivision. Greg was ten minutes away from Don's house, but he could make it in five if every-body would get out of his way. He slowed enough to look for Don's name in his phone.

"Did you get any information out of her?" Don asked, answering the phone.

Don never got worried about the formalities of how to answer a phone. If he knew the number that was calling, he would go straight into having a conversation. Greg hated when he did that. It was Don's way of controlling the conversation and showing the caller that he was the one in charge.

"Don, you have got to get to your house right now. Mary is in danger."

"What? Greg, I don't have time for your shit right now. Do you have anything or not?"

Greg shot through a gas station parking lot to avoid the line at the stop sign.

"Yeah, I have information that the killer is probably already at your house. So quit giving me your shit, and get everybody to your house now," Greg yelled into the phone.

"Shit," was the only response Greg got before the line went dead.

He meandered through the slower traffic. Don's house was still a few minutes away. If they were too late to save Mary, it would be all Greg's fault. He would not forgive himself if she died because he didn't pay attention to what the killer said. It was natural for him to assume he was talking about Shelly and went straight home.

There would be no coming back from this. The killer's escalation would be more than he could handle on his own. Maybe more than the entire Crystal Valley Police Department could handle. He swung into the Ivory Crest subdivision on two wheels. Don lived in an upscale neighborhood. The only police activity they ever saw was Don's unmarked car coming and going from work. Greg pulled into Ivory Crest Court. Police cruisers and nervous onlookers already filled the cul-de-sac. It didn't look like anybody had been inside the house yet. Greg jumped from his car.

"Has anybody been in the house yet?"

The closest uniformed officer walked up to him.

"No, Sir. Detective Murphy instructed us to stay outside until he arrived. We have somebody on all sides of the house. Nobody is getting out."

"Screw that. What if he already left? Follow me."

Greg ran up to the front door and tried the knob, but it was locked. He stepped back and kicked the door. The sound of splintering wood echoed under the porch, but the door barely moved. He reared back and kicked the door three more times before it gave way.

"You three search down here while me and this guy go upstairs."

"Barnes, Sir."

"Whatever. We can introduce ourselves if this goes well," Greg said, and stormed the stairs.

It was warmer on the second floor. Greg pointed Barnes to the master bedroom and continued down the hall. Shouts of "clear" rang through the house from the officers downstairs. Greg walked to the broken window at the end of the hall and looked out. He only saw pieces of broken glass glinting in the sunlight.

The door to Greg's left was the nursery. Don and Mary painted and decorated the spare room five years ago when they found out she was pregnant. That was the happiest Greg could ever remember seeing Don. For seven months, that is all Don would talk about. When he found out he was having a boy, it pushed the proud father over the edge with excitement. Nothing could bring him down from his high.

On a late night in July, Mary started bleeding, and it wouldn't stop. Don rushed her to the hospital, but it was too late. The baby came early and was stillborn. Don was never the same after that; he felt screwed over by life. They were afraid to try to have another child and decided it wasn't in the cards for them and started traveling. They talked about traveling later in life when their son moved out and they both retired, but with nothing keeping them home, they spent every vacation day they had checking destinations off their bucket list.

Greg turned the handle and eased the door open. Mary sat in a rocking chair with her hand still clinging to the knife buried in her chest. Greg dropped his gun and stumbled to Mary's body and felt for a pulse. Officer Barnes walked into the room.

"Dispatch, I need an ambulance at 17 Ivory Crest Court."

"There's no need. She's already gone. We need the crime scene group and the coroner," Greg said. Barnes hesitated and stepped into the hallway.

"Mary. Mary, where are you?" came from the front door.

It was Don. Greg heard thunder coming up the stairs and stepped into the doorway.

"Where is she, Greg? Is she okay?" Don asked, but it was all over Greg's face.

There was no hiding it or breaking it gently. Mary was dead. Don walked toward the nursery and Greg stepped out, blocking the entrance as best he could.

"Don, you don't want to go in there."

"Mary. Mary," Don yelled, trying to see past Greg.

"She's gone, Don. There's nothing we can do."

"No, you're wrong. Now get out of my way, or I will move you out of my way."

Greg half stepped to the side so Don could see into the room, but he was still barring Don from freely walking in.

"No, no, Mary. It can't be her," Don said, and pushed past Greg.

A roar of anguish filled the house. Don walked to Mary on shaky knees and placed both hands on her shoulders. He pulled her hand from the knife and buried his face in her neck and sobbed. When he finally stood, he held her head in his giant hands.

"I'm sorry. I'm so sorry, Mary," he said.

Greg watched from outside the door. He didn't know where to begin on trying to comfort Don. Nothing he could say could ever help. Don saw the note on the changing table and picked it up.

"Life is a beautiful thing that I no longer see. I have surrounded myself with memories that I can no longer fight. I want to be part of the memories. I will see you in the end. Love, N."

Don's body convulsed as another wave of pain and tears wracked his body and he fell to his knees. He looked up at the ceiling and seemed to be listening for an answer from a God he swore off five years ago in the same room. Paramedics ran into the room. When they realized there was nothing they could do for the woman, they attended to the man of the floor. Don pushed their prying hands away.

"How? Greg, how did you know?"

"I ... uh. I was told."

"You were told?" Don forced himself up from his knees. "Were you told by that reporter? Has she known that he was going to kill my wife? I'm going over there right now," he said, and headed for the door. Greg stepped in his way.

"No, Don. It wasn't Morgan who told me."

Don stopped with Greg's hand gently pushing against his chest. If he didn't calm down, he would have a heart attack.

"Then who was it, Greg? You called me and told me to get home. Somebody told you."

"It was him," Greg said, and looked at the floor. "It was the killer. I talked to him on the phone."

"You talked to him? He called you and told you he was going to kill my wife?"

"I talked to him, and he said that he was following somebody and I thought he was talking about Shelly and I went home, and she wasn't there."

Greg was not going to volunteer that he was the one who called the killer. This would be bad enough without going into every last detail.

"And then you realized he was talking about my wife, not yours. And you didn't think to call anybody to let them know on the off chance that you were wrong?"

"I didn't think I was wrong. You would have done the same thing in my place."

"Bullshit. You're always going off on your own. How many times have you talked to him?"

Greg didn't answer. He only looked into Don's hurting eyes. He was lashing out, looking for anybody to blame, and the person who was at fault stood between him and the door.

"You've talked to him more than just once? How long have you been talking to him?" Don yelled and grabbed Greg by his jacket. Greg didn't answer, but he didn't need to, Don could tell from the way he was looking at him it had been a while.

"Since the Cline girl?"

Greg continued to look at Don, longing for him to drop his line of questioning.

"The Martin case?"

Greg looked away from Don.

"Jesus. You've talked to him since the very beginning."

"Look, Don. I can explain. He got my number from my card in her house. He wanted to rub it in my face. He never said anything worth a damn. If he had, I would have told you."

"You mother—" Don started and punched Greg in the mouth before he finished.

Greg fell to the floor. All the officers on the second floor stopped averting their eyes and watched. Greg deserved to get hit, but they would only allow the fight to go so far. They moved toward the two detectives as Don stood over Greg.

"I'm not going to hit this piece of shit again, don't worry about it," Don said to the circling cops and then looked back down at Greg and pointed at him. "Mary is dead because of you. The Cline girl is dead because of you. You need to get the hell out of my house right now. I wouldn't worry about the case anymore. You're finished. When I get done talking to the Captain, the only call you'll be getting is for your badge."

Greg got up off the ground and wiped the blood from his lip.

"Don, look. I know you're upset, but come on. We've been through too much. Let's catch this asshole together."

"I'm going to walk back into that room with my dead wife. If I come back out and you're still here, I promise, I will shoot you," Don said, and walked away.

Greg looked around at the other officers, and they all turned their backs to him. That was it. A jury of fellow officers listened and judged him guilty of all charges. There was nothing left for him to say or do. Greg picked up his gun, and the officers moved their hands to the butts of their guns.

Greg holstered it, and they relaxed and parted as he walked toward the stairs. He didn't know why they would think he might use his gun. Don was the one who threatened him. He walked outside, and the heat enveloped him, but it was welcome from the cold he'd been in. He walked with heavy feet to his car and looked around at the growing crowd of neighbors and news stations. There was nobody at the house representing the newspaper. Apparently, Morgan had not gotten over recent events and decided to sit this one out. He wished he could have stayed on the bench too. There was only one place he belonged now. He headed to his mother-in-law's house. Don was right, he would never work another case again. He needed to see his family. Seeing their smiling faces would show him he hadn't lost everything. Don was the one who would feel that kind of loss tonight.

Chapter Twenty-Eight

The other side of the bed was cool where Shelly had been sleeping last night. Greg rolled over and looked at the alarm clock. It was 11:47. He couldn't remember the last time he slept in that late. After he left Don's house, he rode around town aimlessly. He didn't want to face Shelly and have to tell her somebody killed Mary. They had been friends as long as he and Don had been partners. He especially didn't want to tell her it was his fault she died.

Instead, he drove and stopped at a bar and had a few rounds with the town drunk in Hawthorne County where Shelly's mother lived. When he left the bar, he tried calling The Suicide Killer back. He was going to call him out and tell him to meet him somewhere, and then Greg was going to kill him. But he didn't answer. Not even a serial killer wanted to talk to Greg now. By the time Greg arrived, Shelly already knew. She was still red faced when he walked into the living room, but was void of tears. He sat with her and held her close as a new wave of tears overtook her. Greg cried with her.

Don had called to let her know, but he didn't tell her Greg could have prevented it, he only told her to tell Greg to call the station if she heard from him. Don would let Greg tell Shelly why her friend was dead. Greg didn't tell her anything. He turned his phone off and held her. When they laid down to go to bed, Shelly cried herself to sleep, and Greg listened, helpless. Shelly was asleep for a few hours before Greg finally fell asleep from mental exhaustion.

Greg walked into the kitchen. Shelly sat at the table in her pajamas, her right leg tucked under her, staring at an untouched cup of coffee. Her face was red and blotchy from crying, and a greasy ponytail lay flat against her head. The sight of Shelly startled him. She always took the time to get ready. The last time he remembered her falling apart like this was when her father died ten years prior. Greg hoped she wouldn't stay in this state as long as she had with her dad and immediately felt ashamed and wouldn't look at her for fear she would know what he was thinking.

"Why does Don keep calling trying to find you?" she asked without looking up.

"I don't know. He probably wants me to come in and help with the case."

"Why did you turn your phone off and come out here?"

Shelly was suspicious. It wasn't like Greg to run away from a case, and he definitely wouldn't be running from a case involving a friend. He needed to figure out what he was going to do to find The Suicide Killer and leave before she asked more questions.

"Because, when I saw Mary, all I wanted to do was be alone with my family."

He put his hand on hers. Hope walked into the kitchen and jumped in Greg's lap.

"Morning, Daddy. Why did you come to Grandma's house? I thought you were working hard."

"Good morning, angel. I have been working hard. And I was missing you so much, I decided to drop everything and come see you."

"I miss you too, Daddy," Hope said, and sneezed twice.

"Whoa. Those were some big sneezes from such a little girl. Almost a serial sneezer."

"I'm not little. Mommy says it's all the pollen, but I haven't sneezed that big before. Maybe I'm allergic to you, Daddy," Hope said, pulling away in feigned disgust.

"Yeah, maybe you are," Greg said, half paying attention to his daughter.

The only thing Morgan could tell Greg about the killer was the sneezing fit he had. She told him as he walked out the door and he brushed it off as inconsequential, but it wasn't. When Greg interviewed the barista, he remembered him sneezing six times in a row. The barista had served the guy and given a description, but it was all an attempt to misdirect Greg, and it worked. Greg's body tingled all over like it had fallen asleep. He put his daughter down and stood.

"What's the matter, Daddy?"

"Nothing, Hope, honey. I'm fine. I just started feeling a little sick."

"Yuck. Don't throw up on me," Hope said, and fled from the room.

A concerned look crossed Shelly's face. Greg stumbled to the sink. It was his fault. He knew the killer the entire time. If he'd been paying attention, he could have saved lives and his career. Instead, he played stupid mind games with a killer, and Mary was dead. Everybody would find out he could have stopped it. He would never keep his job and would probably have to move his family away from Crystal Valley. Unless maybe he could track down the barista and stop him. Perhaps he could somehow save his job. He thought about calling Don and felt his cell phone in his pocket through his pants. Even if Don did answer, he wouldn't give Greg a chance to speak. He would yell and scream and tell him to get downtown because the chief wanted to fire him in person. Shelly's death was on Greg alone, and alone he needed to rectify the situation. They would probably still fire him, but maybe he could hold on to some dignity in the process.

"I've gotta go," he finally said, more to his reflection in the window above the sink than to anybody else.

"Go where?"

"I know who he is. I know who killed Mary and all the other women."

"Don't you need to call Don or somebody?"

"Uh, yeah. I'll call on the way back into town," he said, and ran out the door.

He didn't intend on calling anybody. There would be time to explain everything to her later. But for now, he had a twenty-minute ride to figure out how he was going to handle the situation.

Greg parked his car down the road from the coffee shop. He was close enough to tell who was coming and going, but far enough away that nobody should notice him watching. The entire ride back to town he contemplated what he was going to do, and this was all he came up with. Sit outside where he works until he shows up. The rest of the time he thought of ways to drain the life from him as slowly as possible.

When he first arrived, Greg flipped through his notebook until he found the name of the barista he was looking for. The name stood out in bold black ink with a dark circle around it like he knew who the killer was the whole time. He went straight into the shop to confront Bobby, but he wasn't there, so he ordered a coffee and went back to his car. While the girl made his drink, he thought about asking her where Bobby lived, but if she wouldn't or couldn't tell him, he didn't want her to let Bobby know somebody had been asking about him.

It was probably for the best he wasn't at work when Greg got there. He didn't know if he would have been able to keep his cool and not just shoot him when he walked through the door. There would have been no coming back from that with witnesses present.

The sun moved behind the trees in the park, casting long black shadows that seemed to reach out from the gates, threatening to pull anybody within reach back into the depths of the forest. Greg was about to give up for the night when a Bronco pulled up to the shop. The driver double parked in the front spaces and left his high beams on. Greg flipped the sun visor down in his car and tried to see who got out of the vehicle, but was unable. Greg started his car. A blast of warm air hit him in the face and began to cool. He rolled closer to the shopping center, trying to get a better angle from the bright lights of the SUV. The driver didn't stay long, and when he stepped out of the store, Greg saw Bobby for the first time as a killer and wondered how he ever missed it to begin with. Bobby didn't look in his direction. He got into his Bronco and made a U-turn. Greg pulled out behind him.

Greg tried to keep a safe distance from him so Bobby wouldn't see him. It didn't look like he knew he was being followed. He kept driving at a steady speed and didn't make any sudden turns like he was preparing to run. When he interviewed Bobby, he told Greg that he lived in the subdivision behind the park and cut through to get to work faster. Greg had been following him for several miles now, so that was either a lie or Bobby had another destination in mind. The longer Greg followed him, the angrier he grew. Bobby headed in the direction of Greg's house.

Bobby pulled off on the side of the road and killed the lights. Greg pulled into the gas station parking lot a few blocks from the entrance to his subdivision and got out of the car. He cut through the woods between the houses and the gas station and followed a well-worn path the neighborhood kids traveled on their bikes to get snacks at the convenience store.

Greg stood in the shadows of houses belonging to neighbors he never found the time to meet. He tried to keep quiet and hoped they didn't have any dogs that would be more than willing to give up his location to everybody. Down the street, Bobby approached Greg's house. He crossed the street two doors away from Harold and Janice's house. Did he know them? Did he know there was a good chance somebody in that house would see him passing by and decide to find out where he was headed? Without a care in the world, he passed Greg's hiding place. Greg could have reached out and grabbed him, but he hesitated. He wanted to know what Bobby was up to. Nobody was in the house for him to hurt. It would be okay to let him go a little further before Greg took him down. Did Bobby know Greg was waiting for him and cross the street, daring Greg to grab him? A cold chill ran down his back, and he shuddered at the thought of Bobby being that aware.

Greg inched from his hiding spot as Bobby walked up to his front door, turned the knob and walked in like he owned the place. Had the bastard had made a copy of their spare key and could come and go as he pleased? No, he put that key in his office the day 'Stephen' gave Hope a ride home. Did he leave the door unlocked when he left the house? When lights started turning on, Greg growled and emerged from the shadows. The street lamps ticked on as he crossed the street and drew his gun.

Greg skipped around the ruts in the yard and glided up the stairs without making a sound. He walked to the door, turned the knob and continued with his forward momentum. It was locked, and he almost walked face first into the door. Irritated, he looked to the sky and then through the window in the door. He fished his keys out of his pocket and eased the right one into the lock.

The door swung open and Greg quietly walked inside, leaving the door open a crack. He crept through the house, listening for anything that would let him know where Bobby was. The sound of rustling paper came from the kitchen. Greg walked around the corner and saw the intruder standing at his counter.

Greg raised the gun just as Bobby looked up. The two men's eyes locked and Greg pulled the trigger. The clock on the wall shattered as Bobby ducked behind the island.

"Holy shit. You almost blew my damn head off. What is wrong with you?"

"Too bad I missed. Why don't you poke your head up and give me another shot?"

"I thought you would want to at least talk a little bit, not bust in here guns a blazin' like you're John McClane or something."

"Yip—"

"No. Don't say it. You'll only cheapen it now."

Greg inched to the side for a better shot at Bobby, but couldn't see anything. He didn't look armed when he went in the house, but Greg couldn't be sure he wasn't waiting for him to walk around the island into the path of his waiting gun.

"Ah, come on. I gotta have some kind of a one liner," Greg said.

"How about you're not that bad of a guy, and I'm going to let you stand up so we can call it a truce?"

"Nah, I don't like that one. Let's try stand up, or I'm going to walk over there and shoot you in the face?"

"Doesn't really have the one liner ring to it, but I'll stand."

Bobby stuck his hand above the island and waved it around. He stopped moving his hand and dropped all fingers, but his middle one. Greg pointed his gun at his target.

Bobby emerged slowly with his left hand still in the air. Greg smiled and pulled the trigger. The bullet hit Bobby in the right shoulder, knocking him to the floor. Greg walked around the island and stood above Bobby with his gun pointed at his face.

"Ahh," Bobby yelled in anguish. "What the hell, man? Why did you shoot me? You're a cop. You're supposed to say freeze or something. Damn it, that hurts."

"You're a murderer who is breaking and entering into my house. My need to say freeze went out the window long ago."

Bobby rolled on the floor, holding his shoulder.

"Alleged. Alleged murderer, Detective. Plus, you left the door open, so technically I'm just entering."

"Technically, I could shoot you right now, and they would believe you broke in here to attack me."

"Yes, you could do that. But then you wouldn't find out why I'm at your house."

The gun barrel rose with his hesitation. Greg huffed and pointed the gun at Bobby's face again.

"I assume you wanted to harm my family."

"You know what happens when you assume, Detective. I know your family has been staying in Hawthorne County for a while. I *hope* it wasn't because of the misunderstanding at the school."

The way Bobby accented hope disgusted Greg. He pushed the gun in his hand toward Bobby and forced him to lie back against floor. He fingered the trigger and then released it and squeezed again. There was no way he would psych himself out of killing Bobby right now.

A loud crash came from upstairs, and Greg turned from Bobby as he looked up at the ceiling. Bobby pushed off the floor and pinned Greg against the wall with his left shoulder.

Greg chopped his elbow down onto the exit wound the bullet made in Bobby's right shoulder. Bobby yelled, and Greg felt his grasp weaken. Bobby punched Greg in the stomach, knocking the air from his lungs. The gun waved through the air as Greg stumbled forward.

He pulled the trigger, and the bullet hit a framed picture of him and his family. Bobby swung down on Greg's elbow and knocked the gun from his hand.

The pistol slid under the couch, but Bobby didn't go after it. He ran down the hallway and headed up the stairs toward the noises. Greg bent over and put his head between his knees and fought for air.

Slowly, sweet morsels of air forced their way into Greg's lungs. He pulled back, inhaling as much oxygen as his burning lungs would allow. The sudden rush of air caused him to cough. Greg worked his way to the couch and fell to his hands and knees, and felt under the couch for his firearm, but could not reach it. He stood and slid the couch over the hardwood floor, sending it into the glass coffee table and shattering it. He bent down, grabbed the gun and followed Bobby.

Greg got to the top of the stairs and waited to catch his breath.

Normally, he wouldn't be breathing as heavily from climbing the stairs, but the recent gut punch seemed to be having lingering effects. The house was as quiet as if he were alone. Goose flesh rippled across his arms and neck. Out of the three bedrooms on the second floor, Greg knew there was only one Bobby would use to hide in. Greg walked to the master bedroom, took a deep breath, flung the door open and walked in ready to shoot the first thing that moved.

"Whoa, whoa, whoa, Detective. Let's not come in here firing. You don't know who you might hit," Bobby said, trying to hold his right hand up, but only managed to make it waist high.

His other hand pointed a gun at the head of a young brunette woman. The woman lay on Greg's bed with arms and legs tied to the bed frame. Blood red marks wrapped around her wrists and ankles. She had been laying here for a while, fighting the entire time to get free. The bed had been pulled back from the wall, and Bobby stood behind it, shielding himself with the girl.

"What if I just shoot you now?"

"Then you better hope for a head shot. Otherwise, I'll shoot you, and then I'm shooting this lovely lady in the face," he said, running the barrel of his gun through her hair.

The girl screamed through the duct tape on her mouth and tried twisting herself free again.

"You've already taken out a clock and a picture frame. Do you think the third time will be the charm? Cause I'm a bit skeptical at this point."

"Who is she?"

Bobby rolled his eyes and head in an exaggerated motion.

"Why do you care? How does that even matter in your situation?"

"It keeps me human. Keeps me from becoming desensitized in my job and the horrible things people like you do," Greg said.

"Hmm. People like me? She calls herself Hannah if you believe her."

Greg wanted to keep him talking so he would move his gun away from her head.

"Why wouldn't you believe her?"

"Oh, you're going to love this. She works for the local suicide prevention hotline. Those people probably don't use their real names. She was so eager to help in my time of crisis that she broke protocol and met up with me. She just didn't know how she was going to be helping me."

"Let her go. She doesn't have anything to do with this."

"But she does, Detective. Or at least she did. I think she looks a lot like Shelly. How about you? Anyway, I was going to kill her and leave her here for you to find, but then you started following me, and now I have to improvise, so please bear with me."

Greg looked closely at the woman. She did look remarkably similar to his wife. Bobby wanted him to come in and find this girl and think she was Shelly. He looked at the ceiling. The air duct would have been at a perfect angle to see the entire show. Bobby had probably already set everything up to hide in the attic. Bobby knelt down. Only his head and arm draped over the headboard were visible.

"I can read your mind, Detective. You're thinking I was going to hide in the attic and you're right. It would have been a good show too. This is why we make a good pair. I'm obviously the protagonist, and you're the antagonist—"

The gunshot rang out, stopping Bobby in mid-sentence. The girl on the bed screamed like the bullet had hit her. Drywall dust rained down on Bobby's head.

"Damn it, Gregory. You're really pissing me off now. I told you I was going to kill her if you tried to shoot me."

Bobby stood up and Greg put his hands in the air.

"Hey, hey, Bobby, we can talk this out. You don't have to punish her for my mistake. Come on. Point the gun at me, not her."

"Okay, this is how we're going to talk it out," Bobby yelled. "Throw your gun through the window. And it better land outside."

Greg threw his gun through the top window pane, sending shards of broken glass on the comforter and floor. Bobby walked out from behind the bed and picked up the largest piece of glass and put it to the girl's throat.

"Now, I told you what would happen if you tried to shoot me and failed. Again."

"Don't do it. It's not her fault."

"You're right. It's not her fault, but you should have thought about that before you pulled the trigger," Bobby said, and with a quick motion, sliced into the girl's carotid artery.

Blood sprayed into the air, coating the bed and Bobby. The girl's body arched and sent the arterial spray up the walls. She fell back onto the bed limp, blood running from her mouth and the wound in her neck.

"Wow. Old faithful. Am I right?"

The girl spasmed until all the life drained from her body. Bobby chose her because she looked like Shelly. He only wanted Greg to think she was Shelly. Greg was grateful but still had to wonder why he didn't go after his wife like he did with Don's wife. No matter the reason, Greg was to blame for this girl's death. He should have continued to play along with Bobby's game to see where he was going with it. Now, a new game began, and Bobby had the gun.

"You didn't have to do that," Greg said, moving closer to the edge of the bed.

"Yeah, I did. You will never learn if there are no consequences for your actions."

Greg's knee brushed the footboard.

"So what are we going to do now? You don't have a hostage."

"And you don't have a gun," Bobby said, pointing his gun at Greg.

Greg threw his hands up in feigned surrender and moved closer to the edge of the bed. He could tell Bobby was losing his grip on the situation. He moved until he was on the same side of the bed as Bobby.

Bobby was looking around the room like he was trying to find an escape route. Now that his plan backfired, and he was winging it, he was really dangerous. Bobby didn't want to kill Greg. He didn't expect Greg to show up. His only plan was to kill this woman and make Greg think it was his wife. Now, he only wanted to get away with both of them alive, so he could continue with the way things had been. It was a miscalculation when he killed Mary. Everything changed and they could never go back. Even if they both managed to get out of here alive, Greg's career would be over. Now, the only thing Greg had to fight for was his family. Greg moved toward Bobby.

"Greg, I don't want to kill you, but I will."

"I don't think you will," Greg said.

Bobby's face turned like a dog that didn't quite understand its owner. Greg charged Bobby and pushed his left arm in the air. Two shots rang out. Pressure from the gun blast blew Greg's eardrum and his equilibrium went sideways.

He felt Bobby move under him. Greg replanted his feet and lunged at one of the two Bobby's he could see. Bobby tensed as they plowed into the wall.

Bobby wrapped his arm around Greg's neck and brought his elbow down on his neck at the base of his skull. A white flash interrupted Greg's vision. His body went limp, and he fell to the floor. He thought the fall paralyzed him until he felt sharp kicks to his side and legs.

The attack stopped, and Greg pushed himself up. He staggered and fell back against the wall for support. The back of his neck throbbed and electric pulses flowed down his legs. Bobby jumped on the bed to run away.

Greg put his foot against the wall and pushed off for more power as he speared Bobby. He drove his shoulder into his side and used Bobby's momentum to knock him into the floor.

Greg straddled him and pinned his legs down. Fists rained down on Bobby's unprotected face, followed by repeated blows to his stomach.

Blood flew from Bobby's nose. He screamed at Greg, but he ignored him and continued to beat Bobby. Greg lifted his body with his knees and swung down, driving his fist down onto Bobby's gun wound.

Bobby let out a loud screech like a wounded animal. And now Greg had cornered him. The gun bounced in his left hand. He held it in his palm like a rock and blindly swung it. The gun connected with the side of Greg's head and temporarily stunned him. He shook it off and pulled back to hit Bobby again, but the punch went wide right. Bobby reared back and sent the butt of the gun into Greg's face.

Blood gushed from his nose and covered Bobby's face. Another primal scream rang out and the gun connected with his face again. Greg fell to the floor, both of his hands covering his face. Blood ran between his fingers and spilled to the floor. He tried to move, but Bobby was on him.

Bobby used Greg's shoulder to push himself up. He stood above Greg and kicked him in the stomach. Greg's hands automatically moved to protect against the blunt boot attack. Before Bobby delivered another brutal kick, he pulled back and stopped.

The boot stomped the floor beside Greg's face and the gun barrel twisted against his broken nose. Greg screamed. Bobby laughed and pulled Greg's cell phone out of his pocket.

"I told you I don't want to kill you. Now, don't say another word or I will shoot you and then go find that pretty little wife of yours," Bobby said, grinding his pistol into Greg's face.

He scrolled through Greg's phone until he found the number he was looking for. They answered the phone on the second ring.

"Greg, where the hell are you? We—" Don started before Bobby cut him off.

"Whoa, Donnie, calm down. This isn't Greg. You ever think of just saying hello?"

"Then who the hell is this and why are you calling from his phone?"

"This is The Suicide Killer speaking," Bobby said with a laugh.

"What did you do with Greg?"

Bobby pushed all of his weight on Greg as he stood.

"I wasn't going to *do* anything to him, but the asshole attacked me, so something has to be done with him."

"I will find you and—"

"No need for empty threats, Detective. We're at home and eagerly await your arrival," Bobby said, and hung up the phone.

Chapter Twenty-Nine

The last thing Don wanted to do was go and save Greg. Mary was dead because of him. If he would have told everybody from the beginning, like any normal detective would, they could have stopped The Suicide Killer from killing Mary and possibly Laura Cline as well. Now their blood was on Greg's hands too. But this may be his only chance to catch Mary's killer and to hell with Greg Burns. Don was wrestling with what to do when the call of multiple gunshots being reported in Greg's neighborhood came over the radio in his car. Don left his house when they took Mary away, and he hadn't been back since. He stayed in a hotel that night and when he woke this morning, the only thing he could think about doing was getting back to work so he could find her killer. He didn't expect for her killer to find him and then tell him where he was. It was probably a trap, and all the responding officers were about to walk into it. Don picked up the radio.

"This is Detective Don Murphy. All responding officers proceed to 1356 North Oaks Drive. I am in route. Do not enter the house until I arrive."

The radio crackled, and various reports of 10-4 filled the cab of his car. Don drove in silence. The emotionless shock he'd been in for the majority of the day was starting to wear off and anger took its place. Sweat rolled down his face and into his eyes. He turned the air conditioner on high, but it didn't seem to blow cold enough. He rolled down the car window and stuck most of his head outside. The rest of the drive the world came toward him on tilt.

Don arrived at Greg's house to a sea of flashing blue lights. He got out of his car, and six officers surrounded him.

"Okay, listen up everybody. This house is Detective Burns'. He's one of ours. Let's do this right. I need Wilkes and Garner in the house with me. The other four of you spread out around the house and don't let anybody leave."

It made Don's stomach roll to call Greg one of them, but he was willing to use the cop in distress as motivation to assure the killer's capture. Don ran up the front steps, flanked by the two officers. Wilkes stepped up and slammed the Enforcer into the door. Garner went in first, followed by Don and then Wilkes. They walked into the kitchen and into the living room, pointing their guns around corners as they went.

"Looks like we found the shootout. How'd you know?" Wilkes asked.

It was a lie, but Don was nothing like Greg. There would be plenty of time to explain later.

"Lucky guess," Don said.

They walked through the living room, following the path of the fight. Don walked down the hall and motioned for the officers to follow him upstairs. The door to Greg and Shelly's bedroom stood open. Don stepped into the room, and the breath caught in his throat. A young woman laid on the bed covered in blood. Streaks of crimson sprayed up the walls in a grotesque graffiti tag.

"We're going to need an ambulance and the coroner," Don said.

Garner stepped back into the hall and radioed for the extra units. Don walked to the bed and felt the woman's neck for a pulse, even though he knew she was already gone. Her face turned with the pressure of his fingers, and for a split second, he thought it was Shelly. The young woman looked remarkably close to Greg's wife.

"We need to find Burns if he's still here."

A shuffling noise came from the closet. All three cops snapped their guns in the direction of the door. The sound grew louder and sounded like somebody trying to beat their way out of the closet. The two uniformed officers looked at Don, waiting for instructions.

"Come out of there, or we're coming in after you," Don yelled.

The knocks only grew louder and more persistent.

"Wilkes, open the door and fall back."

Officer Wilkes walked to the door and slowly turned the knob so that whoever was behind the door would not hear him. He put three fingers in the air and dropped them one at a time. The final finger dropped with his fist, and he jerked the door open and stumbled back behind Don. At first, there was no movement in the closet. Don and the officers took a step toward the open door, but only saw clothes. A flash from the left side of the closet and a person wearing a black ski mask, dressed in solid black clothes and boots stomped into the room with a gun in his hand.

"Drop your weapon now," Don yelled.

The figure stopped but did not drop the gun. He waved the gun up and down and roared like a muffled bear.

"I said drop the gun now, or I will shoot you."

He dropped to his knees with his hands held in the air. The man's arms quaked like he was having trouble keeping them up. Garner moved toward the man to disarm him, and he dropped his hand holding the gun. Two shots rang out, and Garner jumped back out of the way. Both bullets hit the man in the chest, and he fell on the floor. Don approached him, gun still drawn. He tried to kick the gun out of the suspect's hand, but his entire arm moved with the kick. He bent down and pulled the gun, but his arm moved with it.

"What the hell?"

The gun was taped to his hand. Don rolled him over and pulled off the mask, revealing Greg Burns' face. His mouth had been taped so he couldn't warn them. Don pulled the tape from Greg's mouth, and blood trickled from the corners.

"No, no, no. I didn't know it was you," Don said, patting his face. "Greg, stay with me."

Greg fumbled with the radio at his side.

"Damn it. We've got an officer down. I need the paramedics here now," Don screamed into the radio. "There was nothing I could do. I didn't know it was him."

Wilkes put his hand on Don's shoulder.

"We know you didn't know who he was, Detective. He couldn't drop the gun. I thought he was going to shoot us too."

Don blamed Greg for his wife's death, but he didn't want him to die. Not like this. They had been partners for ten years. He considered Greg family. He held Greg's head in his lap. A folded piece of paper stuck out of Greg's shirt pocket.

Don pulled the paper from Greg's shirt, already knowing it would be another note from the killer.

"I hear the sirens as they echo closer, covering the distance of the night. Are they finally coming for me this time? Know that if I ever made any mistakes that caused pain, they were never in my plan. N."

Don balled up the note and threw it against the wall. Greg began to cough, and Don held him up to keep him from choking on his own blood.

"Don't worry. Help is on the way. You're going to be okay."

Don cursed himself for holding Greg as he was dying, and the only thing he could think to say was the typical false words of hope they had both given many times before. Greg gargled blood and pushed it from his mouth. He was trying to say something, but Don couldn't make it out. He leaned in closer and put his ear up to his mouth.

"Attic," was all Don could make out before Greg died in his arms. Don gently placed Greg's head on one of the pillows lying on the floor.

"What did he say?" Wilkes asked.

Don stood and forced himself not to look at the ceiling as he walked to Wilkes.

"He said attic. I think he means the guy who did this is hiding up there," Don whispered.

The two officers walked out of the room and found the attic entrance. Garner ran up the stairs, followed by two paramedics. Don pulled the door open for the attic. The springs protested every inch he pulled them. The ladder clacked open and Wilkes started up, followed by Don.

Don grabbed the outside rung in time with each step of the officer in front of him. Wilkes stuck his gun through the hole and waved it around. He eased his head through the opening and put his hands on the edge of the entrance to hoist himself into the attic.

A bright flash and gunshot startled Don, and bright red blood fell on his upturned face. Wilkes' body fell down the stairs, carrying Don with it. Don landed on his back with Wilkes' body twitching on top of him. Every tremor of the body covered him with more blood.

He pushed Wilkes off of him and sat against the wall, wiping blood and skull fragments from his face. A loud crash that sounded like a window breaking came from the attic. Don jumped to his feet and raced up the ladder.

He didn't stop at the top to give anybody a chance to aim before they fired. He landed on a piece of plywood acting as flooring between the ceiling rafters and swung his gun in all directions, looking for any movement. The attic was quiet. Don skipped across ceiling rafters to the large window in the back of the attic that looked out over the back yard.

Broken glass jutted like the teeth from a monster shark, leaping from the water with its meal in its mouth. The glass had been cleared from the bottom sill so the killer could climb out. Don could barely make out bloody boot impressions on the wood. It would be a tough escape, but a more athletic person than Don could manage it.

Don watched out the window as the flashing blue lights illuminated the backyard. The only thing he saw were two uniformed police officers looking back at him.

Chapter Thirty

Bobby opened the door to his waiting SUV and fell into the driver's seat. After forty-five minutes of searching, and another thirty by a different officer, Don finally believed that Bobby had gone out the window and gave up the search. When they finally closed the attic door, Bobby slid out from behind a piece of drywall that he'd hung on the bare wall. He hid between two studs in the gable of the roof. Many times the police walked past his hiding spot, and each time he was ready to shoot at any sign that his hiding place had been compromised. Police were still working in the house, and he had to wait a while longer until they finished. He lost track of time, but the dim glow of sunrise forced its way through the attic window when they finally drove away. Bobby emerged from the attic soaked through with sweat. He felt ten pounds lighter.

The screen door slammed as he walked out the back door and down two streets before he turned toward the subdivision exit and his waiting vehicle. He wanted nothing more than to lean the seat back and go to sleep, but he didn't want to end up getting caught because he couldn't stay awake.

It was still too early in the morning for any of the protective mothers to see him when he entered the park and stumbled through the woods. When he reached the edge of the cliff, he pitched over the side and slid to the bottom. Rocks and chunks of red clay fought to hold him back, but he resisted and came to rest at the roots of the fallen tree.

He rubbed his hand over the destroyed heart and then over the newly etched memorial. Danielle's grave looked like a wild animal tried to dig her up. The grave must not have been deep enough to hide her scent. He dropped to his knees and swiped as much dirt as he could back into the hole. Exhaustion threated to overtake him and he resided to return later when he wasn't so tired and fill the hole with rocks and then cover them up with more dirt to make sure nothing found her again.

As much as he enjoyed visiting Danielle, there was somewhere else he thought he needed to be. He climbed back up the hill and back into the park. The mothers were now arriving with their children. Most of them sat in their car and watched him walk across the grass like he was a zombie, coming to feast on their children. The few mothers who were already out of their cars got back in and waited for him to pass. He climbed into his Bronco and spun tires out of the park to give the gawking mothers a bit of a show.

It felt like he'd won the game. That's what it'd been all along, right? One huge game, so it goes. But as with any game, there was the potential for setbacks and he'd had a few of those as well. The loss of Emily and Danielle were more than setbacks to his game. But for each loss he incurred, he'd struck back and enacted justifiable counter moves.

He pulled onto the narrow winding road and followed it to the back of the cemetery. Nobody alive in the cemetery tracked his movements. He placed a handful of wild flowers he didn't remember picking against the headstone.

"I'm sorry," he said, and collapsed on the grave.

He curled up and wrapped his arms around the cool granite. On the breeze, floating through the trees, he heard her sweet voice say, *I knew you would come back for me, my love.*

Acknowledgments

I wrote the dedication for this book before starting these acknowledgments, so now I must proceed through blurry eyes. I promise to try not to be overly sentimental. Ever since my Dad handed me a copy of *Jurassic Park* in sixth-grade and said, "here, I think you would like this," I have been hooked. He was the greatest inspiration for my love of reading and talking about books. Though we didn't read the same genres, we spent many conversations excitedly talking about what we were currently reading. Thanks, Dad.

Now, I need to thank the driving force behind why I have the opportunity to write these words. My wife, Tina, has been so much for me that I am afraid to list anything for fear of leaving something off. If not for her encouragement and support in going to college and then pursing my MFA, I wouldn't be half the writer I am today. She believed in me and had patience with me when I had none for myself.

Thank you Greenlee for showing me what hard work and determination are. You're my hero for so many reasons; for so many ways.

I'd also like to thank my Mom, Taylor, and Katelyn (sorry Taylor's name is first, but he is older than you) for their continued support. Thank you to all my friends and family for the motivation when asking about my book, especially during the submission process.

Thank you to A.A. Medina for creating such an awesome cover for this edition of my first novel.

Thank you to the Columbus State University English Department for enriching my life as well as every student who walks into Arnold Hall. And to the Southern New Hampshire University MFA program for helping me hone my craft.

Finally, to the readers, especially those who have taken the time to read these acknowledgements, I thank you for taking a chance on my book and hope you stick around to see what I come up with next.

About the Author

Zach Lamb is a fictionist who creates thriller, horror, and dark fiction stories. He is the author of The Suicide Killer and Dark Water Sacrifice. Zach has an MFA in creative writing from Southern New Hampshire University. He lives with his wife and kids in the nonfictional town of Ellerslie, Georgia, named after the fictional character Captain Ellerslie from the Waverly Novels.

www.ingramcontent.com/pod-product-compliance
Lightning Source LLC
Chambersburg PA
CBHW020023310726
48970CB00007B/2178